Heroes

Heroes:

An Anthology

Edited by Ashley Cyr

Heroes: An Anthology

Copyright © 2015 by Ashley Cyr

Cover by: John Ryers

ISBN-13: 978-0-9949210-0-0
ISBN-10: 0-9949210-0-0

Bushmead Publishing
www.bushmead.com

Printed in U.S.A

To Nathan Jarmusch,
You are missed.

Table of Contents

An Introduction

Heroes have come under fire lately. The media shows us the worst aspects of humanity every day, and so seldom do we see a hero that isn't plastered up on a movie screen and serving as so much escapist pablum. Politicians throw around the word hero like it has lost all meaning, and they engage in bloody debate over whether an individual is a hero or a monster. In this era of near zero privacy, we see so many heroic offerings that are served up quickly only take a schadenfreude laden fall from succumbing to the fringe benefits that public attention so often brings.

But we still want there to be heroes. With how bad our economy is, how terrifying evil has become in its many forms around the world, so many of us are crying out for a hero. And wouldn't that be nice, to have someone fly in with a billowing cape and winning grin?

Throughout all of this, we've mixed up what it means to be a hero and, I think, forgotten that a hero can come from anywhere. You can be someone's hero if you're a shoulder to cry on when they need it, by giving money to someone in need, by taking the mere moment out of your day to treat someone else with decency. Something so simple as picking up the phone for a friend can be an unknown heroic act; if the call is a last ditch attempt to reach someone, anyone.

We often do not give enough credit to the men and women who are every day heroes – the ones who spend their lives fighting their instincts of self-preservation. This may be the truest measure of heroism the way we commonly talk about it, the willingness to risk and sacrifice for the good of others. Certainly, it is one of the hardest questions we have to grapple with. Most of us will assert, when ensconced in the quotidian safety of our day-to-day, that we would gladly put our lives on the line for some greater good. This is so much more difficult to do when we find ourselves in the position.

Despite all this melancholy about the state of the world and the complaints that maybe all the heroes are gone, there's still hope. We still see some of us willing to put aside our petty squabbles and fear. Maybe that's all it takes, those few bright sparks that put themselves on the line to stand against violence, prejudice, and hatred. Even with flaws, and flawed heroes truly are the most compelling, there are those who will light their souls on fire and hold back all the darkness in the world.

So, now we invite you to take a gander through this collection. Within these pages are different takes on heroes and heroism. There are big damn heroes and every day heroes. There are sword-wielding women and gun-toting men, there are people scraping to get by and members of royalty, there are those looking for a job and there is even a young man wearing his underpants over his bluejeans. Every one of them is a hero, and I hope this inspires you to your own acts of heroism, big or small.

- Tyler Omichinski, September 24, 2015

Sidekicks Wanted – Laura Johnson

SIDEKICKS WANTED

HERO HUNTERS INC.

JOB POSTING: SIDEKICK

Job ID: 09012015
Location: Various
Base Pay: To be discussed
Industry: Heroism/Villainy
Reports to: Hero

DUTIES:
• Fighting evil
• Protecting the innocent
• Rescuing damsels in distress
• Saving the city/world/universe from danger (as required)
• Listening to the Hero explain his origins
• Engaging in witty banter with the Hero

QUALIFICATIONS:
• Possession of a Sidekicking degree from an accredited university*
• Prior Sidekicking experience preferred
• Superpowers are an asset
• Knowledge of weapons and technology
• Sense of humour
• Must be comfortable wearing spandex
• Must be willing to endure rumours of romantic involvement with the Hero
• Must be willing to be kidnapped so the Hero can stage a dramatic rescue
*May be substituted with appropriate experience

Underlings need not apply.

〜∞〜

Frank Mattie was sick of being a minion.

Sure, the pay was great (danger pay and all), travel expenses were covered (on a private jet, no less), and the on-site training had been a phenomenal learning experience (oh, to use that freeze ray again!). Yet, Frank was thinking of settling down, and there was nothing more disconcerting to a potential long-term lover than the very real possibility of his or her spouse dying on the job. (Minions, as you may know, invest heavily into life insurance.)

And nobody had ever heard of a minion getting a happy ending.

With his current Villain recently killed by an up-and-coming Hero hotshot, and the second-in-command on permanent leave, Frank was out of a job. It was certainly time for a change of career. After what happened to poor John... Frankie shuddered. Heroes were getting darker every day, it seemed. No more "incapacitate the henchmen." Now it was all "kill 'em dead."

Heroes have no mercy when you're faceless. You're less than human.

To a Villain, unless you were a pretty high rank – or had some niche skill that made you more useful than the average mook – chances were you'd be in a generic uniform with generic equipment and a monotonous routine. If you were exceptionally lucky, you'd be allowed to fiddle with the Villain's more expensive toys. It made you feel like you, too, had superpowers – but such opportunities were few and far between.

And so when Frank saw the posting for a Hero looking for Sidekick, he jumped on it.

〜∞〜

Frank's palms were sweating as he arrived outside the Hero Hunter building, a glass skyscraper that gleamed in the midsummer sun. He wasn't sure what the appropriate dress code was for a Sidekick position. Hell, he didn't own any spandex. Or a cape. He didn't even have a mask. All he had was his former Underling uniform (his official and politically correct job title), complete with his rank and distinction badges sewn on his left shoulder. The leather was well-worn, with two bullet holes on the right shoulder and claw marks around his ribs.

The bloodstains hadn't come out, alas.

When Frank walked into Hero Hunter's atrium, heads turned and mouths gaped. Perhaps it was the rugged scar that cut across the bridge of his nose (a most unsavoury feature, he'd been told). Perhaps it was his attire. He was, without doubt, a sharp contrast to the clean-cut, cookie-cutter candidates already inside, with their pretty faces – a leather-clad minion in a sea of spandex-sporting Sidekicks.

In fact, he was sure he'd shot himself in the foot with his outfit alone. When he'd applied for the post, he'd hardly expected to be considered.

Underlings did not become Sidekicks.

As Frank approached the front desk, the receptionist gawked at him, then quickly regained her composure. "I'm sorry, sir. I think you've come to the wrong place. We don't recruit Underlings here." She smiled tightly and resumed her typing, fingers *click-click-clicking* at an inhuman speed.

"I have an interview with Xenethera at ten o'clock. Under Frank Mattie? For the Sidekick position?"

She sniffed, *click-click-clicked* for a few seconds on her computer, and stared at the screen. She turned to him again and said, "Please have a seat, Mr. Mattie. Xenethera will be with you shortly."

Frank sat down. On his left: a scruffy, wide-eyed male teen with restless leg syndrome and a sprinkling of acne on his forehead. On his right: a woman in her early twenties dressed for a job at the bank. She was scowling into her smartphone as if it had insulted her.

The gangly teen was summoned first. He shuffled to the designated room, muttering to himself. Fifteen minutes later he emerged, skin pale as the belly of a shark. The woman, when called, strutted to the same room. Confidence radiated from her like from a bonfire. Upon her return to the atrium, however, that fire was gone. She moved stiffly, posture rigid. Through her mask of calm, her lower lip trembled.

This did not bode well for him, but his rent was overdue. If he didn't get this job, he'd have to apply for another Underling position, and his former employer was dead. His supervisor was also dead. And the Head Henchman had vanished. So there went *that* potential reference.

If evil had it easy, they'd obviously never spoken to the minions.

"Mr. Mattie?" called the receptionist. "Xenethera will see you now."

Frank approached the door. He walked with confidence he didn't feel. *You've been in more stressful situations,* he told himself. *Remember the time when the Hero activated the lair's Self-Destruct*[TM] *feature and you were running for your life? This is a walk in the park.* He wasn't convinced; he was terrible at this positive self-talk stuff.

"Do come in, Mr. Mattie." Xenethera spoke with a light accent he couldn't quite place. Eastern European, perhaps. Her black hair had a rainbow sheen to it that reminded him of an oil slick, tied in a severe bun. "What is your name?"

He blinked. Had she not just addressed him? "Uh, Frank Mattie."

"Your *Sidekick* name, Mr. Mattie."

His throat seized as if an invisible hand were slowly crushing his windpipe. "I don't have one. I was expecting to work with the Hero on it if I'm hired."

"I see. Have a seat."

When he sat down, the interviewer peered over her horn-rimmed spectacles at him with neon green eyes, the pupils a trio of black wedges converging around a tiny dot. She removed her glasses and looked at him. For a few seconds she was silent. The soft skin below his temples suddenly itched, and at the back of his mind it felt like someone was rifling through a heap of disorganized folders. Images flashed through his mind, as if a disinterested third party were flipping through a photo album, and nausea gurgled in his stomach.

Then a memory surged to the front of his mind, blotting out reality and Xenethera's intense gaze.

Him, another brick in the wall of faceless goons defying the Hero, firing their weapons with unified screams. Bullets and laser blasts pockmarked the walls and ceiling, deflected by the Hero's armour. The Hero was a glorious sight, cape billowing even in the absence of wind, glowing sword in one hand as he slammed and sliced his way through the throng. Helmets cracked and bones crunched. Blood splattered the walls like a Pollock painting.

It was a losing battle. Frank fled.

The memory faded, and Xenethera's face appeared before him once more. Finally, she sighed.

"You have a most interesting resume. It is not every day that we consider former..." She glanced at the resume on her desk. "*Underlings.*" Another pause. "Why don't we begin there? Tell me, what prompted you to leave your former position?"

"After Dr. Pain's defeat, due to budgeting restrictions and restructuring my job was eliminated. I am seeking a more stable job with long-term potential."

"Is it not your job to prevent the Hero from achieving such things?"

Frank swallowed. "Sometimes, you have to know when to admit that your foe is stronger than you."

"So you fled the fight. Have you considered yellow spandex?"

"I sought backup. I cannot aid my employer if I am dead." He forced his tone to be cordial. He almost added, *If Dr. Pain had not stood his ground, he would be alive to thwart the Hero another day.*

Xenethera's lips twitched. She made a note on a clipboard, then glanced at Frank's resume again. "It says here you worked for--ah, a Nemesis!" Her triangular pupils whirled, though it was unclear her thoughts on the matter. She arched an eyebrow. "How do you feel that experience can benefit the League of Superheroes^{TM}?"

Frank was beginning to understand the emotional reactions from the previous two candidates. He plucked at his collar, inhaled deeply, and said, "A Nemesis is a cut above your typical Villain. My experience with a Nemesis gives me insight into their methods, their way of thinking. I know how they bait Paragons, how they set up traps and the like."

Xenethera's face remained expressionless. "Is that so? Imagine that you had just contested against the Villain. On the one hand, there is a busload of innocent civilians dangling precipitously off the road. On the other side is the Hero's love interest, holding on for dear life. You only have time to rescue one of them. What do you do?"

The questions continued like a barrage of arrows, each a piercing barb in his confidence.

"You do realize," Xenethera eventually said, "that a Sidekick is very different from a *minion*."

Something in Frank snapped. This was not what he had signed up for. If Heroes were like this, hell, maybe returning to Villainy wasn't such a bad idea. He could rise to the rank of Head Henchman eventually, forgo his own life story's love interest, maybe live long enough to retire on an island lair. That was about as cushy a job as they came.

He rose from his chair. "If you didn't see potential in me, I wouldn't be here. You'd have thrown my resume in the shredder and been done with it." The moment the words left his mouth, he regretted them, wished he'd bitten his tongue instead. But more words bubbled at his lips like a vat of roiling acid and he couldn't withhold them. "You want to discriminate against me because I went to the *Underling Academy* instead of *Sidekick School*? Fine. You want to know what they teach Sidekicks there? How to look cool in a cape and spandex. How to deliver cheesy one-liners. How to be funny. Hell, you might as well have joined the circus to learn that.

"You know what they teach Underlings? How to stand up to the Hero without pissing yourself. How to fight in the face of certain defeat. How to take orders even if you don't like them and negotiate your way out of trouble from the Villain, like when the Hero overpowers you and the Villain's debating whether to feed you to the piranhas just because he's in a bad mood. I've operated technology that baffles a Hero. No Sidekick is going to be taught in school how to wield a freeze ray. I can memorize labyrinthine lairs and complex procedures for Code Red. And if it didn't occur to you already, I have personal knowledge of how Villains think and operate. Not stale, outdated textbook theory. But I guess that counts for nothing.

"I thought you Heroes were forgiving, turn-over-a-new-leaf types. If you want to go all holier-than-thou and split hairs over the morality of working for a Villain, fine. Hire Circus Kid. I'll take my talents elsewhere." He half-expected to be shouted at, to be ripped apart by her next words. He was about to turn when he saw a smile tugging at the corner of Xenethera's mouth.

"Finally, some evidence of a backbone. We'll have to work on your snark, of course, but at least there's *something* to work with. All the candidates who walk in here and tremble in their boots in front of *me*, and they think they've enough mettle to be dangled over a vat of acid and threatened with death without pissing their spandex!"

She set down her clipboard and rose. "I'd like to forward you to the next round, the skills practicum, though I am sure you will have no problems there. You will, however, need a Sidekick name. Quite frankly--" She grinned wryly. "I'm afraid 'Frank Mattie' will not do."

Frank thought for a moment. "How about... *Minion*?"

A Warden's Oath
– Shelley Roe

The taverns were often packed to capacity after a good pit fight, and tonight was no exception. Kole wrapped an alcohol-soaked cloth around her bloodied knuckles. Leaning back in her chair, she sipped her ale. The alcohol stung the cut on her lip but the pain began to blur as she downed half the contents.

Just as she emptied her mug, a tavern girl placed a full one in front of her. Kole dug a coin out of the pouch at her waist, sliding it across the table, but the girl waved her off. "He already paid," she said, glancing toward a man who sat at the bar with his back to them. Kole didn't need to see his face. She recognized him from the Warden uniform he wore and the sword at his waist.

Kole groaned. Vaughn. The last man she wanted to see right now. "Send it back," said Kole. "And tell him I said he can shove it up his ass."

The girl's eyebrows rose as she glanced from Kole to Vaughn and back again. She nodded. Kole slid the coin across the table. "For your trouble," she said.

The girl snatched the coin up, slipping it into her apron pocket. She grabbed the mug and crossed the room to the bar, setting it in front of Vaughn. Kole smirked as the tavern girl scurried off without a word. She hadn't really expected her to repeat the message. No one would talk to a Warden like that, not for fear of retribution, but simply because everyone loved and respected the Wardens.

Sending the drink back clearly didn't deter Vaughn. He grabbed the mug, along with his own drink and crossed the room toward her. When he reached her table, he set the mug down in front of her. Vaughn grabbed a chair, taking a seat without an invitation. He hadn't changed much in the past five years. He still had the same defined jaw line and bearing of a man confident in himself and his place in the world. The only difference was the spattering of grey hairs along his temples.

Kole sighed. "I know what you're going to say and I don't want to hear it."

A look of disappointment crossed his features. "You don't belong here, Kole. You're a Warden. You're better than this, better than some pit fighter in some shitty little town in the middle of nowhere."

Kole took a sip of ale from her mug. She'd need an entire barrel to get through this conversation. "That was another life. One I really don't care to talk about." Or think about, for that matter.

Vaughn's presence only served to open old wounds, wounds she'd spent years trying to forget with pit fights and ale. She'd almost succeeded too, until now.

"You think you're the only one who got hurt?"

Kole clenched her fist. "Tavira stabbed me in the back. Literally." She could almost feel the dagger tear through her flesh at the mere mention of it. "I still have the scar to prove it."

Vaughn leaned back in his chair, regarding her in silence. He was probably weighing his words, like he always did. He smirked. "I don't get it. Your partner betrays you and you figure beating people up for coin will make it all better?"

Tavira wasn't just a partner. They'd both been orphaned after earthquakes had devastated a number of cities. The Wardens had rescued them, brought them to Tabarren and given them food, shelter and training. Tavira was the only other girl her age and they quickly became inseparable.

Kole shook her head. "I don't always win. Sometimes they beat me up instead, but it's a hell of a lot better than having to watch my back. Now, what do you want?"

"I need your help."

"With what?" Kole leaned back in her chair, crossing her arms over her chest."An assignment-"

"No." There was no point letting him continue. It would just be a waste of breath. She wasn't a Warden anymore and never would be. It was better that way.

Vaughn sighed. "What happened to you? You're not the same Kole I went through training with. I remember a time when the most important thing to you was living by the Code. Kole, protector of the innocent, defender of the common people. Now you won't even lift a finger to do anything but drink and fight. Have you really become so selfish?"

Kole narrowed her eyes. "I am not selfish. If anything, I did the Wardens a favour by leaving."

"How can you say that? Mason would have wanted you to stay. I wanted you to stay and so did everyone else."

Kole inhaled sharply at the mention of her old trainer's name. His death left a hole in her heart that had never healed. Five years later it still hurt as badly as the day he'd died. No, the day he was murdered. "That's enough." Kole stood. "I don't want to hear another damn word from you. Go back to Tabarren and find someone else to help you with this assignment. There must be dozens of Wardens who'd love to get out of the city for a while."

"Quinn requested you specifically," said Vaughn.

16

Kole snapped her gaze to his. "Why? She knows I left the Wardens."

"Yeah. I reminded her. I also told her I'd have to track you down and even if I found you, you'd probably say no. She said she didn't want anyone else but you. Besides," said Vaughn, "You owe her."

To say she owed Quinn was an understatement. She didn't just owe her some minor favour, she owed her life to Quinn. She was a master healer, highly respected among the Wardens. It had taken nearly every bit of Quinn's energy to keep Kole alive.

"What's the assignment?"

A triumphant grin crept across Vaughn's lips. He knew she couldn't say no. "She wouldn't give me any details. All I know is we're meeting her at the temple in Nareen. She'll explain then."

Kole leaned forward, forearms resting on the table. "One more job," she said. "I'll go with you this one time, but not because of you. I'm only doing it for Quinn. Once this assignment is finished, I'm gone and you have to promise neither you nor any of the other Wardens will bother me ever again."

"You have my word." Vaughn stood. "Meet me in the stables at first light. I'll have a horse for you by then."

Before Kole could say another word, Vaughn had disappeared among the tavern patrons.

∞

True to his word, as Wardens were supposed to be, Vaughn stood in the stables the next morning, saddling a beautiful bay gelding. Tethered nearby was an equally beautiful roan.

"Which one's mine?" asked Kole.

Vaughn turned. "I half expected you to skip town. Glad to know I was wrong. Maybe there's still a Warden in you after all." He tightened the cinch on the bay's saddle. "This one's yours."

She spotted the Wardens brand on the bay's rump. Clearly Vaughn had expected her to agree to the assignment and had procured a mount from the local Warden's Compound. He always was sure of himself.

Kole rubbed the bay's forehead absently. "Keeping one's word isn't solely a Warden trait. I don't like liars, so I make certain not to be one."

Once Vaughn finished with the bay, he grabbed a pack hanging from a nail in the wall and tossed it to her. "Brought you something."

Kole opened the pack. She pulled out a leather jerkin, tunic, and pants. It was her old Warden uniform she'd left folded up on her bed in the barracks when she'd left. "I'm not wearing this. I'm not a Warden anymore." Kole replaced the items, holding the pack out to him.

17

Vaughn shrugged but didn't accept the pack. "I can't make you, but you're acting in the capacity of a Warden. You should dress like one. You got a weapon?"

"A short sword and a few throwing knives, why?" She didn't need to ask. She already knew what he was thinking, so when he pulled the long, slender package from his horse's saddle and handed it to her, she was careful not to cut herself. She set the wrapped package on a bench. Her breath caught in her throat as she pushed the fabric aside to reveal the polished steel of her old sword. The Warden's hawk symbol was engraved onto the hilt, the metal worn away in places from so much use.

Vaughn stepped toward her, leaning against the wall. "I remember watching you practice with it years ago. You were one of the best. You picked it up like it was meant for you, like you'd known how to use it for millennia."

"And I remember it like it was someone else's life."

Kole ran a finger gently over the metal, checking the sharpness of the blade. Years ago, as she'd stood with the other Wardens in front of the giant bonfire, she'd cut her thumb on it as she spoke her oaths, promising to protect the innocent. Defend the weak. Speak the truth. And stand by her brother and sister Wardens against all threats, killing only when necessary. A blood Oath. The white, pearlescent scar still stood out against the tan of her skin.

Vaughn cleared his throat, pulling her from her thoughts. "We'll be travelling through some dangerous territory. I'd suggest you wear the uniform and the sword. Hopefully no one will think messing with a couple of armed Wardens is a good idea."

He had a point. Most thieves and bandits would take one look at them and decide to wait for an easier mark. Besides, Wardens weren't wealthy. If anything, they carried less of value than anyone else aside from the horses and their swords.

"Fine." Kole sounded like a stubborn child even to her own ears. "Just give me some privacy, all right?" She stepped into an empty stall with a wall high enough to hide her from view. Changing into the uniform was like putting on an old glove. She'd expected it to feel strange. Instead, it felt more natural than anything. Finally, she slid the belt around her waist, settling the sword into the scabbard. Kole stepped out of the stall, crossing her arms over her chest.

"Just like old times, huh?" Vaughn couldn't hide the smile tugging at his lips.

Kole rolled her eyes. "Don't get used to it. It's just one job."

"Let's head out. I want to be in Nareen before nightfall."

∽

Sunlight filtered through the trees dappling the forest floor with patches of light and shadows. The thaw had begun to set in, and little mounds of slushy snow still remained at the bases of some of the trees. Kole groaned as she dismounted her horse; her muscles ached and her lower back was stiff. She led the bay toward the bubbling creek, letting him drink while she removed her boots, slipping her swollen feet into the cool water. She sat on a flat rock watching as Vaughn scooped up a handful of water splashing it on his face.

Vaughn smirked. "You're going to be saddle sore tomorrow. See, this is what you get for leaving the Wardens. You get soft."

"Right. Pit fighting makes people soft." She rolled her eyes. "I just haven't ridden a horse in five years."

"It was a little surprising to hear you'd taken up pit fighting. I thought you left the Warden's so you could hunt Tavira down." Vaughn stood, wiping the water from his face with his sleeve.

Kole shrugged. "Pit fighting is the only way I can make coin to travel the country looking for her. Besides, it has the added advantage of keeping me sharp, and I don't have to stay in any one place for long."

Vaughn sniffed. "Do you smell that?"

Kole inhaled, catching the faint smell of smoke on the breeze. "That's not camp fire smoke," she said. She grabbed her boots, hurriedly slipping them on over her wet feet.

She grabbed her mount's lead. Vaughn followed. They mounted up and headed in the direction of the smell of burning wood mixed with something harsh and acrid. In the distance, a thin tendril of dark smoke rose above the tree line. Little specks of black dotted the sky. Whatever was over there had caught the attention of carrion.

Vaughn urged his horse into a gallop before Kole had a chance to suggest caution. He'd managed to get ahead of her and by the time she caught up, he'd reached a clearing. "Slow down," she said. "You don't know what we're walking into." How could he be so reckless?

"Someone might need help," Vaughn said. Of course. Vaughn. Ever the selfless Warden. How could she have expected anything less from him?

As they came around a bend the source of the smoke plume became apparent. An overturned wagon, now burnt down to nearly nothing, smoldered. Crows picked greedily at the corpses of two dead horses, both with arrows sticking out of their throats. The reek of death and waste and the copper tang of blood was thick in the air.

Vaughn dismounted and drew his sword in one fluid motion. Kole drew her own blade, the feel of the hilt familiar in her hands. It was as if she'd never been without the weapon. She crept around the other side of the wagon. More crows pecked at the remains of two burned

19

bodies, one too small to be an adult.

Kole drew one of her throwing knives, flinging it toward the wagon. The blade thunked into the wood, startling the crows enough that they took to the air, some landing in the trees above and others landing nearby, making tentative moves back toward the bodies.

Vaughn reached the corpses before Kole did. He knelt beside the bodies and closed his eyes for a moment, slowly shaking his head. Kole grabbed her knife from the wagon before stepping closer. The bodies were badly burned, but she could tell they were both female, one an adult and the other a girl probably in her teens.

Vaughn glanced up at her. "We won't make Nareen by nightfall. I can't leave them out here to be eaten by wolves and crows."

Kole glanced around. The terrain was dotted with stones, possibly enough to make a cairn large enough for two. "Keep the birds away," said Kole.

She gathered stones and brought them close to the bodies, and when she was too weary to continue, she traded places with Vaughn. By the time the cairn was finished, the sun was setting behind the mountains. Vaughn knelt beside the stones and offered a prayer to speed their souls to the next life.

With the remaining daylight, they found a clearing away from the burial site, several hundred yards downstream and managed a ramshackle camp.

"You think it was bandits?" Kole asked.

Vaughn pulled a few objects from his pack; bread, dried meats, and cheese folded in cloth. "Bandits aren't usually so brutal. Why kill those people? Why kill the horses when they could sell them? It makes no sense."

"We should have left town earlier." Kole moved closer to the fire. "Maybe we could have saved them."

Vaughn stared at her in silence for a time. As usual, he looked like he was carefully weighing his words. "We can't save everyone, Kole. We can only do our best. You couldn't have saved Mason or Emaria and you couldn't have saved the others. Being a Warden means you accept death. You accept that each and every one of us will die someday and you do your best to protect people with the knowledge that you're not a god." He handed her a piece of bread with some of the dried meat and cheese. Of course they weren't gods, but that knowledge didn't make it any easier to accept death, especially not the deaths of people she'd cared about.

Once they reached Nareen, they stabled the horses in the local Warden Compound. The sun was high in the sky and the city bustled with activity. Merchants crowded the streets hocking their wares, and the townspeople were eager to buy from them. Lush fabrics were piled high on a few of the carts; others boasted cures for every ailment imaginable and others sold fresh breads and sweets. Kole followed Vaughn through the throngs, weaving around people, trying to ignore the overzealous merchants.

The Temple of the Order of Caelon stood in the middle of the city so all roads led directly to it like spokes from a wagon wheel. The white stone towers stood like a beacon, offering hope to those who needed it. If an ailment couldn't be cured, the sick would come and pray to Caelon, begging her to save them.

"Why did Quinn come all the way to Nareen?" asked Kole as they neared the temple.

Vaughn shrugged. "She didn't say, but I think she was looking for more people with the Gift. There's always room for healers in the Order."

They reached the stairs of the temple. Unlit torches stood along both sides of the steps, leading up to enormous wooden doors, guarded on either side by Wardens. Vaughn stepped up to one, extending his hand. They clasped each other's forearms in the standard Warden greeting. "I'm here at Elder Quinn's request," said Vaughn.

The Warden nodded. "She's here, but good luck finding her. I'd try the library first." The Warden pulled the door open ushering Kole and Vaughn inside. The circular atrium was cool and silent aside from the fountain in the centre with its statue of the goddess, Caelon, carved from black stone. Containers of plants were placed around the statue and along the walls.

Kole's brows furrowed. "When did Quinn become an elder? She's only a few years older than I am."

"About a year after you left. After Tavira killed Elder Emaria, there was a vacancy. They chose Quinn for the position." Vaughn glanced over at her. "Sorry. I didn't mean to--"

Kole waved him off. "It's fine." It wasn't. Ever since Vaughn showed up in the tavern, she'd been forced to remember that night. She'd lost Mason, her trainer. A man who'd been like a father to her. She'd lost Emaria whom she hadn't known well, but who was so important to the Order that her death was devastating. And, she'd lost her closest friend. Tavira had gone from being her most trusted confidante, to being her most dangerous enemy.

They made their way in silence down corridors, passed rooms that served as living quarters for the healers and larger rooms that housed the ill. Luckily, every temple in every city was designed the same way and locating the library was a simple task.

Vaughn pushed open the door and they stepped inside. The scent of dust and books wafted through the air and small round tables dotted any space devoid of bookshelves. Sitting toward the back of the room, in front of a row of stained glass windows was a young girl with short, dark hair reaching just below her chin. She wore the same beige dress and leather sandals as the rest of the healers of the Order. She looked up from her books, opened her mouth to speak, but stopped when Quinn stepped out from behind a shelf with a stack of books in her arms.

Quinn smiled. She set the books on the table, then crossed the room, pulling Kole into a tight embrace.

"I was almost certain you'd refuse to come." Quinn looked her up and down "What've you been doing all this time? It looks like you've broken your nose a few times."

"Is it that obvious?"

"It's a little crooked," said Vaughn, "But I think it adds character."

Heat flushed Kole's neck and cheeks. "Can we please stop talking about my nose? Vaughn said you requested me for something, so here I am."

Quinn waved the young girl over. Closing the book, the girl stood and crossed the room. Quinn placed a hand on her shoulder. "This is Dove," said Quinn. "She's been training under me for a few years now and she's exceptionally talented, but I've taught her everything I can, which brings me to the reason I requested both of you. I need you to escort us to Tabarren. I've helped the Order recruit and train several healers, but it's time for me to go back and Dove will need to come with me."

Vaughn nodded. "Sounds like an easy enough assignment. Why not just have a few Wardens from Nareen take you?"

Quinn led them to one of the tables and sat down. "There's been trouble on the roads. Bandits have killed a number of people travelling between here and Tabarren. You and Kole are the best fighters the Wardens have ever seen and I don't trust anyone else to make sure we get to Tabarren safely."

Vaughn exchanged a look with Kole and it was clear what he was thinking. "We came across a burned out wagon on the way here. Whoever attacked them killed the occupants."

Kole glanced at Dove. The girl they'd found was about the same age as the young healer. "We'll get you both to Tabarren," said Kole. "I promise."

"We'll leave tomorrow, at first light," said Vaughn.

Quinn smiled. "I've arranged a room for both of you for the night. Supper will be at sundown in the dining hall. I'll show you to your room so you can get some rest before then."

∽∞∾

The dining hall was half full by the time Kole arrived. Dove and Quinn waved her over from a small table near the back of the room. Steam wafted from two trenchers of stew that had been set out for her and Vaughn and the fragrant, savoury scent of cooked pork reminded her how hungry she was.

Dove closed the book she'd been reading, setting it aside. "Where's Vaughn?"

"He went to check on the supplies. Better to get everything ready tonight so we won't have to worry about it tomorrow. He'll be here soon." Kole took a seat. "Are you ready to see Tabarren? It's huge compared to Nareen."

Dove nodded. "Quinn's made me read all about it. I memorized all of the medicinal plants growing around the city, but reading about them in books isn't the same as gathering them in the wild. Will you and Vaughn come with us when we look for plants? Quinn said the Wardens in Tabarren always protect the healers."

"Take a breath, Dove," said Quinn.

The girl spoke so fast Kole had to take a moment to process what she'd just said. "I'm not a Warden anymore, but I'm sure Vaughn will go with you."

Dove's brows furrowed. "But you're wearing a Warden's uniform and you're here with Vaughn, and you're taking us to Tabarren, so why aren't you a Warden?"

"Kole came because I asked her too," Quinn said. "We're old friends. She's doing me a favour, but she's not a Warden anymore and hasn't been for many years."

"Why?" asked Dove. "I mean, why leave the Wardens?"

"It wasn't where I was meant to be anymore."

Quinn set her spoon down on her bowl. "You were born to be a Warden, Kole. You had the compassion, the strength, and the will. You still do, and the Wardens would take you back in a heartbeat."

Kole shook her head. "I told Vaughn this was a onetime thing. Once you're both safely in Tabarren, I'm done."

"And what will you do then? Go back to pit fighting?"

Kole raised her eyebrows. "How did you–"

"Vaughn told me everything. He also said you're going to get yourself killed if you keep it up. Kole, please. Forget about Tavira and just go back to being a Warden. Stop running from something that wasn't your fault."

Kole let out a short, humourless laugh. "It was my fault. I should have seen it coming. It's my duty to find her and keep her from hurting anyone else."

"In all this time, all you've done is travel from city to city. Have you even come close to finding her or has this all been a means of running from your past? Tavira's betrayal wasn't your fault. Stop being a

23

coward and return to where you belong." Quinn's voice was pleading.

Kole slammed her fist into the table. "I am not a coward." She stood abruptly, her chair falling over and clattering to the stone floor. She turned and stormed from the room, nearly slamming into Vaughn as she turned a corner.

He grabbed her shoulders to steady her. "Slow down. Where are you going in such a hurry?"

Kole shrugged out of his grip. "I need some air. Quinn and Dove are waiting for you."

She brushed past him, grateful when she didn't hear the sound of his boots following her.

Kole hurried through the temple's corridors until she found the entrance, slipping outside where she discovered the sun had set over the village. She sat down on the steps, leaning against a pillar. This one last job was going to drive her crazy, but once it was over, she'd never have to worry about the Wardens again, or about Quinn requesting her assistance or Vaughn showing up at some tavern when she least expected it.

Moments later, the door to the temple creaked open, then closed. Kole rolled her eyes. Vaughn always had to meddle, always had to have the last word, but not this time. "I don't want to hear another damn word about Tavira or about Mason or Emaria and I sure as hells don't need to hear you tell me to let it go."

She turned to see Dove standing on the steps above her.

Kole sighed. "I'm sorry," she said. "I thought you were Vaughn."

Dove sat on the steps beside her. "You're hurt," she said.

"I'm not hurt. I'm just angry," said Kole.

"It's the same thing," said Dove. "Let me heal you."

The girl reached for her hand, but Kole jerked away. "I said I'm fine."

Dove hesitated, but grabbed her hand anyway. Warmth radiated up Kole's arm and buzzed all long her body. Dove closed her eyes, her breathing settling into a rhythmic flow.

"Close your eyes," said Dove. She sounded far away, like a voice calling through her mind. Kole realized Dove hadn't opened her mouth to speak the words. Sighing, Kole closed her eyes, but she could still see. It just wasn't the steps of the temple in Nareen she was seeing.

She was standing over Mason's bloody body in the Temple in Tabarren, kneeling over him, her fingers checking the pulse at his neck but there was nothing. There was the scuff of a boot behind her. "Go find a healer! Hurry!" Kole shouted, but before she could turn, she felt cold steel sink into her back, separating flesh. Pain shot down her arm. Kole stood, turning to find Tavira standing there with the bloody dagger in her hands.

"You killed him? Why?"

Kole's legs buckled and she dropped to her hands and knees. Warm blood spread along her back through the fabric of her tunic.

A look of sorrow flashed through Tavira's eyes, but she blinked it away. "I'm sorry. I didn't want to, but he got in the way and so did you. If you hadn't come here, I wouldn't have had to hurt you."

Tavira turned and stalked out of the room into the night. Kole felt her strength leave her. She gasped, pulling away from Dove, breaking contact. The vision dissolved, leaving nausea to rise in her gut. Hot tears streamed down her face. She turned to Dove and saw understanding in the young girl's eyes.

"I'm sorry," said Dove. "But you've kept it in so long it was wounding you from inside. You have to let it go." She spoke like a woman far beyond her years.

"It still hurts. Whatever you did changed nothing. You just ripped it open again," Kole spat, wiping at the tears dampening her cheeks. "You can't heal that. It doesn't go away until Tavira is dead."

"If Tavira dies, you'll find something else to chase. Vaughn and Quinn were right. You can't keep hunting her down. This isn't what you were meant to be. You were meant to be a Warden. To protect people."

Kole stood and Dove moved to follow her. "Just leave me alone! I don't know what you think you're doing, but stop," she snapped.

"I'm sorry," Dove stepped out of her way. "I couldn't just leave the wound unhealed."

Kole ignored her. She turned her back, heading inside the Temple; to the only place she could be alone for a while. She stormed through the corridors to the room she shared with Vaughn, brushing at the tears running down her cheeks. Relief flooded her when she found it empty.

Night had passed in a sleepless blur of tossing and turning, and Kole felt the lack of sleep even now, late in the afternoon. Tabarren wasn't far. The thaw had only just begun to take hold on the forests outside of the city, and while there was still snow on the ground, it was now a brownish slush. Water dripped from the tree branches like rain. The sun peeked from behind the tops of the trees. Just enough daylight for them to reach the city before darkness fell. Vaughn rode at the head of the group while Kole rode behind, keeping Quinn and

Dove safely between them.

Dove glanced behind her, slowing her horse to match Kole's pace. "I'm sorry about last night. I didn't mean to upset you. I only wanted to help you. Please don't hate me." Her voice cracked and her eyes were wide with worry.

Kole sighed. It was impossible to be mad at Dove. "I don't hate you. I know you were only trying to help, but next time you do that to someone, warn them."

Dove nodded. "I will. I promise."

Dove's horse hesitated, its ears perking and the whites of its eyes blazing. Kole slowed her mount, peering through the tightly packed trees. There was nothing she could see, but a horse didn't react to nothing. Something or someone was out there.

"Kole?" Dove's voice was thick with worry.

Kole spoke just loud enough for Dove to hear. "Get to the front with Vaughn. Now. Tell him someone's out there." Dove nodded, and didn't argue. She urged her horse forward.

The crunch of a boot in the snow nearby broke the quiet of the forest. Kole reached for her sword as an arrow slammed into her mount's throat. The horse screamed, rising up on its hind legs as another arrow pierced its flesh. Kole pulled on the reins to regain control, but the horse reared again. Arrows whipped past her, slamming into nearby trees, spraying bark into her eyes.

The horse lost its footing and started to go down. Kole jumped clear, landing hard in the slushy snow. Groaning, she pulled herself to her feet, drawing her sword. Vaughn's horse was down with arrows in its throat and so was Quinn's mount. Just like the horses they found with the wagon the day before. Quinn held the reins of Dove's mount as Vaughn helped her off the only horse still alive.

Shapes appeared through the mist, moving toward them. Kole backed toward Vaughn and the others, keeping her eyes on the advancing enemies. Another arrow whipped past Vaughn, slamming into Quinn's throat and dropping the healer to the ground. Dove screamed. She dropped to her knees, her shaking hands hovering over Quinn's wound. There was too much blood. Quinn released a final, shuddery breath and Dove screamed again, sobbing.

Kole swallowed back the bile rising in her throat. She counted no less than ten men emerging from the woods, swords drawn.

"Get her out of here!" Vaughn shouted.

"You can't take this many." She couldn't leave him. Vaughn was a well-trained warrior, but he couldn't handle ten men.

Vaughn drew his sword. "Getting Dove to Tabarren is the assignment, now do your job!"

Kole grabbed Dove's arm, pulling her to her feet. "Come on!"

Dove shook her head. "Please. Not without Quinn." Tears ran

26

down her cheeks.

"She's gone," said Kole, voice thick with tears she fought back. "Come on."

Kole dragged Dove toward the trees, away from the advancing men. The sound of steel clashed against steel, but as long as Kole could hear them it meant Vaughn was still alive.

∞

Kole and Dove ran toward a clearing up ahead. Before they could reach it, a cloaked figure stepped out from the trees, bow raised and arrow aimed right at Kole's chest.

"Kole?" The figure lowered the bow, then pushed back the hood of her cloak. "I thought you left the Wardens years ago."

"Tavira," Kole breathed. She pushed Dove behind her.

Kole kept her eyes trained on Tavira, and her sword at the ready. With her free hand, she slipped her dagger from its sheath and passed it to Dove. "I left so I could hunt you down."

Tavira smiled. "I'm right here."

"You killed Quinn." Heat rushed through Kole's veins. Her grip on her sword tightened. "Why?"

Tavira glanced at Dove. "Your girl is an exceptional talent. My men need a good healer. Quinn was in the way. Just hand her over and no harm will come to her. I need her skills, not her death."

"Run," Kole told Dove. "Follow the road."

She'd need to buy the girl some time. Without bothering to see if Dove had followed her orders, Kole closed the distance between her and Tavira, coming in close so she couldn't use her bow. Tavira threw the bow to the ground and drew her sword, slashing toward Kole's throat, the blade whistling past her neck. Kole blocked the blow with her blade. Their blades clashed and Kole's arms began to tire from the weight of her sword and Tavira's relentless onslaught.

If nothing else, pit fighting had hardened Kole and given her the stamina to fight longer, but her sword skills had suffered while Tavira's seemed to have improved. Tavira raised her blade, slashing downward, but Kole blocked the blow. She slammed her shoulder into Tavira's gut, knocking her to the ground. A move she'd learned while pit fighting.

Kole pulled her dagger, kneeling over Tavira, her knee pinning her sword arm. She held the blade against Tavira's throat, the edge nicking her flesh, drawing a thin trickle of blood. "You killed Mason," said Kole, her voice low, almost a growl. "You killed Emaria. You killed Quinn. Give me one good reason I shouldn't slit your throat and leave you for the wolves."

Tavira smirked. "You can't do it. I can see it in your eyes right now, Kole. You were never the strong one. You can't kill me."

Kole pressed the blade deeper, drawing a bit more blood. Tavira squirmed.

Tavira closed her eyes. "Do it then. It won't bring them back."

If Tavira dies, you'll just find something else to chase. You have to let it go. Dove's voice filled her mind.

"Do it," said Tavira.

She couldn't. She couldn't kill the woman she'd known since childhood. Dove was right. The pain wouldn't go away with Tavira's death, but maybe it would heal when she faced the justice of the court and they decided her punishment.

Dove's shrill scream echoed through the forest. Kole pulled her arm back, slamming her fist into Tavira's jaw hard enough to knock her out. Kole jumped to her feet and ran toward the sound of the scream.

Dove stood in a clearing on a frozen pond covered with a layer of slushy snow. Kole ran toward her, the sound of the ice creaking as she neared.

"Dove..." Kole said, her heart pounded in her chest. "Very very slowly, I want you to lie down on the ice."

Dove's face was red and streaked with tears. She nodded as she lowered herself to the ice.

"Good." Kole reached the edge of the pond and dropped to her hands and knees. "I'm going to crawl halfway to you and you're going to crawl toward me too, all right?"

Dove nodded again. She got to her hands and knees and crawled forward. Kole did the same. Suddenly, a loud creak broke the quiet. Dove froze. She looked at Kole, tears streaming down her face as she shivered.

"Keep moving toward me," said Kole. "Don't listen to anything but my voice."

Kole moved toward Dove, reaching for her hand. "You're almost here."

The ice cracked plunging Dove into the water from the waist down. She screamed. Kole lunged and grabbed her hand. "I've got you."

"Don't let go," Dove cried.

"I won't."

Slowly, Kole pulled Dove from the ice, backing toward the bank. When they reached solid ground, Dove collapsed into Kole's arms, sobbing. The snow crunched behind her and Kole turned. Relief flooded her as she saw Vaughn, leading Dove's horse toward them.

Blood dripped from his nose and off his chin; he was covered in cuts and scrapes. Vaughn dropped the horse's reins.

"We have to go back and find Tavira. I hit her hard enough to knock her out for a while, but she won't be down for long."

28

"She's gone," he said. "I spotted boot prints in the snow."

Kole closed her eyes. "I had her. I could have killed her, but..." She glanced down at Dove, still shivering in her arms and the words died on her lips.

"Doesn't matter," said Vaughn. "You saved Dove. That's all Quinn wanted, now let's get her to Tabarren."

Kole nodded, grudgingly, and helped Dove to her feet.

꩜

The taverns were often packed after a good pit fight, and tonight was no exception. Judging by the conversations of the nearby patrons, it had been one to see. Kole stared at the thin cut on her index finger right beside the scar from when she'd taken her oaths the first time. She rewrapped the alcohol-soaked cloth around it and sipped her ale.

It had been four days. Quinn's funeral had drawn the attendance of nearly the entire city of Tabarren, but the loss still weighed heavily on Kole. Dove had thrown herself into her training as a means of distracting herself from the loss, always engrossed in her books or searching out medicinal herbs outside the city walls. Vaughn, too, had found ways to keep himself busy sparring with other Wardens or taking simple assignments within Tabarren.

Just as she emptied her mug, someone placed a full one in front of her. Kole looked up as Vaughn pulled out a chair, taking a seat across from her.

"I heard they let you back in," he said. "Quinn would be happy to know you're wearing the uniform again."

Kole sighed. "I wish she could have been here." She unwrapped the bandage and held her finger out to Vaughn. "I took my oath this afternoon."

Vaughn reached for her hand, drawing it closer so he could see her finger better. "You went a bit deep, didn't you? It almost needs to be stitched."

Kole shrugged. "I figured it would stick this time, if I cut a little deeper."

"It better." Vaughn grinned. "I can't have my new partner breaking her oaths."

Kole raised her eyebrows. "You want me to be your partner? After everything that happened? Even after I left the Wardens?"

Vaughn leaned back in his seat. "It takes a strong person to do what you did, Kole. You had Tavira right where you wanted her, but you gave up on your vengeance in order to save Dove. I trust you with my life and I know we can work well together. Now it's up to you. Do you accept?"

Kole leaned back in her seat, crossing her arms over her chest, the hint of a smile playing at her lips. "I'd be honoured."

Nix - C. P. Roelke

"Why don't you tell us a story, little lass, I hear you've inherited your father's silver tongue," Jarl Destin inquired of me as our hunting party trotted through the forest. We had just finished coursing a stag and were headed back to the Jarl's mead hall. Our party included the Jarl's two sons, Oliver and Balin, some bondsmen, and my brother Germaine. I sat behind my brother, my arms wrapped around his waist, the only female of the group. Leaning back a bit so I would not be speaking into Germaine's back, I addressed the others in the party.

"This is a story my father used to tell us when we were children," I disclosed as I began. "There once was a woman who lived by herself in a small house near a pond. Every morning, when the woman would go out to gather water, she would see a beautiful white horse drinking from the pond. One day the woman approached the horse, and holding out her hand, she patted it as it nuzzled against her. From that day on they became friends, spending each morning together at the pond.

"After a few years the woman found herself a husband. She brought him to meet the horse and that was the last time she saw it. Every morning thereafter, when she would go to gather her water, the banks of the pond were empty. One morning, while his wife was at the pond gathering water, the husband chopped firewood near their house. Stopping to wipe the sweat from his brow, the husband looked up to find the horse standing nearby, staring at him. Enchanted by its gaze he stood motionless as it walked towards him, slowly shifting from the shape of a horse into that of a radiant, unclothed woman. When she reached him she gave him a bewitching kiss and beckoned for him to follow her. He followed her to the banks of the pond and out into the water.

"As she gathered her water, the woman saw her husband walk out into the water and disappear beneath the surface. Unable to swim, she stood on the banks of the water calling his name, but he never returned. Distraught, she threw herself to the ground and bitterly wept herself to sleep. Waking in the middle of the night, she saw the light of the moon reflected on the surface of the pond, beckoning her. She stood up and began to walk out into the water until it pulled her under, hoping to find her husband again on the other side," I finished and a somber silence fell over the party.

"That is a most woeful story, little one," Jarl Destin uttered,

31

breaking the silence.

"I had forgotten about that story, Lynd," Germaine murmured so only I could hear.

"Let's hear more about these girls that spend their time walking around unclothed. You wouldn't happen to be one of those girls, would you Lynd?" The Jarl's younger son, Balin, asked, leering at me. Blushing at the uncouth remark, I dropped my eyes to the ground.

"You spend entirely too much time thinking about unclothed girls and not enough time actually finding yourself one," Jarl Destin retorted, eliciting a few snickers from some of the bondsmen.

"Father, do you hear that?" Balin's older brother, Oliver, interjected as the pound of hooves sounded somewhere nearby.

"It's moving closer, ready yourselves, it might be another stag," The Jarl said in a loud whisper. We waited in silence, tensed for action. A moment later a horse, with silvery-white hair that seemed to shimmer in the sunlight, galloped out of a nearby thicket directly in front of Jarl Destin. The Jarl's horse reared at the sudden commotion, bucking the Jarl from the saddle. He landed in a heap on the ground, surrounded by stamping hooves. The two horses danced around, kicking at each other, their hooves pummelling him. After a few furious seconds of fighting the Jarl's horse cowered back and the white horse galloped on its way. One of the bondsmen jumped down from his horse, hurried over to the Jarl, and tried to help him to his feet.

"Get off," Jarl Destin shouted and pushed himself to his feet, one of his arms dangling by his side with an unnatural bend. "Bastard broke my arm. Whoever brings me that horse will be given the honour of drinking from my cup at tonight's feast."

"I shall get it for you, father," Oliver said and spurred his horse to a gallop, chasing the silvery steed. Balin, Germaine, and a few of the bondsmen followed suit and I gripped my brother tightly around the waist to prevent myself from toppling over backwards at the sudden burst of speed. We kept the pace for a full quarter of an hour until we reached the mouth of a small seaside cavern. Oliver had pulled up and dismounted where its opening was hidden among the rocks on the beach.

"It went inside. I will go in after it, the rest of you wait here to take it should it get past me," He ordered the party of horsemen that had gathered around him, including my brother and Balin. Then he handed the reins of his horse to one of those still mounted and disappeared through the mouth of the cave.

"If it does come out without you, I will capture it and take the glory for myself, brother, be warned," Balin shouted after him. The jest elicited a few chuckles from the other men. "Well, you heard him, form up."

At his word, our party formed a half-circle around the opening of the cave, ropes at the ready. We waited like that for the better part of an hour, at which point the tide had noticeably risen.

"Should we go in to look for him, Balin?" My brother asked as a wave washed over the horses's hooves and through the mouth of the cave.

"Let us wait a bit, Germaine."

"But the tide is coming in; if he is inside during high tide he'll likely drown."

"My brother is a capable man. You watch, any moment now he'll come flying out of this cave atop that white horse, like Mani being pursued across the night sky."

Another wave rolled past us into the cave, and when it receded again the body of a man floated out with it, face down, giving the lie to Balin's statement. The body was pinned along some rocks, bumping into them with a soft slap every time a ripple flowed through the water. My brother jumped down off his horse and splashed his way across the knee deep water to the body. When he reached it, I saw him turn the body over and inspect its face. Letting out a wail, he dropped to his knees, the water covering him to his waist, and frantically shook the body by the shoulders. Goosebumps ran across my skin at the sight and I felt my mouth go dry.

"Is it..." Balin began to shout, but his voice faltered.

"It is your brother," Germaine shouted back, his voice cracking with sorrow. He stood up and began to pull Oliver's body across the water towards us. As they neared us, I could see Oliver's dark hair floating aimlessly on the surface of the water, like dead seaweed. He had purple bruises on his neck, but the rest of his skin was ashen. At the sight I felt a surge of bile rise up and burn the back of my throat, but I swallowed it back down; it was the first time I had actually seen a corpse. Balin and a few of the other men jumped down into the water and splashed across it to meet Germaine. I stayed atop Germaine's horse, frozen in place from shock.

"Lash him onto my horse," Balin instructed the others. I watched the men lift Oliver's body up out of the water and pull him across the back of his brother's horse, face down, and lash him with leather straps. When that was finished, Germaine climbed back up in front of me. His eyes were red at the edges and I saw a pair of tears roll down his cheeks and drip off his chin. The Jarl's sons were his constant companions; he thought of them as brothers, and now one of them was dead.

Balin spurred his horse away from the cavern and back towards home. The rest of us followed behind him in somber silence. Hoof beats and the increasingly distant wash of waves onto the shore were the only sounds that accompanied our ride inland. The sound of our arrival brought a crowd out of the mead hall, including the Jarl and the

33

rest of his family. Balin dismounted from his horse and walked towards his father.

"Father, my brother is dead," He bawled.

"What? Did you say my son is dead?" Jarl Destin asked, his voice full of incredulity.

"Aye, father."

"How? That's impossible. Not a man such as him, his little finger has more fortitude and spirit than you possess in your entire body."

"I don't know how it happened, father."

"How don't you know, you were there weren't you? Aren't you good for anything? Bring me my son and let me look upon him."

At his command my brother and several men from our party got down off of their horses, unstrapped Oliver's body, and carried him to the front of the mead hall. They laid him down on his back at his father's feet. His mother, Asta, let out a wail and some of the others who had gathered gasped when they saw his face. Dark purple splotches striped across his throat in what appeared to be a handprint. His eyes bulged out of his head like those of a squeezed fish, bloodshot and glassy. He had seemingly been strangled to death.

"Who did this to my son?" The Jarl bellowed.

"I told you, father, we don't know," Balin croaked, his voice cracking with emotion.

"Then tell me what you do know," Jarl Destin demanded and Balin relayed what we witnessed at the cave.

"Well, it's obvious then, isn't it? Someone, or something, in that cave murdered your brother," The Jarl said to his son, and then cast his gaze upon the rest of us. "The man who brings me the head of whoever did this shall be given all the property Oliver is leaving behind and will be named my successor upon my death. Now, let us return to the feast, I have much drinking to do."

"But father, with Oliver gone I'm supposed to be next in line," Balin protested.

"If you want it you'll have to prove your worth, because right now all I see is a spoiled little weakling."

Jarl Destin led most of the crowd back into the feast, but a few of us stayed behind, including my brother and Balin. A pair of bondsmen dragged Oliver's body away to be prepared for his funeral. When they disappeared into the gathering darkness, Balin turned to my brother.

"On the morrow I intend to return to the coast to avenge my brother's death," He said and added with a mutter to himself, "and show my father the kind of man I truly am."

"My axe is yours," Germaine replied.

"We ride at daybreak," Balin said, grabbed his horse by the bridle, and walked off towards the stables.

"I'm sorry, Germ," I whispered to my brother, calling him by my

34

pet name for him.

"So am I, little sister, so am I," He replied. I could hear the sorrow in his voice and it made my heart ache for him.

"Do you want to go to the feast?" I asked, lamely, unable to think of anything to say to console him.

"You may if you wish, but I must return home and prepare for tomorrow."

"I don't want to, I just thought you might. Let's go home."

We rode Germaine's horse back towards the coast to our home. It was a seaside turf house built by our father years before either of us was born. As a young man our father left his homeland and their dishonest Jarl behind to search for a land ruled by someone he could have faith in. His search ended when he met Jarl Destin and they became fast friends. Our father became one of the Jarl's retainers and made him wealthy through his many maritime trading voyages. A few years ago he died at sea during a storm. As he was returning home from one of his voyages the waves dashed his boat against the shore, destroying it. Now the two of us live in the house with only our mother.

When we arrived at home, Germaine took his horse around back to stable it and I headed inside to make us up some supper. As I was placing a pot of leftover fish stew on the hearth to reheat, my mother walked up behind me.

"Back so soon? I thought you would still be at the feast."

"We didn't go to the feast. Oliver was murdered tonight. Germ and Balin are headed out at dawn to bring his killer to justice."

"Oh my... Asta must be devastated. A mother outliving her son is a terrible thing, especially one as full of life as Oliver. Where is your brother?"

"He's stabling the horse."

"How is he taking it?"

"He's sad. I could hear it in his voice."

"Do you think he wants to talk about it?"

"It's Germ, mother, of course he doesn't."

"He's always been long-suffering, just like your father was."

Early the next morning, when it was still dark out, I was woken by a noise. It took me a moment to figure out what had woke me up, but when I realized it was the sound of my brother's footsteps as he walked out of the house, I jumped up off of my sleeping mat and dressed hastily. I ran out of the house and when I found Germ he already had his jerkin and axe on and was saddling his horse.

"Go back to bed, little sister, you're not coming along."

"Yes I am."

"You're not going into that cave with us; you don't even have an axe and armour."

"I won't go in the cave, but I'm still coming along."

"And do what, stand outside and wait for us?"

"Precisely, I intend to stand vigil for you outside that cavern."

"You're being ridiculous, Lynd."

"I don't care."

"You're terribly stubborn, you know that?"

"It certainly runs in the family."

"I suppose it does at that. Fine, get up here then, it is time we are on our way," He sighed as he climbed up into the saddle and held a hand out to me. I grabbed him by the wrist and he pulled me up and set me down behind him. We rode slowly, but steadily through the darkness. We reached the edge of the Jarl's property as the sky was just beginning to lighten on the horizon. Balin sat atop his horse, waiting for us.

"What are you doing here, little one?" He asked when he saw me.

"She's going to stand vigil for us," My brother answered for me.

"Aren't you kind-hearted."

"Thank you," I replied and hid my face behind Germ's shoulder as my cheeks reddened.

"Let's be off, shall we?" Balin asked, but did not wait for an answer, and spurred his horse to a gallop toward the coast. We took off after him, keeping close behind, galloping the whole way. When we reached the cavern we slipped down from our mounts and my brother and Balin gathered up their gear.

"There is some fodder for the horses in the saddlebags and a bit of dried meat you can have too. If we aren't back out by the sundown, go straight to Jarl Destin and tell him what happened. Understood?" Germaine demanded of me.

"I understand," I replied.

"Wish me luck, little sister."

"Come back to me, Germ," I breathed, reaching up and wrapping my arms around the back of his neck. Then I pulled his face down, gave him a quick peck on the cheek, and let him go. I stood there and watched them disappear through the mouth of the cavern, then sat down on a rock to wait. All day I sat there and stared into the shadows of the cave, but the pair did not return.

During the evening, when the tide began to come in, I searched around for a safe place to go with the horses. Eventually I found a ledge high above the sea. It was just large enough to hold the three of us and I led the horses up to it by way of a steep, narrow path. Sitting with my feet dangling over the edge, I watched the tide come in and prayed fervently that it would not fill the cavern and drown my brother. The water stopped rising about halfway up the full height of the cavern. Hopefully that was not high enough to drown someone as tall as Germaine. As I continued my vigil, the rhythmic lap of the waves against the shore combined with my early awakening to lull me to sleep as the sun set beneath the sea.

An indeterminate amount of time later I was woken up by the whickering of a horse. I opened my eyes and found myself in moonlit darkness, confused as to my whereabouts. It took me a moment to remember where I was and why I was there, but when I did I sat up, careful to avoid the edge of the cliff, and rubbed the sleep out of my eyes. When my vision adjusted to the darkness, I looked around to check on the horses and let out a surprised scream that I quickly stifled out of fear.

The horses were bedded down on a small patch of weeds that had fought their way up through a crack in the rock. In the space between the two horses stood another horse, the silvery-white one we had chased to the sea the day before. It shimmered with an eerie whiteness, as if one of Mani's steeds stood before me. Even its eyes were white, looking like a pair of giant pearls, and they appeared to be staring straight through me and into the depths of my very being.

I sat there, frozen, overcome by an indescribable fear. It was just a horse, so it should not frighten me, but there was something wrong about this one, I could feel it. The beast took a step forward, its hoof making a sharp clack against the flat rock. I scooted back a couple of inches and it took another step closer to me, so I scooted back again.

This continued for several feet until I felt my fingers slide over the edge of the cliff. Panicking, I stopped moving and folded my knees to my chest, trying to make myself smaller. The horse took one more step, its nose stopping within an inch of my face. It pierced me with its pearlescent gaze and I could feel the hot breath from its nostrils blasting against my cheeks. After an eternal moment, it lowered its head and nudged me in the chest with its nose, pushing me past the precipice. I felt myself go into a free-fall and snatched at the rock face with my hands, scrabbling to latch onto something, anything. Rocks banged against my wrists and hands. One of the stones sent a sharp pain shooting down one of my fingers.

Finally, after a few frightening seconds, my fingers tangled in the roots of a weed sticking out of the side of the cliff, stopping my fall. I took several deep breaths, and then looked around to assess my position. I was approximately one-third of the way down the rock face. The quickest way to safety seemed to be to climb back to the top instead of going the rest of the way down, so I began the ascent. Making sure to scope out each handhold thoroughly, I made slow and steady progress. My arms burned from supporting my weight for so long and every time I pulled myself up with my right hand I felt that sharp pain shoot through my finger again.

When I finally made it to the top, I pulled myself up over the edge with shaking arms and collapsed onto my back, breathing heavily. As my breathing slowed I sat up and looked around. The white horse was gone, but the other two were still there, sleeping. My little finger on my right hand throbbed and I had trouble bending it, but I did not have enough light to see how bad it actually was. I walked over to the horses and lay down between them for warmth, curling my body around my injured hand. The fright and exhaustion caught up to me and I wept myself to sleep.

Something jostled me awake and I opened my eyes to see that the sun was now high in the sky. Germaine's horse stood over me, its face near my chest. Balin's horse had disappeared. The horse bumped me in the chest with its nose, indicating that it wanted some fodder.

"I'm awake, I'm awake," I moaned, pushing it away and standing up. My finger still throbbed so I took a look at it. It was very swollen and purple. I tried to bend it, but the slightest movement shot bolts of pain up my hand and wrist. Digging through the saddlebags, I grabbed a few handfuls of fodder and tossed it to the horse, and then I pulled out some dried meat for myself. As I broke the night's fast I sat at the edge of the cliff and watched for Germaine and Balin, but they still did not return. When I finished eating I climbed up onto Germaine's horse and rode inland to Jarl Destin's longhouse. At the door to the house one of the Jarl's retainers, Carr, halted me. He was an unkind man that had been bitterly jealous of my father's relationship with Jarl Destin.

"And where do you think you're going, little one?" He asked.

"I have an urgent message for the Jarl."

"The Jarl is sleeping off his mead, doesn't want to be disturbed."

"This is urgent, I need to see him now, Carr."

"I've told you to get out of here once; you'll regret making me tell you twice. Piss off."

"But it's about his son. He might be dead."

"He knows about his son's death, he's..."

"No," I said, cutting him off, "Not..." His hand lashed out and smacked me across the face, stopping me mid-sentence. My eyes watered at the sting in my cheek.

"If you don't move along immediately I will give you another."

I pulled on the reins, turning the horse about, and took off at a gallop. Speeding back towards home my mind raced as I desperately tried to figure out what to do next. By the time I made it to the house I had determined a course of action. I hopped off the horse, ran into the house, and opened a small wooden jewelry box that sat next to my sleeping mat. The box contained a small silver brooch with a sliver of sapphire in the centre, the kind of thing most girls my age would love to possess. While other girls braided flowers into their hair and giggled as they watched boys spar, I preferred to cut my hair short and join the sparring, but the brooch was an exception. It was the last gift my father gave me before he died, bringing it back for me after a months-long

38

trading voyage.

I pinned the brooch onto my hair and ran out of the house, snatching up an old jerkin of Germaine's on the way out the door. My mother shouted something from inside the house, but I did not stop to listen. I hopped back onto the horse and hastened into the nearby village and pulled the horse to a stop in front of a smithy. The blacksmith was in the midst of dousing the fire in his forge when I walked into his stall.

"Just closin' up shop for supper, sorry lass," The blacksmith explained when he saw me.

"Please, I need some equipment tonight. I can pay well," I begged.

"What with, exactly?" He asked, giving me an appraising look that seemed to indicate that he found me wanting.

"I'll give you this," I said, unpinning the brooch and holding it out to him. He grabbed it out of my hand and examined it closely.

"What are you looking to get for this?"

"Just an axe and a dagger."

"Wait here," He said, walked off, and rummaged around in a corner. A few moments later he came back carrying a rusty axe and a dagger.

"That's it?" I blurted.

"'Tis the best I can offer ya, and a generous offer at that. The misses has her name day comin' up and she would be happier'n a sow in slop to get that brooch to show off 'round the bale fire."

"You can't give me anything else?"

"It's a fine dagger. Sharp too. The axe's better'n nothin'. What ya see is what ya get. Take it or leave it."

"Fine, hand it over," I huffed and snatched the equipment out of his hand when he held it out to me. Walking out of his stall I stuffed the axe and dagger into a saddlebag, and then climbed back onto the horse. Spurring it to a gallop, I rode at a break-neck pace back to the seaside cavern.

Outside the mouth of the cave I hitched the horse on the highest ground I could find, pulled my equipment out of the saddlebag and donned it. Germaine's old jerkin was too big for me; hanging down past my knees, but it would have to suffice. I lit a torch I found among Germaine's things in the bags, said a quick prayer, and entered the cave to find my brother.

Wading through thigh deep water, I worked my way into the darkness. Progress was slow because I had to fight both the resistance of the water and the heaviness of my armour. Everything about the cave was wet. Water ran down the walls in dark rivulets. Moss grew across the ceiling, shiny with moisture, and dripped water down upon my head and shoulders. It even smelled wet; in much the same way the air does on a drizzly autumn day, but with an added hint of salt and rotting fish. As I moved deeper into the cavern the passage became shorter and narrower until I was crouched down and shuffling sideways, water up to my chest. Germaine and Balin must have had an incredibly difficult time getting through that part of the passage.

I squeezed through a small opening into another segment of the cave and found that I had much more space, so I stood up. As I did so I felt something brush the top of my head. Looking up I saw a man's corpse hanging above me; I had bumped into its feet. The thought of its dead, clammy skin against mine revolted me, but I had to know who it was, so I reached up and pulled the body down into the water with one hand. Water splashed against me, making my torch sputter for a frightening second, but it did not douse the fire completely. I plunged my hand into the water, grabbing the corpse by the hair, and tried to pull it to the surface. Its scalp came free in my hand and I quickly dropped it, heaving. My breakfast came up and floated atop the water. When I recovered, I grabbed the body under the armpits and pulled it up. Examining the face closely, I determined that it was not my brother or Balin; just some unknown victim of whatever dwelt in the cavern.

Moving on, I continued into the depths of the cave. I began to hear the sound of rushing water which became louder the deeper I waded into the darkness. Walking around a bend, I entered a large cavern with an opening in the ceiling. A waterfall poured through the opening and down into a deep, inky-black pool. Moonlight shone through the opening, casting an ethereal glow onto the waterfall. I felt like I was seeing the moon weeping into the maw of Hel: it was breathtaking.

Looking around the cavern for any signs of my brother I saw two men chained to the wall. I ran over to them as fast my legs could carry me, stumbling on my jerkin the whole way. When I got to the wall I saw that the two men were Germaine and Balin. They were chained at the wrists and ankles in a standing position, completely naked. Both of them were unconscious.

"Germ! Wake up," I shouted, shaking him, but he did not open his eyes. The roar of the waterfall made it impossible for me to hear if he was still breathing, so I watched his chest. I saw it rise and fall shallowly. Casting about for something to break the shackles with I glimpsed something emerging from the dark pool at the base of the waterfall. I froze in place out of fear.

A head broke the surface of the water and continued to rise until a naked woman stood before me, waist deep in the pool. Her long, silver hair hung down over her breasts and water cascaded down her body in shimmering rivulets. She was gorgeous. Stepping out of the pool she walked towards me, singing a beautiful melody. I tried to back away from her, but I tripped on the edge of the jerkin and crashed to the ground, sprawled on my back. When she reached me she dropped to her hands and knees and crawled over me until we were face to face. She stared into my eyes, our lips only inches apart, and continued to sing her melody. A silver choker that was wrapped around her neck appeared to glow with its own light and glinted off her eyes, making them blaze. The intensity of her eyes frightened me and I tried to scramble away from her, but I bumped into the wall of the cavern. She gave me a surprised look, and then slid a hand up along my thigh.

"I see," She mused and her features began to melt and reform until I was staring into the eyes of the most beautiful man I had ever seen. He started to sing a serene melody and I lost myself in the shining pools of his sapphire eyes, aching with the desire to taste those lips that were so maddeningly close to mine. Arching my back, I felt a tickle as the edges of our lips brushed each other. He slid a hand up to my neck and stroked the side of it with a finger, then his gaze went hard and he clamped his hand over my throat, cutting of my air.

I panicked, breaking out of the trance he had me in, and grabbed his wrist, trying to pull his hand away from my throat. He had an iron-clad grip that I could not get to budge an inch. Reaching down to my waist I groped around until I found the hilt of my dagger. Wrapping my hand around it, I slipped it out of its sheath, and plunged the blade into one of his eyes. He let out an ear-rending scream, lifted me a few inches off the ground, and dashed my skull against the stone floor with a sickening crack. Sparks of lightning flashed across my vision and my body convulsed, trying to throw up, but my vomit was held back by the hand wrapped around my throat. His grip tightened and I thought I felt something pop in my neck. Desperate to get him to let go before I suffocated, I clawed at his face with my fingernails. His skin was so wet that my fingers slid down his cheeks to his neck. They caught on the silver choker as they slipped down his neck, pulling it away from his body.

Suddenly I could breathe again. I gulped air, each breath burning my throat like a searing wind. Coughing, I sat up and looked around the cavern, wondering what had happened. The man was gone, but the silvery-white horse that had pushed me off the cliff stood cowering in the corner. It stared at me, whinnying and stamping its hooves against the stone, one of its eyes bleeding profusely. My dagger sat on the ground at its feet. Trying to figure out why it was so fearful, I looked down at myself and saw that the silver choker was tangled between my fingers. I held it up to examine it more closely and the horse whinnied louder.

"Quiet down you stupid horse," I rasped. The horse stopped whinnying. I looked at it again, still cowering in the corner, but it was doing so silently. Getting an idea I spoke again. "Come to me." The horse began to walk towards me.

"Stop," I commanded and it stood still. "Stay there."

41

Pushing myself to my feet I walked over to Germaine and Balin. Their shackles had released and their bodies were lying on the hard, wet ground. I dropped to my knees next to Germaine and tried to shake him awake. As I was trying to revive him, something solid bashed into the back of my skull and my whole world went black.

I woke up in some sort of sick bed with Germaine standing next to it, holding my hand. My injured finger had a fresh binding lashed around it. A deep, dull pain throbbed at the back of my head.

"Hey there, Germ," I whispered to my brother.

"Oh Lynd, thank heavens. I was afraid that you would never wake."

"Thick-headedness runs in the family, as you know," I said with a smile.

"What were you thinking, coming after us like that, little sister?"

"When you didn't return I tried to speak to Jarl Destin like you told me to, but they wouldn't let me in. I didn't know what else to do."

"Well it's a good thing Balin broke free of his shackles or all three of us would be dead right now."

"What do you mean?"

"That creature in the cave, whatever it is, was about to kill you, but Balin escaped his chains and stopped it before it could finish the job. They seem to think the silvery steed is some sort of shape shifter. Balin claims it can be controlled by a collar or necklace or something of the like. He also said he found this in the cave, told me he saw you holding it," Germaine explained as he set a sheathed dagger on my lap. "Where did you get that?"

"But..."

"But what, little sister?"

"That doesn't make any sense."

"What doesn't?"

"The whole thing. I found you and Balin shackled in the cavern with the creature. It attacked and I accidentally pulled the necklace off. Somehow that freed you from the shackles, I think. Then...then everything went black."

"You probably just dreamed it."

"It wasn't a dream, Germ."

"You're sure?"

"I'm sure."

"Odd," Germ intoned, seemingly lost in thought.

"What?" I asked.

"Oh, it's probably nothing. Get a little more rest. We're going to a feast in Balin's honour this evening," He informed me and walked out of the room.

That night we attended the feast at Jarl Destin's mead hall. My mother forced me to wear a dress instead of my preferred shirt and pants. Germaine and I sat at the end of the head table with the Jarl's family. Early on in the festivities I saw Germaine and Balin move off into a corner of the hall. They appeared to have a heated conversation, and then Germaine stormed back to the table with a scowl on his face. A few minutes later Balin called for silence in the hall and stood in front of the head table, facing his father.

"Kith and kin," He shouted, "This is a most bittersweet occasion; bitter because we are still in mourning over the passing of my brother, who was murdered a few days past, and sweet because his murderer has been brought to justice. Oliver has been avenged."

The crowd cheered his words.

"So in honour of my brother, on this, the day of his vindication," He continued, "I would like to put said justice into my father's hands."

Balin held the silver choker out to Jarl Destin who accepted it and stood up.

"My son is most honourable, is he not? Now, to the dancing," The Jarl announced and music began to play. Pairs of men and women began to form up at the centre of the hall, twirling about the floor. Germaine leaned in close to me and whispered in my ear.

"Let's go, while they're distracted by the dancing."

"What, why?" I asked.

"I'll tell you outside. Quickly now," He replied, stood up, and walked to the door. I hopped up and chased after him. Outside, at the stables, he climbed into the saddle of his horse and then pulled me up behind him.

"What's going on, Germ?" I asked.

"I confronted Balin about what happened in the cavern because of what you told me," He replied. "He admitted the truth of what you said. It seems he knocked you out inside the cave so as to take the glory himself. He also told me he intends to take you as his wife, as retribution for wronging you. It has apparently already been arranged with mother, but I'm not going to let that snake have you. We're leaving this place tonight."

"I'm so sorry, Germ, I didn't mean to put you in this position."

"Don't be, little sister, don't be."

We rode out of town in silence. When we had covered several leagues, Germaine pulled the horse to stop in a scrub of trees on the outskirts of a forest. As we were setting up camp for the night we heard the thunder of hooves somewhere nearby.

"Get behind me, Lynd," Germaine commanded as he gripped his axe. I did what he asked and we stood there in a tense silence, waiting. A few moments later several mounted spearmen, led by Balin, formed up around us.

"Where are you taking my betrothed, Germaine?" Balin asked.

"Far away from you," My brother replied.

43

"Why, might I ask, would you do something so foolish?"

"Because you were a brother to me and you betrayed us," Germaine bellowed. "I won't let her be beholden to a man like you."

"You must understand; I couldn't let my father hand what rightfully belongs to me over to someone else. This way I keep what is deservedly mine but your sister still gets rewarded for her bravery. Now why don't you return with us and we'll forget about this little lapse in judgement."

"Never."

"If you come back with us now I will keep my promise to you and wed her, but if you continue in your obstinacy I will be forced to break my promise. In which case I shall wed my brother's widow and take your little sister for some sport on the side. I will have her one way or another. You choose."

"Over my dead body."

"It pains me to hear that, but it shall be as you wish."

Balin signalled to the others with a wave of his hand and they closed in on my brother, stabbing at him with the spears. Germaine swung his axe, cutting the heads off of a pair of spears, but a second pair struck true, catching him in the thigh and shoulder. He grabbed the one stuck in his thigh and pulled on it, yanking its wielder to the ground, and then buried the blade of his axe into the base of the man's skull. Another spear came at Germaine's head, but he parried it with his forearm.

As I rushed towards the fray, intending to fight alongside my brother, I felt someone snatch me under the armpits and pull me across a saddle. Twisting my body to see who had grabbed me, I found myself staring up at the face of Balin. He held me pinned against the saddle in front of him with one hand and worked the reins with the other. We were galloping away from the battle, back towards the Jarl's estate. I looked at Germaine and saw him take another spear thrust to the chest. I screamed his name and tried to wriggle off of the horse, but Balin held me fast. Then we went around a bend in the road and my brother disappeared from view.

Desperate to help my brother I struggled with all the strength in my body to try to break free from Balin's grasp and a few seconds later heard something pop. Balin grunted and yanked his hand to his chest, releasing me. I slipped off the horse and crashed to the ground in a heap. Hopping to my feet I drew my dagger and whirled around. Balin halted his horse and turned to face me, cradling one of his hands to his chest.

"You're more trouble than you're worth," He hissed and used his uninjured hand to pull out his axe. Holding on with nothing but his knees he spurred the horse forward, swinging the axe at me. I spun to avoid the blow, slashing my dagger toward him at the same time. The

44

axe grazed my shoulder, slicing it open, but I felt my dagger catch on something solid a moment later. Balin screamed and toppled from his horse, his axe skittering away across the dirt. The hand that had held it hung limply, blood flowing freely from its wrist.

"What did you do?" He whined. "I can't move my fingers."

"Your tendons were severed, most likely. No need to worry though, you'll bleed out in a few hours and it will no longer be a problem."

"Lynd, please. Don't let me die like this. Show me some mercy, I beg you. End it quickly," He whimpered. I picked his axe up off the ground and strode over to where he lay.

"A swift death is too good for you," I spat and walked over to where his horse was stamping around. Grabbing its reins, I patted it on the neck until it was calm, then climbed up into the saddle and sped back up the road to help Germaine.

"Please, Lynd. Please," I heard him wail as I rode around the bend in the road.

Back at our camp I leaped off the horse and sprinted into the fray. Germaine had dispatched all but two of the spearmen, but he had been pierced by several more spear thrusts. A large hole in his chest sprayed frothy blood every time he let out a breath. He had managed to unhorse both of the spearmen, but they had him backed against a tree. Running up behind one of the spearmen, I buried Balin's axe between his shoulder blades and kept running towards the other spearman. When I reached him I lowered my shoulder and tackled him to the ground, knocking the spear out of his hands. I rolled away and as I was pushing myself back to my feet I saw Germaine decapitate the spearman with a single blow of his axe. Germaine fell back against the tree and slid to the ground.

"Germ!" I screamed and ran up to him. "Are you okay?"

"Never been better, little sister, just need to catch my breath," He coughed and blood flowed down his chin.

"We'll just wait for you to catch your breath, then we'll finish setting up camp, okay?" I chatted, trying to sound reassuring, but the hot tears streaming down my cheeks belied the truth.

"Why don't you go on ahead? On the other side of this forest is a town. Just follow the road. You can wait for me there. I'll catch up to you on the other side," He gurgled, his eyes beginning to lose focus. I leaned forward, kissing him on the forehead.

"See you on the other side, Germ. I love you," I whispered and climbed into the saddle of his horse.

Vows of the Penitent – Thomas Atwood

Water dripped from the ceiling of the cave, its constant patter the only sound that broke the reverent silence of the crypt. Alric descended the stone stairs, blind to the statues of ancient kings that stared down at him. His fathers and forefathers, men who had all ruled the countryside for miles around, inspected him as he descended to the basement. Alric felt shame and disappointment burning into him with each step he took, and the still monuments seemed to be glaring in anger as the stone door to his wife's tomb creaked open.

A massive gargoyle loomed over the coffins, its mouth frozen in a permanent scowl. Two alabaster coffins, barely larger than a footlocker, flanked a massive granite monument. A woman's slumbering form was carved with immaculate care, showing every strand of hair, every freckle of the woman who lay there. Alric stood over the statue and gripped the woman's cold stone hand as tears ran down his cheek.

"My dearest Caitlin," he whispered, it's been seven years, yet I still feel your loss every day. Erik would have been a knight by now, and Eagon would have been your loyal page, running the house for you. If I had just been there, if you had me to protect you..." Alric sank to his knees, weeping openly as his tears fell like rain on the cold stone. Age's old guilt overwhelmed him, wrapping around his neck like an anchor. A lump formed in his throat at the memory of past events and he couldn't bring himself to gaze at her stone visage. He opened his mouth to beg for forgiveness, but the words couldn't leave his tongue. He was lost, of no use to anyone. How could he protect anyone when he let his wife and sons die?

A figure behind him cleared its throat, and Alric turned to see his brother Aegon standing at the door of the tomb. A flowing white beard hung around his knees, and faded brown robes covered his bent frame as he hobbled over to Alric.

"Begging your majesty's pardon..." he started, but Alric held his hand up, silencing him.

"I am no king. Do not address me in such a manner."

"How shall I address you then? You control the last bit of land that hasn't been burned, desecrated or twisted for Morgana's amusement." The monk walked over to the crypt and set a hand on the monument.

"I remember when you first brought her here. Many thought you were mad, you know. A knight from an ancient line of Kings marrying a no-name, low ranking noble from across the channel. We thought she was some sort of enchantress. Still, she was the only who could still that temper of yours or bring a smile to your face after a long campaign." He nodded as he walked away. "She was a good woman."

"What is it you wish of me, Aegon?"

"I wish for you to come with me, brother. There is something you must see."

"It can wait."

"It cannot. The world does not stop while you weep, brother. There are important matters to attend to, important decisions to be made."

"Than make them. You are the elder brother, so rule."

"I cannot; you know the law as well as I. Only a man who can wield a sword is able to sit on the throne. You passed the tests of knighthood; I did not. Besides," he said with a huff as he plopped himself down on the stairs, "I bloody well don't want to. Call it the virtues of growing older, but I've reached the age where all I want is a good ale, a pretty lass, and to wake up the next morning. You'll be there in a decade or so, if you're lucky. Now come with me, we need to discuss the Morgana threat."

"There is no Morgana threat. Her armies lay banished far to the north. They may have managed to kill Arthur, but that does not make them a threat."

"No, it just means that every knight and warrior has retreated to defend their homeland, letting her pick them off one by one. The danger is closer than you think. Riders have come from the Riverlands."

"What?" Alric stated, turning in surprise as he raised a single eyebrow. "What do you know?"

"Do I look like a wizard? A man who can just pluck answers from the air? I ran to find you as soon as I heard, and you've been sitting on your arse this entire time! Come," he commanded, struggling to ascend the steps.

Alric scowled and followed his brother. The two emerged from the crypt just in time for the midday sun to shine down on the emerald fields surrounding them. Two horses, one as black as night and the other white as opal, stood next to each other. Gleaming steel barding lay on the two, with a verdant flag displaying a gold, two headed snake on either side. Alric vaulted onto his horse, as his brother struggled, cursing and flailing to mount his. The two rode off, horses breaking into a run as they crested down the hill. They rode in silence, the wind rushing through Alric's platinum hair and goatee.

A massive plume of smoke greeted them. It rose, foreboding over the horizon, twisting and coiling like a massive, ebon snake. Flames rose from countless houses, consuming like a thousand hungry mouths. The air ran rancid with the smell of burning and desecrated corpses, and Alric rode into the town square, shock running through him as he surveyed the carnage. Everywhere they went, they were greeted with the pungent smell of human waste and scorched flesh.

"This...this is impossible," he whispered, struggling to come to terms with the devastation surrounding him.

"Inevitable you mean. Without a strong leader to hold the nobles together, Morgana has been running unchecked. Her armies are vast; she can't be stopped by a few dozen men and soldiers. The people need a hero, a symbol." Aegon gasped as he looked in the centre of town. A pile of bodies lay stacked there, the rotted and burned remains of the dozens of men, women and children the army slew on their way through the village.

"They need something to believe in," Aegon stated, tears welling at the deplorable sight.

A single scream echoed in the night, causing the brothers to turn. A woman struggled to run forward into a blazing building, barely held back by the two men who stood next to her. A young boy screamed and wailed for his mother, a massive beam of wood separating them.

"Come!" Alric shouted, rushing toward the building. Fire blazed inside as he leapt over the debris and dirt that stood in front of the entrance of the house. Hot air surged into his lungs, making each breath he took a struggle. Flames licked at his arms and legs, leaving bright red burns. Ignoring the searing pain, he wrapped his arms along the wooden beam that separated him from the child. With a yell of defiance, he pulled, struggling to yank it out of the way. Time after time he struggled as the conflagration threatened to consume him. Each struggle, however, was fruitless as the beam remained where it was.

"Brother! Get out of there!" Aegon's frantic voice cried.

"I won't leave a child to die! Go, get everyone else to safety!"

Sweat poured down the man's face, and the smoke cleared for an instant. A silvery light appeared at the end of the hall, and as Alric watched, his wife and sons seemed to walk through the smoke. Bathed in pale light, they smiled at him, waving and cheering at him as he struggled. They beckoned Alric to them, and as the last ounce of strength seemed to vanish from Alric's limbs, he smiled, eager to join them.

A shattering thunk echoed through the beam, and Alric looked in shock as his brother struck the beam of wood with an axe. Aegon's axe descended on the wood time and time again, each time tearing into the barrier.

"Brother?"

"Some men fight with their strength, others choose to use their wits," he said, arms trembling as he struggled to hack through the brittle wood. "Besides, if you choose to risk your fool life to save a peasant child, I can't very well just stand there and have you make me look the coward." He handed his brother an axe, and the two struggled to cut the beam away. In a manner of seconds, the beam was cut in two and fell out of the way. Alric rushed forward, scooping the child in his arms as the ceiling collapsed around him. He ran out of the building, setting the child on the ground as he and his brother collapsed, panting under the effort.

"Thank you, oh thank you milord," the peasant woman sobbed, hugging him as he pulled himself to his feet. Alric simply nodded and watched as they raced away, taking one last look at their destroyed homes.

"Your heroics are rubbing off on me," Aegon said, struggling to pull himself off the ground. "In my sixty years on this earth I have never worked so hard." Alric ignored him, staring out at the devastation as he rubbed his eyebrows. "What the hell were you thinking? You could have been killed!"

"Were you willing to stand by and watch that child die?" Alric grumbled in response. "This was all my fault."

"Really? Was it your sword that cut these men down? Was it your torch that set these homes ablaze?"

"You know it wasn't., but my blades weren't there to stop them." Alric sighed. "I should have been here."

"We have one hundred men and maybe six knights under our command. We would have made little difference." Aegon sighed and laid his hand on his brother's shoulder. "Brother, our father decided to give up our kingdom, and join our fate with Uther's. When your family died, you insisted we separate from the realm." Alric opened his mouth to argue, but Aegon held up a hand, stopping him. "I understand your motives. Serving Arthur took you away from your family, and you believe that if you were home you could have protected them. I understand why you did that, but brother, look around you. How many lives are being lost while we do nothing?"

"It's not that simple. If I order my men to fight, they could join the fallen, along with their families."

"Morgana is already killing any who stand in her way. She's already to the Riverlands. How long until she marches on Camelot? Once she's finished with them, what's to stop her from attacking us? We'd be facing one army, with countless men, who control territory on all sides of us. There's a word for that: surrounded."

Alric set his jaw, a stubborn glare lighting in his eyes like a campfire.

"At least consider my words brother," Aegon pleaded.

"I will consider them. At home." Alric looked around in disgust, fingers running through his platinum hair. "There's nothing more we

49

can do here."

The ride home was uneventful, with neither brother willing to risk the other's anger by mentioning the day's events. Finally, the iron gates of Dragonclaw came into view, causing Alric to smile at the sight of his ancestral home. A magnificent scarlet dragon lay on the tallest tower, its still body sitting with Alric's father's sword still driven into its heart. The walls were made out of black steel, and no army had ever successfully breached the walls of Dragonclaw.

Alric rode down the cobblestone streets, waving his hand in greeting to his subjects who swarmed from their homes. Pikeman clapped their fists to their breastplate, and peasants surged the streets, spilling flower petals on the ground in front of them. Children clamoured over themselves all to catch a gaze of the Lord of the city and cried in delight when they did. Alric boomed with laughter as his people swarmed around him, offering food, roses and wine. He turned down all offers but greeted each man and woman with a smile.

Alric and Aegon stabled their horses and walked inside the castle. A serving maid walked over to them, a nervous smile on her face.

"Ah, Emir," Alric said, giving her a wide, beaming smile. "It's good to see you again. Please track down the stable hands and have them see to my horse. Also, tell the kitchens to have a meal ready. I'm famished. Some of that bread they baked earlier this morning, perhaps, roast boar, and ale. As much ale as they can find."

"I'm...I'm sorry, milord..."

"Don't be sorry. If we're out of ale, than some of the wine should do in a pinch," he said, giving her a friendly wink. The young woman trembled, her emerald eyes staring at the ground as she backed away. "Is something wrong? What frightens you?"

"A man rode in while you were gone," she stuttered. "He's taken over the household and demands to see you."

"Who is he?"

"He didn't say. He wears armour. as black as midnight and has a hanged man on his shield. He threatened us, milord."

"Gregor," Alric grumbled, glancing at his brother.

"Always nice to have a house guest even if it is Morgana's lap dog," Aegon quipped.

"Where is the man now?"

"He's in the banquet hall milord."

"Good work, child," Aegon said as Alric rushed to the hall. A large man sat at the head of the table, leaning back in the rosewood chair reserved for Alric. A roast boar lay in front of him, and he ripped the meat from the animal with his bare hands, letting the juice drip down his chin as he indulged himself. He tore into the assembled feast of bread, meat and stew like a man at his last meal. He wiped the food from his armour. as he saw Alric walking up, chuckling at the sight of the old knight and running his fingers through his sandy red hair.

"Alric, the twin-fang," he said in greeting, not bothering to stand. "I helped myself to some of your fine hospitality. I hope you don't mind."

"I mind you terrifying my household," Alric grumbled.

"Your household moves too slowly and lacks the proper respect." A serving woman walked by, setting a tray of food in front of Gregor. A large, crimson welt covered her eye and she whimpered as she backed away.

"My lessons caused no permanent damage," he assured.

"You come into my house without invitation. You command my staff, and beat my servants. What have I done to deserve such dishonour?"

"No dishonour intended, old man," he stated, wiping his hands on a linen cloth as he stood. "I come with a message."

"What message is that?"

"Morgana is pleased with your split from Arthur. Your forces withdrawing has made it easier to take this land despite it being done for poor reasons. I've come here to welcome you into the fold."

"And what does that mean exactly?"

"We're sacking Camelot," the burly knight stated, a massive grin on his face. "Our forces are already marshaled, and in a matter of time we will have conquered her. The largest city in Albion will be ours. We will be kings. No one will dare challenge us. We will have what we want, when we want it. No more codes and honour. Gold, treasure, women, land, anything your heart desires friend. All with the most powerful spellcasters this world has ever seen backing us up. We will be masterless men, free and unfettered."

"Masterless men," Alric scoffed. "You mean dogs, fit for little more than the table scraps that Morgana wishes to throw to us."

"You will have to bend a knee before the rightful queen, yes."

"The rightful queen? What makes her that?"

"She was Uther's firstborn."

"And she was so deranged and power hungry that even Uther would acknowledge her claim," Alric replied, a smirk crawling across his face.

"You served a man who pulled a stone from a boulder! Yet you care about her claim."

"I served Arthur because he was noble and true. He offered justice to these lands."

"We will give the same justice, old man."

"I have seen the justice you give!" Alric shouted, slamming his fist down on the table. "I have seen the bodies, stacked toward the heavens, and discarded as if they were nothing. I have seen the flames consume the innocent merely because they had something you wanted. Your army is a plague across this land. You claim you

51

offer justice yet I see nothing but evil and oppression. You sicken me."

"You dare speak to me in such a tone!" Gregor shouted, standing bolt upright and casting the chair to his side. "Do you know who I am? I have killed countless of your precious knights. I have caused an ocean of their blood to flow from the end of my axe. I have crushed their skulls, split open their torsos, and placed their heads on the top of my wall. You dare insult me, sir?"

Alric moved until he was standing within an inch of the other knight, a confident, knowing smile on his face. "Please give Morgana my regards, and tell her that it is my deepest regret that I will not be joining her crusade. I doubt my wife would have approved of the alliance."

"Fine. Foolish old man," Gregor snapped, lifting his battleaxe from the ground. "Pathetic. You refuse your chance for glory because a harlot would disapprove."

Alric stopped, fury boiling through his veins as he glared at Gregor. "What did you say?"

"I said your wife was a harlot, and your children were motherless dogs. They deserved to be slaughtered, because their weak, pathetic excuse for a father wasn't there to protect them. How did it feel, sir knight, to walk into your dining hall and find their corpses littering the ground?"

Alric reached toward his waist and in a single motion pulled both swords from their scabbards. Ailing hands creaked and pain shot through his knuckles as he gripped them tight. Weariness still settled on him from the day's excursion. Still, despite the trappings of age, strength and purpose flowed through his old bones at the feel of them. Memories of a thousand battles flowed through him, and he glared at Gregor, hate burning in his eyes.

"Draw your weapon, knight," he hissed in command.

"Have you gone daft?"

"Hardly. You are not leaving this castle alive, and I will not have it said that I butchered you. Come at me with your axe, fool, and we'll see which of us is pathetic."

"You have no armour., nothing to protect you when I split your skull like a melon. All you have is your two tiny blades."

"I need no armour. to protect me, and these tiny blades have seen more combat than you can dream of. Come at me, coward. I will take your head to the gates of Camelot. I will cast it down before all of Morgana's men, so they know that the best warrior she can find was slain by a weak, old man."

Gregor shouted as he ripped off the leather protecting the head of the axe. He stomped toward Alric, fire burning in his eyes as he swung the weapon as if it weighed nothing. Alric watched, unmoving, both weapons pointed at his opponent, waiting. In a flash, the axe split the air, the swings causing the air to chime as they cut through the space between them. Time and time again he struck, but each time Alric danced out of reach, just a hair's breadth from his enemy's blade. Gregor howled in fury and swung the weapon down with inhuman power. The weapon struck the stone where Alric was mere moments ago. The head of the axe shattered stone, sending grey dust flying through the air like a cloud.

Alric spun like a dancer, cutting through the gap in the man's greaves. Blood flowed from the wound, and in an instant he cut open the man's other leg, sending him crashing to the ground. Gregor howled in pain as he struggled to rise from his knees, looking at Alric in fear.

"You fought bravely," he said, wiping the bead of sweat from his brow. "No matter what can be said of you, you gave it your all. Sadly, patience is a gift given only to those with experience."

"Are you going to keep your promise, knight?" Gregor jeered. "Are you going to use my lifeless body to mock my countrymen?"

Alric sighed. "No, those words were spoken in anger. You will be laid to rest, given the proper rituals, and I pray you will have some measure of peace."

"You're pathetic," Gregor sneered. "What kind of weakling shows honour to his enemies?"

Alric gave a shout, sending his weapon straight for the man's neck. The sound of shattering bone filled the air as the sword cut a large hole into his neck. The weapon swung repeatedly, eventually cutting through the last remnants of the man's neck. His head rolled across the floor, and Alric sighed as he wiped the blood from his blade.

"I do not do it for you," he said, staring at the lifeless head. "It is something I do for myself."

"I see our guest was rude," Aegon quipped, staring at the lifeless body in front of him."You do know this will have repercussions."

"I'm aware," Alric stated. "Have the priests remove the body, and give him the proper rites."

"Of course. But what now? Shall I have the knights ready themselves and marshal our forces?

"No, but fetch my armour.," Alric commanded a nearby servant who ran to obey the command. The duo walked to Alric's chambers as servants followed, carrying pieces of his armour. in tow.

His brother stared at him, stunned as his squires dressed him in his armour. Alric watched in the mirror, and nodded at his squire who raced away.

"So what's your plan?"

"I go to Camelot. I find the witch, and I kill her."

"That's...that's a bad plan, my friend."

"It's the only one we have."

"Let our men stand beside you! Send our knights! Send me with you!" Aegon stood in front of him, barring his way. "It's suicide if you go."

"Perhaps, but if I send our men, they will be killed. If I go alone then maybe I can bring some peace to this land."

"You're my brother," Aegon replied, tears streaming down his face. "I don't want you to go."

"I have to."

Aegon clapped his brother on the back and slunk out of the room, giving his brother one last glance before he ducked away. Alric sighed and walked over to the portrait hanging on his wall. His wife and sons, immortalized forever.

"Hello, my darling Caitlin," he whispered, the wind flowing through the window, as if in response. "I'm sorry. I've used the grief of losing you to hide away from the world. I've let everything turn to ash around me. I wish I could have been there to protect you from those brigands. I wish I could have seen my sons grow up and known the men they would have become. I know you must be ashamed of me, wherever you are. I will make it right, my love. I will make everything right."

Alric walked out to the stables, mounting his horse as he squirmed uncomfortably. The armour., which once felt like a second skin, weighed down on his old bones. With the flick of his reins, the horse bolted down the cobblestone streets, racing toward Camelot.

The days seemed to pass in an instant, but Alric didn't dare to slow down. He rode through the day and night, taking precious few moments to rest his horse, his eyes ever-focused on the horizon, looking for the tall spires of his destination. Horse and rider were both exhausted, with sweat coating his old stallion's mane. Still they rode, racing through the countryside like the wind, cutting through towns, cities, and around castles with a mad fervour. On the fourth day, Alric found the once proud spires of Camelot. He let out a small sigh of relief as he saw them, and frowned as he closed near the gates.

The heads of old friends lay impaled on spikes across the battlements, a look of shock and grief frozen on their rotting faces. Knights dangled in iron cages, their emaciated bodies shaking at their restraints fruitlessly. Men in leather masks grinned with sadistic glee as they jabbed at them, piercing their skin with dull spears. Alric rode to the front gate, only for two men to cross spears in front of him and glare up.

"I'm here to discuss the Lady Morgana's proposal. Announce me," he commanded.

"Who are you?" one of the men hissed.

"Lord Alric of Dragonclaw, keeper of the north, steward of the Riverlands, and champion of the king."

"Former king," the man corrected.

"As you say. Now announce me, before I leave your desiccated corpses to announce my presence."

The two men walked off, leaving Alric to hitch his horse outside the gate. He walked down the familiar city streets, frowning at what the city had changed into. Men in armour. dragged screaming women from their homes, only for their companions to toss lit torches inside, causing the home to erupt in flame. The thriving market was no more, and trade stands were tossed aside, leaving the stench of rotting food to waft from the streets. Craftsmen, once offering a smile and hearty greeting, were chained to their tables, their bleary-eyed gazes not bothering to look up from their work. Men stood in chains, heads hung low, as they were marched to the headsman's block. Soldiers, who once stood tall and proud, were stripped to their waists, filth covered rags displaying skin marred with dozens of cuts and bruises. Alric watched in shame as the Headsman's axe crashed again and again on the condemned man, finally managing to saw through the poor man's neck. He'd kick the body aside, and gesture for the next in line.

The nearest man in line caught Alric's gaze, and he gasped at the site. Kay, the king's brother, walked with them, a proud and surly look still on his face. He refused to walk forward, only for the guards to descend on him with clubs. Alric pushed the men aside, blades pointed at them as he walked over to his old friend.

"Alric," the man gasped. "What...what are you doing here?"

"Saving your life, it would seem," Alric returned, beaming at him. He turned to the guards, a savage scowl on his face. "Free this man at once. Fetch him proper clothes, armour., and his weapon."

"This man stands convicted of treason against the queen. You can't just..."

"Oh I can, and I will," Alric stated, pointing his sword at the man's chest. "Do you know who I am, boy?" The man nodded nervously. "Good, then you know I am here to surrender my lands and my service to your queen. So you will see us to the castle, you will have my friend fed, clothed, armed and armoured. He is also going to swear his service to the queen."

The man's face turned deathly pale at the sight of the armed Alric, fidgeting as he unfastened Kay's restraints and leading them into the castle. The pair navigated the halls, finally coming to a small chamber. Alric heard Kay give a sigh of comfort as the servants led him to a cramped bathing room, closing the door behind them. Alric watched as he stepped out, a frown on his face as a plate of bread and fruit was slid in front of him.

"I won't surrender to that witch, Alric," he stated, tearing a hunk of bread off with his teeth.

"I know, old friend."

"If you decide to serve her, be warned: I plan to kill her today, along with anyone who stands in my way."

"I figured as much, and we are twin in purpose. That is why I rescued you."

"Do you have a plan?"

"A ghost of one. Morgana is a proud woman. She will be intent on mocking us before she accepts our service. With a bit of luck, the time will present itself for us to strike."

"You're serious? You plan to kill Morgana in her own throne room?"

"Unless you have a better plan."

Kay let out a loud, merry laugh as he clapped his friend on the back, his other hand gripping his warhammer tight. "We are madmen, old friend. Madmen with a desperate plan."

"Indeed," Alric stated, returning his friend's smile. "I fear we will not live to see the morrow."

"Just as well. What man desires to live forever?"

The pair waited, and after several long moments a servant walked in, bowing her head at them. "The queen will see you now."

They nodded, and walked down the familiar path to the throne room. The round table where friends had once congregated to share ale and food was split in two. The chairs that surrounded it were piled unceremoniously on top, and a low flame flickered as the monument was slowly consumed. The plaques, indicating the place settings of the noblest men Alric had known, were nailed into the wall. Desecrated corpses hung beside them, the swinging bodies of the knights they served with.

Alric barely managed to hide his disgust as Morgana stepped into the throne room. Her lips curled into a smile, her fingers running across the stone as she gazed at every tapestry and piece of art with a satisfied grin. She stared out with a face as beautiful and cold as a winter storm, her magic keeping her youthful despite the years. Everything from her robes to the gemmed rings on her fingers spoke of opulence, and her ruby lips spread in a greedy grin as she saw the throne.

"It's mine; it's finally mine..." she whispered, running her fingers over it as if it was an old lover. "Finally, everything I've been owed is mine." Two men in armour. flanked her as she sat down, surveying the throne room.

"You were around in the days of Uther, weren't you, Alric?" Morgana asked, a mocking look levelled at the knight.

"I remember very little, your grace," Alric paused, waiting for the doors to close. "I was barely a squire when Uther died."

"Did you ever think you would kneel before me?" she asked, leaping up to walk a hairs breadth from him.

"I did not, your grace."

"Of course you didn't," she said, scoffing. "No, you and your knights would rather follow a boy whose only qualification was pulling a sword from a bloody boulder than serve me. A woman could never hold power in your eyes. I was the firstborn, I was the rightful heir, and all of this should have been mine!" She hissed each word like a coiled serpent as she walked away from him.

"Uther wouldn't let me inherit, however. He felt the kingdom was too wild to be ruled by a mere woman. Well, look at this woman now. I've killed anyone who ever stood in my way, burned their kingdoms to ash, and scattered their bones to the four winds. Tell me, Alric, what do you think? Should I have been the heir instead of Arthur?" She spat Arthur's name out like a curse, watching the old knight's reaction carefully.

"I do not think you wish to hear my answer to that, your grace," Alric replied, watching as Kay moved to a nearby pillar. The queen gave a curt nod, and her soldiers sealed the heavy wood doors.

"Why is that?"

"Because I think you are a spoiled, horrible witch. You believe strength gives you the right to rule. You believe that because you slaughter peasants and spill the blood of honourable men, others should fear and respect you. Arthur ruled with compassion and wisdom; every man from the lowest peasant to the highest lord lived in peace and dignity under the man's rule. You will turn Albion to nothing more than a graveyard, and I will be damned if I let you rule for one second longer."

Morgana reeled back as if she was slapped, and with a fearsome howl, Kay slammed his warhammer into the nearby guard, caving in his breastplate. Morgana spun, eyes mad with rage at the betrayal. Alric pulled his blades at the distraction, cutting both guards' throats in the blink of an eye. Blood flowed from both men, staining the floor a brilliant crimson. Alric stood in front of Morgana, a slight grin on his face as he pointed his weapon at the sorceress.

"I'm afraid we've misled you, your grace," he stated, the last words a cruel jest. "I trust you are not too displeased."

Morgana snarled in response and merely flicked a finger in the direction of Kay. A blast of wind erupted from her, slamming into Kay hard enough to send him flying through the stone pillar. He struggled to rise, but golden restraints formed in the air, binding him.

"Stay," Morgana hissed. "I'm impressed. I wouldn't have expected such deception from the noble Knights of the Round Table."

"If it makes you feel any better, my lady, I've been retired for some time now."

"And you've emerged from retirement to die by my hand. I've been waiting a long time to kill all of you."

"Best be hurrying then. I'd hate to delay your triumph."

"Burn," Morgana commanded as white hot flame emerged from her hands. Alric rolled across the floor, and grabbed one of the guard's shields. Flame met steel, turning the metal red hot. Alric grunted as the steel burned into his arms, sizzling as it began to peel his skin away. The smell of melting flesh filled the room gagging him. He pressed forward, ignoring the heat of the flame, and his struggle to breathe in the hot air. He pressed forward until he was within arm's reach of Morgana. With a mighty cry, he slammed the shield against her. She rolled, the skin on her face sizzling and blackened as she howled in pain and rage. The perfection of her beauty was marred by blackened and burnt flesh. Alric drove the shield down at her, but she narrowly dodged.

"Alric Twin Fang using a shield. Will wonders never cease?" she asked, conjuring a gleaming, silver sword from the air.

"A man must add some variety to his life, otherwise it tends to get dull."

"That life ends today, old man!"

"If all my enemies have is a touch of flame, I believe I will live to be a ripe old age."

"Fortunately that is not all I possess!" Steel clashed against steel, and the two danced across the throne room. Alric knew every inch of the castle, every column and every piece of stone. He led Morgana into each, his swords moving with blinding speed. Morgana's speed and youth began to overpower him, however, and he cried out in pain as the woman cut a narrow gash in him. She cut him again and again, her sword always finding the chinks in his armour. With sweeping strikes, she cut at the leather straps in his armour. until the steel clattered along the floor.

"Is this all you have, old man? I had hoped for a bit of a challenge," Morgana gloated as she tossed his breastplate away with the flick of her sword.

"I am a bit rusty," Alric admitted. He groaned in pain as her sword bit deep into his shoulder. The razor cut the skin on his arm, but his eyes gleamed with fire despite the pain. He grabbed the woman's sword and tossed her. She flew into a pillar, and his fist struck her again and again. Bone shattered under Alric's assault, and her blood began to flow as he struggled to keep her pinned. Her sword lashed out, biting deep into his side, and cutting through his torso. Alric collapsed on the ground, barely holding onto consciousness as he pressed against the wound, frightened as the scarlet liquid fled his body. He stared, helpless, as Morgana walked over to him, chuckling.

"For a moment, you had me frightened, old man. You hit stronger than your age would have me believe," she said, wiping the trail of blood away from her skin. "Still, you could never defeat me."

"I already have, my lady," he stated, choking on each breath.

"Why is that? Do you think history will remember any of this? What do you think history will know of Arthur and his knights after I have ground you and the others into dust?"

"They will know that few stood against many and that the righteous stood against the wicked. You have already lost, Morgana. You are merely prepared to kill to achieve your ambitions, while I..."

Morgana snarled in frustration at the man and thrust her sword deep into his chest. The weapon dragged against Alric's sternum, and he used the delay to catch the blade. Morgana thrust forward with all her strength, determined to kill the knight. Alric gathered the last of his strength and yanked the weapon from her hands.

"While I am prepared to die for mine," he whispered, ferocity lining every word. He pressed his hand to his chest, desperate to stop the bleeding as Morgana collapsed to the ground. Alric limped over to where Kay lay pinned, and grinned in relief as the restraints vanished from him.

"We did it, old friend," he croaked, victory and relief gleaming in his eyes.

"We did it," Kay agreed. "Come, we must get you to the healer."

Alric nodded, but his legs gave out, sending him collapsing to the floor. He moaned in pain as he struggled to rise. His body refused, however, and the last of his strength began to flee his body. A white haze covered the world, slowly encroaching on his vision of the throne room.

"I fear....I fear it is too late for that," he whispered, each word a struggle, each breath a laborious effort.

"Nonsense," Kay replied, holding his friend's hand. "You are going to get up. You're going to get up, the healer is going to stitch you, and you will continue to serve for many decades."

"I cannot obey that command...old friend..." Alric whispered, leaning his head against the cool floor.

"Yes you will!" Kay shouted. "You will get up now! You cannot die!" Tears flowed down Kay's cheeks as he shook his friend, desperate for him to stand up. "Please. I need you."

"You do not. You will be fine without me." Alric gripped the man's hand fiercely, looking up into Kay's sapphire eyes as they glistened with tears. "I leave the realm in the hands of a great man." A spasm of pain wracked through him, and he cried out.

"Promise me one thing," Alric asked, his voice barely a whisper.

"Anything."

"When I die, lay me in my family's tomb. Don't bury me beneath the stone of the castle with the other knights. Let me be with my family where I belong."

"I promise," Kay said, prompting Alric's lips to curl into a smile. The white haze covered everything, and in the distance he heard

Caitlin's voice calling. He looked and found his wife in a magnificent white robe, her ruby hair flowing like flame and her smile beaming with the same light it always had. Erik and Eagon played near her, Erik swinging his makeshift sword and Eagon with his books cradled carefully in his arms. Alric reached out to them and breathed his last.

Wren in the Mist – Beth Hammond

Betrayal

Thomas didn't mean for it to happen. The bleak afternoon stood frozen as he knelt over the dead bird's body, a small brown wren. If he'd listened to her, no, if she'd believed him. "Nothing," that is what he had to give.

"Why did you have to stay? Why couldn't you just leave me alone?" His words were soft and anguished. But he was more hurt than angry. You could see it in the set of his shoulders, the way his hand trembled as it hovered over the little wren's body.

A cold wind picked up but he didn't feel it. He stared at the bird for a long while, rocking rhythmically. His hand moved to the pocket of his ragged coat. Even that small solid object he'd carried with him for years gave him no comfort. Nothing could now. She was gone, and with her, hope.

"You should have listened to her." A hard voice sounded from behind.

Thomas turned to the tall thin man standing over him. He was dressed in a grey robe too thin for the chill in the air. His thick black hair and beard rustled in the breeze, and his eyes struck Thomas hard, as they looked him over searchingly. Thomas didn't stand. He nodded and looked back at the bird. He swiped his sleeve across his face and sniffed. An arrow pierced her middle; a small trickle of blood seeped from her beak. Her lifeless eyes stared into the air, and he could swear her expression spoke of betrayal.

Ten Years Earlier

Thomas stared and his mouth hung open.

"Close your mouth Thomas. You look simple, gawking like that." His mother whispered and chuckled softly.

Thomas blinked and closed his mouth. "What's gawking?" he asked, his eyes still fixed on the milling people and costumed performers. His mother ruffled his hair.

"What you were doing. Save some of the looking for us." She smiled and leaned down to bring her eyes level with his. She pulled a copper flitter from her pocket and pressed it into his hand. His eyes went wide. "Go buy yourself something good to eat." His mother winked, and Thomas's smile spread from ear to ear. He scurried off through the masses toward a cart selling sweets.

He waited in line and gaped at the crowd. In all his life he had never seen so many people, so many colourful outfits. This was the first time the travelling band had been this way since he was born. The copper in his hand was a stark reminder of how special today was. They didn't have many flitters to spare.

His eyes swept past a wagon at the edge of the cluster of excitement. The wagon appeared older than the others, its wood bleached grey and scrollwork carved deep at the top corners. Like frost growing on glass, a cold sensation slid down his arms causing his hair to stand. He wasn't sure why. The carriage seemed out of place like a winter tree standing in a field of spring flowers. His eyes roamed the lines of the carving trying to make sense of the whirling design. The picture that came to mind was water, though he didn't understand why as the design didn't look like water. It looked more like writing. He had seen writing before, though he wasn't schooled for it.

Movement caught his attention. A small brown-haired girl peeked from behind the wagon. She was thin. Her hair flew in tangled strands around a dirt-smeared face. She smiled and it changed the shape of her eyes, creasing them into half moons. He glanced back to see if she was smiling at someone else. No, she was smiling at him. Heat crept up his face and he shoved hands into deep pockets. He smiled back. The girl wore a tattered dress, and her feet were bare. It didn't appear she was with anyone as he scanned the crowd for her family. The thought concerned him. He looked back to her but she had ducked behind the wagon, her feet visible under the chassis.

Next!" a large ruddy-faced woman barked from behind the sweets cart. He jumped at the deep tone and urgency with which she called to him. She eyed him impatiently over a rather large nose. "What'll you have?" Her crass condescendence matched her furrowed brows. He stepped forward and pulled the flitter from his pocket. It sat in his palm like a decision, as he looked from it to the tart, then over to the bare feet visible beneath the wagon. His mouth watered as the scent of apples and pastry trailed past. "Let's go boy. I've not got all day." Thomas blinked at the grouchy woman. With a breath of resignation he put the flitter back in his pocket and walked out of the line. He paused at the back of the wagon.

"Hello," he called timidly.

The girl looked from behind the wagon and her face came into view. The first thing he noticed this close were her eyes. They were saucer-shaped and a rich golden brown. Dark lashes dusted her checks when she blinked. Then she smiled. The dirt on her face looked out of place like a vagabond trailing a royal parade so transformed her face became.

"Are you here with your family?" He spoke as if to a wild animal, afraid he might send her running and with her the sun might follow.

Her smile fell. She dipped her chin and smoothed her tattered dress. The effort was in vain as the dress was far beyond fixing. She had to be close to his age, not more than twelve years. When she started to back away his heart sank.

"Are you hungry?" Thomas asked, desperate to keep her there. She stopped inching away and searched his face. The air went still and he felt exposed, as if she could see into the depths of his young soul. He cleared his throat and looked away. He shoved a hand in his pocket and pulled out the flitter. The tremble in his hand made him self-conscious but he held the coin out to her anyway. The smile on her face as she glanced from his hand to him was enough to make his awkwardness worthwhile.

"Here." He didn't recognize his own voice, so strong and sure, though his body felt weak.

"Thank you." Her voice was like water. As she reached for the coin her hand brushed his. A tingling warmth moved up his arm. He blinked and looked from his hand to her.

"You are good," she said.

He opened his mouth to reply but was cut off by the sound of stomping hooves and the crack of wood struck by metal. The air erupted into a flurry of screams and fleeing feet. A man on a horse wearing a shiny metal suit nearly knocked him over. He dove under the cart, reaching for the girl to pull her to safety but she was gone. He hadn't seen her leave but she wasn't there anymore. Only a small puddle of water remained, steam rising from its centre. There wasn't time to find that odd as he watched bodies fall to the ground from the trepid safety of his hiding place.

Carts toppled. Animals ran in circles, calling wildly. He covered his head, trying to block out the sounds. After what seemed like an eternity it went quiet. It was the kind of silence that followed a raging storm. With a clenched gut and tense muscles he stayed frozen, afraid to move lest his disturbance of the air make the violence start again. He let out the breath he was holding and braced himself. Nothing happened. That was slightly reassuring so he opened his eyes and brought his arms slowly from his head.

His mind refused to process the deadly scene. There was no reference from his past to pull from, having never seen anything like it. Bodies littered the ground; carts and wagons were burned in varying degrees. Belongings were strewn about the ground kicked and trampled by the horse bound men. He lay there for a good long while to be sure the men wearing metal suits and wielding swords were gone.

When his mind started to clear he took a deep breath of relief. But it was short-lived relief as a thought sliced through his thin veil of innocence. His family. With his heart in his throat he scrambled from under the cart. He hit his head and tore his shirt on the rough wood. A word escaped his mouth that he was not supposed to use, and guilt racked him as he rubbed at the knot forming at the back of his skull. Then he saw them. A choking sob sounded strange and the desperate cry startled him. But he was the only one alive. It was he who made the noise though he had no control over it. He walked toward them without knowledge of his own movement. A stinging jolt shot up his legs as his knees hit the ground, but he didn't care. They were gone. They were gone...they were gone.

The day went on with no regard for the tragedy before him. Shadows grew long, and the air chilled, yet still he sat. His empty stare revealed the secrets of his heart. They were things he dared not say aloud. The last of the light slunk toward the horizon and his eyes moved to a wagon still glowing with embers from a dying flame. Primal need took hold, and he moved to the warmth. Night was the messenger solidifying his deepest fear. There would be no gentle nudge to wake him from this nightmare. He curled into a ball, and drifted into a restless sleep, his cheeks wet from defeated tears.

He woke to the tittering call of a wren, and for the briefest moment his heart was happy in answer to her call. He peeled one eye open. It resisted, swollen and raw. As his eye focused he remembered, and the weight of it crushed his chest. New tears welled and he clenched his eyes shut against reality. But that was no better. He sighed and opened both eyes. A wren sat a few feet from where he lay, pecking at some spilled grain scattered amongst the carnage. He watched her for a moment, letting his mind go numb. She pecked and looked, pecked and looked. Then, her tiny bird head turned to him. A small object glinted from her beak. She hopped toward him. He stayed very still, waiting, watching. She inched forward. He could see it now. The object in her beak was a coin, a copper flitter. She held it carefully and cocked her head as if waiting.

"Here, don't eat that bird." He sat up and motioned to the bird. She flew off in a flurry of wings. He watched her fly until he could see her no more. He sighed and looked down. There, on the ground, she had left the flitter. Tears sprung to his eyes anew. He picked up the coin, placed it in his pocket, said one last farewell to the dead, and trudged away.

Thomas didn't see the old man standing in the shadows watching him walk away. The wren circled overhead, and lit on the old man's shoulder. He didn't flinch; he kept his eyes in the direction the boy had gone. She chirped.

"Yes, when it is time, little one," he said. Though it wasn't clear whether he was speaking to her, or about the boy.

∞

The Here and Now

The inn was dank and dirty, but the ale was just as wet. Thomas's legs still burned from the pace he'd kept over the last few days. He'd worn out his welcome in the last town. He knew when to leave well enough alone. Well enough had gained him several nice rings and a coin pouch with enough weight to be worth the dog bite on his hand. He swallowed another long drink and looked at the wound on his hand. It would heal, but likely leave a scar. He added gloves to his mental list of 'need to acquire' items.

"Have another mister?" the barmaid said, a coy smile playing on her full lips. Her eyes twinkled as if telling a joke. Her dirty blond hair clung to her cheeks, tinged pink with the heat of the room. One long strand trailed down her neck, clinging to the skin her low cut dress revealed. Thomas shifted in his seat and kept his eyes toward the bustling room. He held one hand up and shook his head. Out of the corner of his eye he saw the barmaid push her chest out further. "Are you sure?" The words were low and full of promise. Thomas looked at her and donned his most gruesome smile. His blue eyes flashed wild, and his teeth gleamed white.

"Are you sure?" he asked. His tone was like a blade, low but piercing through the clatter in the room. Her eyes went wide and her mouth parted. She shook her head meekly and backed away. Thomas watched her move along to another table, less balanced than she had been before. He finished his drink in one long swallow, wiped a sleeve across his face, and leaned back.

He couldn't stay here long. The barmaid whispered to a table full of men while casting sneers in his direction. The men eyed him over their own drinks. His appearance revealed nothing as he sat easily, one leg propped on the chair across from him and arms folded comfortably over his chest. But the uneasiness he felt inside was a counterpoint to his demeanour. He stretched, scratched the stubble on his chin, and pulled a few coins from his pouch. He let the coins clatter to the table as he stood to leave. He didn't glance back as he prowled towards the door.

The cool night air was a welcome change from the stale stench of the inn. He breathed deeply and looked to the sky. It was a clear night, good for travel if you had the need. By the looks of the men inside, he needed to. Which direction though? North was out of the question. He'd just come from there. East was no better. The cattle herd he'd lifted, and then sold to the next town over, was still fresh news. West then. The inn door slammed open, jolting Thomas from his decision. Three men exited purposefully. A tall stocky man was the first to catch Thomas's eye.

"Hoy boy," he called in mock friendliness. Thomas bristled at the title boy. The man smiled showing brown, stained teeth. There were remnants of his dinner clinging to his beard as if waiting to be served as a second course.

"Can I help you?" Thomas asked. His tone was friendly enough, but his shoulders squared and his hand went to the hilt of the dagger worn tight against his waist.

"Oh well then, you just might." The tall bearded man's eyes flicked to the hand at Thomas's hip. His eyes twinkled and his smile grew wider. The other two men flanked the tall man. They said nothing, and their faces remained stoic, almost bored.

"I was just wondering you see," the bearded man moved closer to Thomas with an easy stride, his hands making a placating gesture, "I saw the nice weight to your coin pouch." He stopped and rubbed a hand over his beard freeing the crumbs from their perch. "Seeing as my friends and I have fallen on hard times, would you mind making a small donation to our cause?" His brows rose in question and he smiled again.

Thomas nodded amiably, "I see," he said and reached for his pouch. He shook the bag once, and the hard coins made a hefty jingle. "What cause is yours then?" he asked, dipping one hand in the bag. The bearded man's eyes went steel. Thomas saw it before he moved. The shift of his eyes, and set of his brow told him he was going to charge. In one fluid motion Thomas pulled a slender blade from his pouch. With a flick of his wrist the blade left his hand and found its mark in the bearded man's left eye. The bearded man clutched his face and howled. Thomas didn't wait for the other men to react. He ran into the tree line. Swift like a shadow, ducking and dodging the underbrush, he made his way. He ran east for a solid mile before he turned to the west. Sure, they could track him in the daylight, but tonight they would be looking for him in the wrong direction. It would give him enough time to gain ground, and cover his tracks once first light hit.

Based on the placement of the moon he'd been running for two solid hours. He slowed to a brisk walk and finally to a shuffle. The men had lost him. He moved faster than most and those men were well into their middle years. He stopped and looked up at a break in the trees. This was his life. Always running, breaking away just in the nick of time.

He shook his head and ran a hand over his face. He would love nothing more than to find a pile of pine boughs and sleep. But he had made that mistake before. He traced a finger over the long thin scar on his left wrist. They had tried to take his hand when he'd been caught lifting pouches several years ago. If he had only kept running the night before and not given in to sleep he wouldn't have the scar now. Lucky for him the town square had been packed that day. An overturned apple cart caused a distraction just as the blade made contact with his skin. He'd broken free and run for a day straight.

He shook his head and grunted. One boot trudged in front of the other, pushing further west. When at last the sun showed the first signs of life he ducked into a thicket of underbrush and fell like a rock. He drifted into a dreamless sleep, his hand clutching the hilt of his dagger.

When he woke the sun was setting. His bladder was full otherwise he might have slept on through. He lay there for a moment blinking up at the boughs of low shrubs then his eyes flew wide when the smell of smoke registered. Someone had a camp nearby. He rolled to his stomach and inched forward until he could see a clearing up a ways. There in the distance an orange glow indicated a camp. A dark figure sat hunched near the glowing embers. He scooted backward into the underbrush and stood. He skirted the perimeter of the clearing, his dagger unsheathed and at the ready. There would be more men, he was sure of it. On his third pass around a chill pricked the bottom of his neck and crept along his shoulders. His breath came ragged as he pressed his back to a large tree. There were no others. The man sitting at the fire, now just a few yards from the tree, said something softly. *He's talking to himself.* Thomas wondered at the sanity of the man. It was full dark now. Thomas peered around the tree. The man seemed to be looking in his direction. He ducked back and held his breath.

"There is no one but me." The man's voice was soft but carried over the air effortlessly.

Thomas clinched his eyes shut and gripped his blade tighter.

"Come. Sit by the fire and share a meal with me." The man sounded amused.

Thomas swung from behind the tree to face the fire. He stood in the shadows for a time watching, his eyes darting around the edges of the camp.

"Look, it's just me. Come over here and sit or be on your way. You're making me nervous with your circling and heavy breathing."

Thomas sniffed and raised his chin. He did not breath heavily.

He inched closer. The man kept his eyes on the fire as Thomas approached. He was tall and thin with a long black beard. His garb was grey and his hood left his eyes in shadow. When Thomas stopped just inside the light of the fire the man lifted his chin. His steel blue eyes swept over Thomas from his boots to his eyes and lingered there for a moment before he nodded.

"Have a bite," the man said as he ladled stew into a bowl. He held it out to Thomas.

Thomas watched him for a moment, unmoving. The man grunted and sat it on a rock to the side.

"I'll not force you to eat but I'm hungry." He retrieved another bowl from his pack and proceeded to eat, unfazed. Thomas's stomach growled loudly as the smell of the stew reached his nose. The old man snorted and shook his head.

"You're a stubborn one."

Thomas scratched the back of his neck and shrugged. With a crooked smile he retrieved the offered bowl, sitting opposite the old man. The first swallow of stew was a mixture of pain and pleasure as it slipped down his throat. It made him light headed. He raised the bowl in a grateful gesture.

"Thank you. Thomas is the name."

"You're welcome Thomas." The way the old man said his name made him flinch. He said it like a familiar name, one that he knew, that he said often. The old man took down his hood. A medallion hanging from a chain around his neck shimmered in the firelight. The shape of the medallion was odd, like old writing. Thomas looked up. A strange emotion flashed in the old man's eyes when he looked up and smiled, returning the raised bowl gesture. He looked back down and the medallion slid back under his robe. The peculiar feeling it gave Thomas dissipated.

Thomas finished eating and thanked the man again.

"I need to be off. What can I offer you for the meal?"

The man shook is head and waved a hand. "No need."

Thomas stood and nodded farewell.

The man narrowed his eyes. "Good will to you and know this... a bird's advice is worth heeding." The old man touched the tip of his nose as if sharing a secret.

Thomas nodded politely and backed away grateful for the food, but also grateful to be leaving the company of the strange old man.

∞

The Bird Knows

He woke the next morning to the sound of a woman's voice. "Thomas you need to go." He opened his eyes to the sound of hooves, at least three horses. He sat up and bolted deeper into the woods. As he ducked under branches away from the worn path, his shirt caught on a branch and tore. He slipped on wet leaves and tumbled down a steep bank, landing in a creek. He would have liked to think it was a graceful fall but the loud splash followed by a dull crack of his head against a rock suggested otherwise. He cursed and sat up, rubbing at the bump on his head. Someone giggled. He shook his head and grunted.

"They are gone. They didn't see you," a voice like water said.

Thomas jolted to stand and swung around, his shirt half torn and wet hair plastered over his eyes. He pushed it back and looked around. No one.

"Who are you? Show your self." His voice cracked.

A small brown wren flitted from a nearby branch and landed on a rock in the stream. Its head cocked to the side and he could swear it smiled.

"Shoo." Thomas flapped an arm and looked around for the woman who was hiding.

"That's awfully rude when it was you who asked for me to show myself."

Thomas blinked dumbly at the bird. Her wings were tucked, as if perched on her hips, and her eyes narrowed. Thomas cleared his throat.

"Look, I realize you may have never heard a bird speak before but I can assure you it was me. Also, you were about to get yourself in trouble falling asleep on the edge of that path up there. You really should be more careful, Thomas."

Thomas blinked again and rubbed gingerly at the lump on his head. He must have hit it harder than he thought. He shook his head and made his way to the bank. The bird made an indignant noise when he walked away.

Some time later he stopped to peel wet boots from his feet. He lit a small fire and set his things near it to dry. With his arms folded over his knees he stared at the fire.

"Thomas, why have you chosen to live this way?"

Thomas closed his eyes and groaned. Damn, he was delusional. He sighed and looked up. There it was, his bird of madness. He wondered if talking back would solidify his insanity or perhaps make it fade away like lyrics stuck in your head. If he could just finish the ridiculous song and dance perhaps it would leave his mind. He lifted his head and forced a smile. The edges of his eyes tilted up, painting his face crazy. It was a weapon, a trick of the trade. No one wanted to mess with you if you appeared insane.

"Well, let's see. I was orphaned at the age of twelve. I had no skills, no family, and nowhere to go." He shrugged a shoulder and arched his brows up and down quickly to enhance the lunacy act. "I just went where I could, took what I needed. The longer I did it, the better I got." There. He told the bird what she wanted to know. Maybe she would leave.

The bird tilted her head to one side. "It was never your only choice Thomas. This isn't what you were meant to be."

It started in the pit of his stomach: the slow, seeping anger, colouring his face red. "Choice? You think this was my choice? You know nothing. You're a bird. A blasted talking bird. And furthermore," he held up a finger in determination, "you're only a talking bird because I hit my head. Now go."

The bird shook her head. She shook her head! Good lord he was out of his mind.

"No, you need me now, Thomas. I've left you alone for far too long. I tried to tell him but..." She stopped as if she'd said too much.

Thomas narrowed his eyes and pressed his lips in a hard line. No, he would not be baited by a bird. He didn't care. He ignored her. He put on his still-wet boots, tamped down the fire and kept moving west.

He felt her there, ever persistent. She followed. Oh, sure she fell back a ways, but the unmistakable sound of tiny wings as she darted from tree to tree cut through the air, practically smacking Thomas on the back of the head every 200 feet. He continued to ignore her. At least that's what he told himself, though his mind was ever tuned to her location. He dreaded hearing her speak again. He hoped she would speak again, and then hated himself for wanting to hear her speak again. That game went on for several hours: the flitting of wings behind him, the bracing himself to hear her say something.

"Why!" Thomas's voice cracked and the sound of it sent several birds into flight from a nearby tree. He rolled his eyes. It wasn't so much a question as a means to break the silence.

He sat down heavily on the bank of the small stream he'd been following. The water felt good as it washed down his throat. He hadn't realized how thirsty he had become, focusing on not focusing on the bird. Staring at the water as it meandered through the thick underbrush didn't help the situation, but he didn't feel like walking anymore. So he sat.

"I know you're still there. I can feel your black eyes staring at me." He said this under his breath. The soft flutter of wings stirred a momentary breeze against his neck and he shivered despite the fact he wasn't cold.

"My eyes are brown thank you very much. And I wasn't staring at

70

you. You aren't that much to look at, you know." She said primly. If a bird could purse her beak, she did.

Thomas couldn't help it. He laughed. When he stopped he took the time to really look at the bird. She did have brown eyes. They weren't the typical black beads he'd always known a bird to have. He furrowed his brow.

"So little wren, am I the only one who hears you or do you go around driving everyone mad who will listen?" It was the wren's turn to laugh. The sound of it flowed over Thomas like a lost emotion. His breath stuttered and he cleared his throat to cover it.

"No I've only ever spoken to one other."

"Why?" Thomas furrowed his brow and rubbed the back of his neck.

"Thomas, my purpose is to help you help me. I'm trapped and it will be you who sets it right."

"Sets what right? What do you mean trapped?"

"I," Wren stammered unsure of how to answer, "I honestly don't know. I think I knew once. Your name is clear in my memory. Your face," Wren snorted, "that image is burned into my brain." She shook her head. "But how I came to be... I think he told me once but it's like sand through a sifter. The memories faded." She stayed quiet for a moment and Thomas stared at her incredulously. Wren sighed. "It's like this: you must give to receive, or something like that. I'm giving you help and then you, in turn, will help me." She seemed satisfied with that, the curt bob of her head a clear indication.

Thomas waved a hand flat. "You've got the wrong person, Wren." He stood and brushed the dirt from his britches. "I don't need help and I've got nothing to give."

The next few weeks were strange. Thomas kept travelling west. Wren kept following. He ducked into a few small towns to purchase gloves, a new shirt, and a larger travel sack to store things he had "acquired" along the way. Every night, Wren waited for him. He refused to admit that the company of the odd bird was a comfort. He denied that he had let someone into his walled-off world. She was annoying. She spoke her mind too often. He had to bite his tongue on more than one occasion lest he say something inappropriate for a woman's ears, even if the 'woman' was a bird. One night in particular he came to the woods a little worse for wear.

"Honestly Thomas, I don't know why you feel the need to go into places like that." Wren looked down her beak at the swollen eye he held a wet rag over. Thomas shrugged a shoulder.

"The other guy looks worse." He flexed his fist and winced.

Wren made a noise clearly indicating her disapproval. "You're going to get yourself killed before I can figure out how you're supposed to save me."

71

Thomas grunted. "I told you. I'm not saving you."

"No I don't suppose you will. You're too busy trying to get yourself killed." Wren looked at Thomas with penetrating brown eyes. "You don't want me here do you?"

"What was your first clue, my constant annoyance at your pointing out my flaws," he ticked off one finger, "my denial of your need to be saved," he ticked off another finger, "or my attempt to shake you every time I go into the woods?" His words came out harsh as he ticked off the third finger. Wren blinked once but said nothing in return. Thomas felt guilty for the severity of his tone the moment she flitted away.

It had been days since he had seen any sign of Wren. She was gone. "Good." He lied to himself. A sinking sense of loneliness grew deeper with each passing day. He found himself wandering with no purpose. He must have drifted too far in the wrong direction because he ran into a camp. There, sitting around a fire, was a travelling band of outlaws. One looked familiar and wore an eye-patch over his left eye. It was an eye-patch made necessary from a knife to the eye. Thomas swallowed. He backed up slowly and made for the nearest underbrush. That's when he stepped on a branch. Thomas winced. The eye-patched bastard looked up, his right eye narrowing. The look of recognition dawned on his face and Thomas waved a hand in awkward greeting before turning to run. Eye-patch man followed. A prolific string of promises spewed from his mouth, something about 'maiming' and 'left alive to watch the animals feast on your flesh'. Why was eye-patch man so fast? Honestly, he had never heard half the words the man was using. Thomas huffed, sliding over and under branches.

After a while the air grew still and Thomas slowed. Tipping his head back and forth, he strained to hear the sound of someone else. The quiet was shattered by the unmistakable twang of a bowstring preceded a brown swoop, a hard thwack and distinct thud. Shouts from a distance called to eye-patch man. Footsteps sounded in retreat. Thomas blinked, looking down at his chest, certain to find an arrow jutting from his heart. Instead he saw her, Wren, on the ground with the arrow through her middle.

∽

Salvation

"She saved you." The bearded man pointed out. He was dressed in the same thin grey robe as the night he'd come upon him in the woods. His medallion was obscured under fabric but Thomas knew it was there. The look the man gave was hard but did not reflect the same anguish, the same sorrow, Thomas felt right now. Then it hit him: a bird's advice is worth heeding.

Thomas spoke through clenched teeth. "It was you. You told her I would save her."

The man nodded and touched his nose. "You will." He turned and disappeared into the tree line.

Thomas turned his eyes back to Wren. His gut roiled at the sight. He leaned over and retched. He wiped his mouth and scooped Wren up, holding her in his hands at a loss for what to do. Staring at her wouldn't bring her back to life.

He dug a bird-sized hole and placed her in the grave. Kneeling over the hole he let tears stream down his face. He didn't want to cover her with dirt. He had, somewhere in the back of his mind, wished she had been right, that his life had purpose. That he was good. That he might have saved her.

He reached in his pocket and pulled out the only thing left that meant something to him. The flitter his mother had given him just moments before she was killed. He dropped the coin in the hole and methodically covered her with dirt.

He woke later, curled next to the fresh grave, shivering. His clothes were wet. He looked up and blinked. Water surrounded him on all sides. A swollen, seeping puddle centred on the grave. He rubbed his eyes as mist began to rise from the middle. It formed a long cylinder drifting upward. The puddle continued to gather into the growing mist until all of the water from the ground collected in the air, knitting into an opaque form. He was dry, he dimly noted, as he stared at the illuminated vapour silhouette. Brown hair like a halo floated above a face, soft and sweet. Warm brown eyes blinked from the veil of clouds as she stepped forward. Dark lashes danced on her cheeks. Bare feet peaked beneath a tattered dress. She held out her hand palm up. In her hand, glinting like the sun was his copper flitter.

"You are good." Wren said.

The old man watched from afar, a smile tugging at his lips. The medallion on his neck transformed into a different pattern for another purpose. Thomas and Wren did not see him fade into nothing. They didn't see the mist drift on the wind cast toward a silent call.

All of the choices Thomas had made, the bad decisions borne from desperate fears dissipated. This was it. He could see it now as clearly as the first day they met so many years ago. She was the light he almost touched. Now his light touched hers, mingling into a promise. He was, after years of drifting in empty silence, home.

With a peace he'd never known, and a long forgotten emotion blooming in his heart, he reached out and closed her hand over the coin. "It's for you."

Blood Lines – Lindsay Toomey

When I was young, I was taken from my parents and put up for adoption. One day, my adoptive parents came to visit me. They said they had been looking for someone just like me to join their family. They went away and then they came back again and told me that I would be going to live with them. I would have a house, and a bed, and a yard and we would play and be happy forever.

It took some getting used to, but I started staying in my own bed and sleeping through the night. I wasn't used to sleeping alone and it was scary. I also worried that my new parents didn't love me. My daddy was always away on business trips and my mummy worked long hours away from home. But soon I learned my new routine and became comfortable and happy.

In the morning, mummy would wake up and feed me breakfast. She would play with me and talk to me as she got ready for work. When she was ready to leave, she would take me to daycare. I would play and sleep and snack and then before I knew it, mummy was back to pick me up and take me home again. This was our life for a very long time. Mummy and daddy provided me with a good home and it didn't take long for me to realize that I was loved very much.

My parents took me to see my grandparents. It was a very long drive, but when we got there I got to play with my cousins and my grandparents had special treats for me. They had a big backyard and my cousins and I played for out there for hours. By the end of the first day, I was so tired that I fell asleep in my mummy's arms.

The next day I woke up feeling a little bit under the weather, but I still played with my family outside and had a fun time. I had a cut in my mouth. It would not stop bleeding. By the end of the day, I was feeling very sick. Mummy made sure I had lots to drink and that I ate all my dinner. She told me to go to sleep and get as much rest as I could and that I would feel better in the morning.

I woke up and I did not feel better. I felt worse. I did not want to play outside with my cousins or have any of the treats my grandparents gave me. I just wanted to lay on the couch with mummy. My mouth was still bleeding. It was time to go home, but mummy and daddy looked worried and decided to take me to the hospital before we left.

They took me to an emergency clinic. It was cold and I was scared but mummy and daddy were beside me the entire time. The doctors took away some of my blood. It hurt, but mummy said, "Shh, buddy, you'll be alright," and I was. The nurses brought me some water to drink and some more blankets while we waited for the results of my test. I was tired and fell asleep.

When I woke up mummy and daddy were talking to the doctor. He said that from the results, it looked like I had gotten into some rat poison. Mummy looked really sad. She looked as white as a sheet of paper. She saw me looking at her and smiled. She walked over, stoked my head, and told me not to worry; they were going to take care of me.

The doctor put yellow medicine in the same pointy thing they used to take some of my blood. He said I might feel a pinch. It was more than a pinch, but I was brave and didn't speak. Mummy stroked my head some more. Daddy asked the doctor if it would be okay to take me home and explained that the drive would be long. The doctor said it would be okay and that I would probably sleep the whole time.

He was right. I woke up and we were almost home. I heard mummy and daddy talking in hushed tones and it was comforting. I fell back asleep and woke up again in the morning, in my bed, with my toys and mummy sitting next to me.

I didn't feel any better or any worse. I felt the same. My mouth was still bleeding. Mummy made me get up and have some breakfast. She had made my favourite, bacon. I ate, even though I didn't really feel like it. Mummy told daddy that she was going to stay home with me because I still didn't look very good. Daddy agreed it was a good idea, stroked my head, and then left for work.

I didn't do much more that day other than sit with mummy. She put on a couple of shows and I drifted in and out of sleep while she stroked my head and back. This is how we stayed all day. When daddy came home, mummy said she had an appointment and would be back in a few hours. When I saw that mummy was leaving, I got up to say goodbye. I felt weird. I was wobbly. It was getting dark. I felt something hard. I was asleep.

c✪⁊

I was getting my coat on to leave and Steve was getting up to say goodbye. He didn't look too steady on his legs, but I attributed that to the fact that he had been lying down all day. He wobbled and swayed and walked headlong into the wall. I panicked and ran to him. I lifted his little body in my arms. It felt like a lifetime, but he finally came to. He was in bad shape. Without waiting a moment, Gord, Steve's dad, and I whisked him out to the car and we were on our way to the emergency room.

It felt like an eternity getting there. Finally, we arrived and I ran in with Steve and he was immediately placed in a room. The doctor came in, took his temperature, and took more blood for a test. Steve was given IV fluids into his forearm. He was lethargic and quiet. He curled up on my lap while I rocked him back and forth waiting for the results of his test.

The results were in. His white blood cell count was through the roof. His red blood cell and platelet counts were dangerously low. The doctors and nurses acted quickly injecting IV steroids, sucralfate (stomach lining protectors), vitamin K, and immune suppressants. Steve was in rough shape and the prognosis wasn't good.

We tried to stay strong and positive and kept a constant vigil at his side. It was hard and we were panicking. We had chosen Steve. He was ours, we loved him and wanted to protect him, but there didn't seem like much we could do. We held on to each other and made it through the night. The doctors suggested that we go get some rest and let Steve do the same. Reluctantly, we went home leaving Steve with his beeping machines and IV-pricked arms.

We got home and I had a hot shower. I couldn't sleep. I paced and paced and paced some more. I couldn't sit there and do nothing. I called the hospital for an update. Steve was resting and they had done another blood test. The results weren't in, but they would call us when they were.

I paced some more. And some more. And then some more.

Finally, the phone rang. I pounced on it. The results were in and Steve was worse. His blood was the consistency of water. His body was failing him and time was running out. We headed to the hospital gripping hands and praying to any god that would listen that our little one would be okay.

The journey to the hospital seemed to take an eternity. It is amazing what you'll consider doing to reach a loved one when they need you. Red lights? Look both ways, then go. Speed limits? They're just suggestions.

We arrived and Steve was still with us. We rushed into his room. He looked awful. I held him tight. I never wanted to let go. The doctors came in and explained what was happening. They had finally diagnosed Steve. He had thrombocytopenia, a condition in which the patient's platelet count is very low. We were told this was why Steve's mouth wouldn't stop bleeding; his blood couldn't clot. The doctor went on to explain that he was susceptible to the disease because he had a weakened immune system.

Steve was in bad shape. The treatment that he had been going through was exactly what the treatment was for thrombocytopenia. Because it took so long to figure out what was wrong with Steve, they were passed the point of the medicines in their current dosages helping. It was looking grim and our hearts were breaking.

I held on to Steve's nearly lifeless body trying to anchor him to the here and now. The doctor had one more piece of bad news for us. There was a treatment that we hadn't tried. Steve needed a blood transfusion. I was elated. Of course we would do it. That wasn't bad news; that was wonderful news. Then the hammer was dropped on us in one final defeating blow. The hospital had the tools for the job, but not the much-needed life-saving blood. The closest facility that could do the treatment was four hours away and the way things were looking, Steve didn't have that kind of time.

I went limp. Hugging Steve even tighter than before, this time in an effort to anchor myself to the here and now, I sobbed. How could this have happened? Through tear-filled eyes, I looked at the doctor and one more time asked if there was anything more we could do. He was going to increase Steve's dosages in a last ditch effort to bring up his platelet and red blood cell count, beyond that, there was nothing left to do.

I hadn't let go of him. I couldn't let go of him. I don't know how long I stayed like that. It could have been minutes or hours. Memories were flooding through my mind. The doctor came back through the door. The new dosage should have had an effect by then and they were going do another blood test. I released him long enough for them to extract some more blood from Steve's already battered arm and then hugged him in tightly again. And then we waited.

They had pushed the test through and we had the results within an hour. He hadn't improved. My heart sank. That was it; our last hope of saving Steve had vanished. I held him tight and felt his chest rise and fall. I told him I was sorry. I didn't protect him and I couldn't save him.

A nurse, Amber, who had always been very kind and gentle with Steve, came in and rested her hand on my shoulder. "I have some good news," she said, "I was able to find a blood donor for Steve. He is here and more than willing to help." I looked up at her, disbelief colouring my face. A blood donor was here, ready, and willing to save the life of a perfect stranger.

Steve was quickly whisked away and prepared for the transfusion. I couldn't believe what was happening. The doctor explained that they would do one round and then do a blood test. Because of the size of the room, we weren't allowed to go with Steve and had to wait outside. The procedure would take a few of hours, so we rushed home to shower and get something to eat.

When we got back to the hospital, Amber reported that Steve had been very brave and that the transfusion went well, but that they were still waiting for the results of his latest blood test. We were allowed to go in to wait with him. He was awake and more energetic than I had seen him in the last few days. I was elated. Just then the doctor came in with the results. Everything had improved. His white blood cell count had come down and his red blood cell and platelet counts had gone up. He wasn't out of the woods, but it was a great improvement.

The doctor recommended a second transfusion that would hopefully get all his blood counts back into the normal range. We agreed to the second transfusion and hugged and kissed Steve. One more transfusion and one more test. We could make it through this. Again Steve went into the small room. This time we waited outside for him. Trying not to pace, but failing miserably, we held hands and waited. Finally it was done and the results were in and we were thrilled. Steve had pulled through.

After we got the results, Amber came in and told us that the Steve's donor was there and if we wanted, she would bring him in. I looked at Steve, then Gord, and then back at Amber. Of course we wanted to meet the stranger that saved Steve. I wanted nothing more than to thank him for such a selfless and brave act. I nodded at Amber, trying to keep the tears from spilling out of my eyes.

In a minute Amber was back and trailing behind her was a beautiful boy. His name was Zeus. I knelt down and stroked his head and let my tears flow. "Thank-you, thank-you" I whispered. In that moment, Steve caught sight of Zeus and jumped out of his cot and ran to his new friend and lifesaver. They rolled on the floor together, tangled in tubes and tails wagging looking for all the world like they had been friends forever.

Heroes come in every shape and form. Our hero was the six-year-old German Shepherd named Zeus, who selflessly gave a piece of himself to save our dog's life.

Capeless – John Ryers

I held three tickets in my trembling hands, the envelope they came in ripped into a thousand pieces and strewn about my quasi-tidy room. I picked a few bits of envelope from my braided hair and stared at the tickets and the stoic image of a masked man dressed all in red printed on them.

They say that heroes walk among us. Capeless. Unseen. They say they're unknown to the little people milling about their everyday lives and that we're blind to their heroics until they don their mask to beat the living snot out of evildoers. But that's a load of crap. Heroes are very much caped and very much seen, especially in the case of the Blood Revenger, played by the dreamy and exceptionally muscular Marcen Weston. He was everything a hero should be, and I was going to meet him.

Marcen rarely did meet-and-greets with his fans, so when he tweeted that he'd be stopping by the grand opening of the Skylark Razor, an obscenely tall skyscraper slash condo slash store-type monstrosity just five hours away from my bedroom, I knew it was my destiny to shake his hand. Or you know, have dinner with him and walk along the beach strip where he'd propose and whisper secrets about Season Three in my ear, because after that Season Two finale, he owed me. Us. He owed us.

I picked up the phone beside my bed, the corded, pink one with the faded, half-peeling My Little Pony stickers on it and dialled Jess, Best Friend Number One. I had my cell but reception in our area sucked, and this was important news that required a hardwire to the world. She answered and I didn't even say hello, I just said, "They came." A squeal came from the other end, the kind that only dogs and other sixteen-year-old girls with tickets to a Marcen Weston meet-and-greet can hear. We hung up immediately and I dialled Megan, Best Friend Number Two, but only because I organized my best friends in alphabetical order and not by some hierarchy of loyalty like most of the other girls in high school did. More squeals. More oh-emm-gees. More hanging up.

I ran out of my room and down the stairs, nearly crashing into my dad who was coming upstairs with Mathew, my annoying 7-year-old brother. "Slow down, Katherine. You're gonna kill yourself," Dad said and Mathew parroted my dad as I made it to the first floor in just four bounds, and rounded the corner into the kitchen. Mom was there reading the paper and eating toast smeared with disgusting marmalade. She looked up over her reading glasses and I showed her the tickets, trying to speak words but only able to express myself with excited grunts and mumbles. "I'm glad they came," she said, not fully grasping the awesomeness of the situation. "Now get something to eat before you're late for school."

As if I'd be late on a momentous day like today. I grabbed a protein bar and an apple (two things I hadn't planned on eating but took to prevent the disdainful head shake I knew was coming if I didn't do something to appease her) and picked the bits of envelope from my haphazard hair. I then began the daily ritual of searching for my schoolbooks, which always seemed to evade me in the mornings.

"Looking for these?" my dad said, holding said books in his hands.

"Looking for these?" Matty mimicked again, standing there with his over-sized, Blood Revenger-themed backpack. He was a fan too but in that lame little-kid way that didn't appreciate the talent or looks of the acting god that played my hero every Sunday night at nine o'clock. Eight central.

"I need you to take Mathew to school this morning," Dad said, fully squelching my momentum. "I've got an interview this morning."

Dad had been out of work for a few months since his company had - air quotes - restructured. There'd been a lot of that going on. Megan's mom had been "restructured" a few months before my dad and had received her first job offer just last week. Still, it didn't mean I wanted a little-brother tagging along this morning, ruining the epic Marcen Weston ticket reveal. I waved Matty over with an impatient sigh, loud enough to make my feelings on the matter known. "Thank-you, Katherine," my mom said without looking up from her crossword puzzle.

Jess pulled up in her car which she had lovingly named Rust On Wheels, and Matty and I climbed into the back while Megan sat in the front. I withheld the tickets for a little bit, teasing them as if I didn't know what they were talking about but that got old pretty quick, so I whipped the tickets out, making sure to keep them pinched between my fingers so they wouldn't blow out the window.

"This is so perfect," Megan said. "What a sweet farewell this'll be."

Megan's mom's new job came with a catch. It required Best Friend Number Two to move out of state. A move that happened exactly one day after the Marcen Weston event.

Jess snatched her ticket out of my fingers. "Do you think he'll be like, dressed as the Blood Revenger or just as his alter-ego, Warren Wilby?"

I grabbed the tickets back. I'd been the one to stay on the phone until 2am to order them, so that meant I was their devoted protector and even Best Friend Number One or Two would not possess them until the actual meet-and-greet this coming Saturday. "I think he'll just be good ol' Marcen Weston," I said. "Good ol', muscle-ly, five-o'clock shadowy, blue-eyed Marcen." God my hero was gorgeous.

I walked Matty to his classroom, begrudgingly reminding him I'd meet him there at the end of the day for the ride home, said good-bye to Megan and walked to Chemistry class with Jess for first period. Morning classes seemed to drag but lunch flew by as usual, especially since we were planning out the road trip. Jess despised the Rust On Wheels, but to me, it was a luxury sedan that'd bring me so close to Marcen that we'd probably share breaths of air between us.

I thought on this through the last periods of the day, then retrieved the annoyance when the final bell rang. Matty held a paper in his hand with a painting that looked like ketchup and mustard had exploded all over it. "It's the Blood Revenger using his blood powers."

I rolled my eyes, but he didn't notice. He just stared at his painting with a goofy grin and never said a word the entire way home, which is exactly the way all little brothers should be.

⚜

The rest of the week went in much of the same manner, each day seeming longer and longer until Friday finally came. Or as I referred to it, the day before Marcen Weston day. Jess had missed school that day but she sometimes took Fridays off if we had something big planned. I could think of nothing bigger than tomorrow.

That evening, just before dinner, I'd just finished washing my hair and noticed three missed calls from Megan on my cell. Someone was obviously excited.

I called her back and she answered during the first ring, sobbing into her phone. She was crying so hard she had that heaving, jumpy breath that forced sentences out one word at a time. "I. Can't. Go."

"What do you mean you can't go?"

When she finally calmed down enough to speak properly, she informed me that her mom's new employer had pushed up the start date and that Megan and her family were leaving tonight. Since her mom had been looking for a job for so long, she wasn't about to risk it for anything. And anything included Marcen Weston. I found myself crying with her by the end of it all. Not having Best Friend Number Two beside me as I met my hero was bad enough, but knowing our good-byes would happen over the phone and not in person was even worse. We said all we could to say to each other, then stayed on our phones in silence until the batteries died.

When I'd charged the phone back up enough to break the news to Best Friend Number One, I called Jess. It rang until voicemail picked up, so I hung up and waited the obligatory ten seconds before calling back. Upon second attempt, someone picked up who at first I'd assumed was her brother. When I asked to speak to Jess, she revealed that it was in fact, her. "I'm dying, Katie," she croaked into the receiver.

"Can you maybe die tomorrow night?" I asked, hoping she'd laugh and say, but of course Katie, because I know I'm your ride to the Skylark Razor, but she just coughed and hacked up what sounded like a bucket of phlegm into the receiver. Gross.

"I've had a fever of, like, a hundred and eighty all day," she said. "I can barely see let alone drive the Rust On Wheels."

I felt exactly like the Blood Revenger in the season two finale. Two of his most trusted allies joined forces and betrayed him, leaving him in an abandoned warehouse while it burned to the ground then exploded in a wide angle shot that cut to credits. Marcen would do something heroic in the Season Three premiere to save his skin, and I had no doubt his perfect mind would figure out a way. I tried explaining this to Jess, but she only said, "I'm sorry Katie," then her voice pulled away from the phone and it sounded like she barfed. She returned a few seconds later. "I can't."

"Fine," I said and hung up without saying good-bye.

I stood there for a moment with my cell in my hand, staring at my reflection in the lifeless, black screen. I thought about Marcen. I thought of how it would've been such an awesome road trip and thought of the memories my two best friends and I would've had of our last time together. Then I did what any hero would do in that situation: I cried.

A gentle knock came at the door ten minutes later. "Dinner's ready, kiddo," my dad said on the other side. He knew the rules of engagement: much like vampires, he was not to enter my room unless invited, but when I never answered, he nudged the door open a crack. "Katherine? Everything alright in here?"

"Fine," I said. And then like an idiot, I sniffled. Daughters crying superseded the vampire invitation rule and my dad pushed open the door with fatherly concern in his eyes. I'd managed to wipe away the tears in time, but my eyes still felt puffy and red, betraying the cool, calm exterior I was trying desperately to portray.

I explained the situation and he gave me a one-armed hug around the shoulder, kissing the top of my head before helping me to my feet. "Come on," he said, ushering me out of the room. "It's meatloaf. Your favourite."

We both gave a brief, hesitant laugh, knowing full well that meatloaf was exactly no one's favourite, then headed into the kitchen.

Matty and my mom were already seated. She looked at me the same way my dad had when he came into my room, but he gave her a little head shake which in parent-speak meant, I'll tell you how lame our daughter is later.

I ate in morose silence. My parents talked a little bit about my dad's interview the other day and how he thought it went really well and expected to get an e-mail about it tomorrow. Maybe one of us would have a happy Saturday. Matty was busy not-eating his dinner and I was doing my best to chew through the gloriousness of under-sauced meatloaf when my dad looked over and said, "I'll take you."

"Take me?" I asked.

"To the Blood Avenger guy."

"Revenger, Dad. And I don't think—"

"Oh come on. You've been looking forward to this all week and it looks like you've got a couple extra tickets for your old man and little brother. The three of us can head out to the Skylark Razor and meet this Marcen character. Would you like that, Matty?"

Matty raised his fork with a cheer and a piece of meatloaf flew from it, landing on my plate. A boiling rage filled my chest at the thought of one of my best friend's tickets going to that little brat and the other going to my father who couldn't even pronounce Marcen's name correctly. Though in his defence, most adults pronounced his name with a hard C.

The whole idea of a five-hour road trip with those two almost made me regret ever getting the tickets in the first place, but then my hero's beautiful face popped into my head and whispered, "The sacrifice of one, for sake of the many," which was what the Blood Revenger always said to the villains after they'd given him a sound and thorough beating. So I'd do the same and sacrifice my sanity for the sake of meeting Marcen. "Alright," I conceded with a fake smile. "Sounds good." I excused myself from the table and retreated back to my room for the remainder of the night.

⚬∞⚬

Morning came quickly and for once the annoying death knell of my alarm wasn't so depressing; today was Marcen Weston day. I showered and put a little more effort into my braids this morning, adding the same blood-red flower to my hair that the Blood Revenger would always leave on his enemies after thwarting their evil plans. A dab of perfume on my wrists and a bit of lip gloss (just in case) and I was ready to go.

My dad was already up, checking his e-mail on his laptop at the kitchen table. Mom was getting Matty's jacket on and applying a thick coat of sunscreen despite a thunderstorm in the forecast. "Anything

84

yet?" she asked my dad, who'd been checking for a response from his potential employer relentlessly. Dad shook his head, closed the laptop and tucked it under his arm. "Ready to meet your hero, kiddo?"

I was so ready. Ever since the pilot episode, I'd dreamt of meeting Marcen. His character worked as a geeky investor on Wall Street until he discovered his employers doing a little insider trading. Before he could alert the authorities, they'd kidnapped him and drowned him in a vat of genetically altered blood, then threw him out of a fifty-seventh storey window where he splattered on the sidewalk below. Little did they know the blood they drowned him in could repair even the most gruesome wounds, and before they could get the cover-up story of his suicide onto the evening news, he'd healed and vanished into the shadows, vowing revenge on them all. Hence, his alter ego was born, as was my undying love for the greatest man I'd ever almost-known.

"Hellooo?" my dad said, waving his hand in front of my face. "Earth to Katherine."

"I'm ready," I said. "Can we go? I don't want to be late."

"It's 8:00 a.m.," my mom said. "The event isn't over until 4 o'clock. You'll be fine." She kissed my father and wished him luck but I couldn't be sure if the luck was for a potential job offer or his five-hour sentence of designated-driver-of-children. Either way, he said thanks, returned the kiss and we were on our way.

∽∽

I was already on the third encore of Taylor Swift's album, RED (eyes closed, indulged in a sea of lyrical genius), when I felt the car pull off the freeway and slow. I cracked an eyelid and saw Matty with his face pressed up against the front passenger window, my dad telling him to get his little butt back in the seat until we came to a stop. We were still a couple of hours away from reaching the Skylark Razor, but since dad drove like a NASCAR finalist, we'd gained enough time to stop for lunch. As anxious as I was to get to the meet-and-greet, I had to admit unpretzeling from the backseat felt pretty damn good.

My dad pulled into a spot outside a little strip mall containing a thrift shop, currency exchange and little dive of a diner he said he used go to when he was in high school. With the threat of rain imminent, the diner was packed, so we were forced to take our chances on the patio outside and sat on one of the decrepit picnic tables with a tattered, yellow umbrella. I sat carefully on the bench between a bit of bird poop and a carving of someone's initials in a heart. A blue-haired waitress who looked about a hundred and sixty years old came and took our order.

While we waited, Dad flipped open his laptop and attached his

85

little antenna doohickey to the side so he could check his e-mail. Matty played with his Blood Revenger action figures and I popped my earphones back in until the food arrived. I thought we'd eat fast and be on our way, but my dad decided he'd pick a fight with me. Not on purpose of course, but any time anyone questions my benevolent hero, they best bring their sparring gloves.

"So how old is this Marken guy?" Dad said.

"Marcen, Dad. MARRRR. SENNN."

He ignored the phonetic lesson and asked the question again. "He's twenty-five, Dad. His birthday is April 14th, 1990. He's an Aries (which I might add is a sign that goes exceptionally well with my fiery Sagittarius personality). He has beautiful blue eyes and dark brown hair and a little dimple that always pops up when he does his signature smirk at overconfident bad guys."

"If he's so beautiful, why does he wear the mask?" Dad asked, pointing at Matty's action figure. "I mean, it covers his whole face except for the eye holes."

"He does it to protect his loved ones. Don't you know anything about being heroic?"

Dad shrugged. "I don't really get the allure."

I let out an audible sigh of frustration and grabbed his laptop. I pulled up the Heropedia website and found the entry for Blood Revenger which contained every snippet of information on both the Blood Revenger and the beautiful creature who played him on TV. "Here," I said and turned the laptop back to him. "You're going to earn your ticket, Dad. I'm going over to that tree to finish my lunch in peace. During said peaceful lunch, I want you to pore over this information and acclimate yourself to the world of Marcen Weston. When you're done, we shall continue on to the Skylark Razor, and by then you should be worthy to stand in the presence of a true hero and his fans."

"Yes, ma'am," Dad said with a little salute. He chewed on his cheeseburger and read while I retreated to the tree as promised. The Blood Revenger had to deal with annoying sidekicks on more than one occasion, and this felt very similar to that. His sidekicks always had a habit of disappearing before the season finales though. I wouldn't be so lucky.

I was finishing up the last bit of fries when Matty shuffled up to my feet and looked down at me. "Dad says to watch me until he gets back."

I peered around the annoyance and saw my dad heading into the thrift shop. "Really?"

Matty shrugged and plopped down beside me, then continued to play with his Blood Revenger until about ten minutes later when my dad finally emerged from the shop with a large paper bag. He waved and I tapped an imaginary watch on my wrist.

Thunder boomed as he opened the car doors for us and a few raindrops hit me in the forehead as I fought Matty for the front seat. I won, but the victory was short-lived. We'd wasted more time on lunch than I thought we would and dad would have to drive extra NASCARy in order for us to get a decent spot in line.

Traffic ground to a halt about half an hour from our destination. The storm had hit with full force and even though sheets of water rolled down the windshield, you could still see the epic Skylark Razor towering over the rest of the city in the distance. It taunted me. It was so close yet with bumper to bumper traffic blocking the way, so very, very far away. It really made me wish we had the Crimson Jet, the Blood Revenger's personal, aerial transport system. We'd just fly above all these cars and land right beside the desk Marcen was signing posters at.

My dad drummed his fingers on the steering wheel as we crept along, ever patient. He seemed a little quieter now, but he was most likely mapping out the best route to the tower once we got out of this mess.

The storm began to ease enough to downgrade the wiper speed from frantic to fast, and through the blots of water pelting the windshield, I saw a car up ahead with its hazard lights flashing. It'd pulled off to the side, but everyone driving by had to have a look to see what was going on. This would certainly threaten a timely arrival to the meet-and-greet.

When it was our turn to ogle, my dad slowed almost to a stop. A man stood outside the car with an obviously flat tire and some sort of L-shaped bar in his hand. His other hand was scratching his head.

We drove past but then pulled sharply off the road a few car lengths in front of it. "What are you doing?" I asked, my voice an octave higher. "We're already late as it is."

"He needs help, Katherine," my dad said. "Watch your brother. I'll be right back."

My dad grabbed the thrift store paper bag and threw it into the trunk, then walked over to the drenched man. I watched my father in the side-view mirror as he gave the man a quick handshake before setting to work on the wheel. My dad had worked as a mechanic's assistant during high school and knew his way around a car pretty well, but still, the clock was ticking and even as he removed the flat and began securing the spare, I knew our window for a good spot in line had closed. Now it was just a matter of actually getting there before the whole damn thing was over.

What seemed like eighty-three years later, my dad finally returned.

He plopped down in the driver's seat, combed his fingers through his soaked hair and gave a satisfied sigh. "All set," he said and started the car. "They're going to follow us. He's got three boys with him about Matty's age and they're going to the meet-and-greet as well."

"Fantastic," I said. "Then we can all miss it together."

"Katherine," my dad said in his I'm-about-to-lecture-you tone, "there are more important things in life than meeting some television star. The sacrifice of one, for the sake of the many? Ring a bell?"

Oh no he did not just quote the Blood Revenger to me while we were on our way to missing the Blood Revenger. It made me regret ever forcing him to soak up all those nuggets of goodness on Heropedia. "You're not even doing his voice right," was all I responded with. He tried a few other voices and on his fifth attempt, Matty perked up and told him he'd gotten it right. I had to admit the impression was pretty good, but I was too pissed off to say it out loud. I couldn't even listen to Ms. Swift anymore, so I just sat there, staring out the side window, hoping beyond hope that we'd make it on time.

∽

I should have known something was wrong when we found a parking spot in the fourth row. There was still fifteen minutes left of the meet-and-greet, but it was eerily quiet. The family dad had helped with the flat parked right beside us and we all piled out of the cars.

Three boys around the same age as Matty scrambled around the vehicles, swarming like flies in their little Blood Revenger costumes. Blood Revenger's suit was relatively simple to recreate because on the show, he'd made it mostly out of different shades of red clothes he'd found around the house he lived in before his attempted murder. Dress shirts and ties and pants, either originally red or dyed to match were fitted to Marcen's lovely physique, and the villains often didn't take him seriously until they were picking their teeth up off the ground. The kids made quick friends with Matty. It would've been a cute moment if not for the sense of impending doom in the pit of my stomach.

I bolted up the Skylark Razor stairs with everyone else taking their sweet-ass time behind me. The tower itself seemed to disappear into the clearing sky and I shaded my eyes from the blinding afternoon sun as I stared up at it, waiting for the slowpokes to join me. "Come on, old man," I called down to my father. He shook his head, then helped Matty when he stumbled on the second last step before the grand entrance.

Normally the Skylark Razor would have locked entrance doors, protected by a concierge who would sit behind a desk and let the people in, but because it was the grand opening, the doors were propped open with nothing blocking the way but a few coloured streamers and some helium balloons bouncing off the glass. I ran into the main lobby and marvelled at the expansive marble floors covering an area nearly the size of an ice rink. Stores now open to the general public lined both sides, their managers (or assistant managers or whomever drew the short straw) stood at the entrances peddling free samples of various crap.

A large temporary railing was setup across the middle of the marble causeway. On the other side of the railing was the concierge desk. The desk that Marcen Weston was supposed to be sitting at. The desk he was supposed to be signing autographs from; shaking hands from and asking for my number from. But there was no Marcen Weston at the desk. The only things left were a few small posters of the Blood Revenger, a couple pens and a half-empty bottle of Perrier.

"What the actual fu–"

"Katherine!" my dad said, cutting off my emotional explosion with a stern look and nod toward the boys. Whatever. While they peered over the railing with slight confusion, all I could do to keep from knocking the whole damn railing down was swear or cry. Neither seemed appropriate to do in public so I chose the former and swore. In my head. Many times.

I was working my way through a flurry of mental expletives when a group of men dressed in suits exited a store at the opposite end of the lobby. They were walking very close to each other, tightly packed and laughing, slapping backs as they moved across the lobby. About halfway across the marble expanse, their little man-huddle separated slightly and my heart skipped a beat. It was Marcen Weston, surrounded by what was probably his entourage, security and publicists.

"Marcen!" I screamed without thinking, and for a brief second, I felt a bit embarrassed by how shrill and juvenile my voice sounded. The boys jumped up and down at the railing, waving furiously as Marcen stopped and looked over at us. I found myself waving too, like an imbecile, but I'd be damned if the little twerps got his attention before I did. One of the men whispered something in Marcen's ear. He looked down at his watch, then back up to the man and shook his head. They both laughed and continued across the lobby with the others in tow, leaving through a door on the other side.

"He left," I said to no one in particular.

He effing left. Without so much as a wave back to one of his greatest fans. A fan who spent a five-hour car ride with her annoying brother and non-fan father to get here. A fan who bought both the DVD and Blu-ray versions of Season One just because the cases came with different artwork. He just, left. There were no such things as heroes; only asshats who played them on TV.

My shock and stunned silence was interrupted by Matty's hope-dashed sniffles. His three new friends joined in, creating a symphony of angry-boy-cries. The other father just stood there staring at my dad with a look of, oh God what do we do now? What do we do with a pissed-off sixteen-year-old girl and four distraught, mini Blood Revengers?

"I'm really sorry," my dad said. His words felt genuine and he looked legitimately saddened by the situation, but his condolences did little to alleviate my heartbreak. He continued to console. "I know what it's like to have your heart set on something, only to have it snuffed out at the last moment."

I didn't really know what he was talking about. I didn't really care. He crouched down beside Matty and gave him a hug, but that only made him cry harder. The other dad tried to do the same, but two of his three boys rejected the comfort and pulled away with angry grunts and more tears. My dad patted my shoulder a couple times. "I'll go pull the car around. Be right back."

I didn't answer as he left.

Several minutes and a few gallons of Matty tears later, he looked back past me toward the entrance and his watery eyes widened. The other boys did the same and one of them pointed, shouting, "Blood Revenger!"

I froze, suddenly feeling star-struck and unable to face my hero. Had it all been an act? Had Marcen just played the too-cool-for-fans douchebag on the outside, only to don his Blood Revenger suit and sneak up from behind?

"Good afternoon, citizens," he said, and although the voice was nearly perfect to the untrained ear, I knew instantly it wasn't Marcen Weston but in fact, my father. This made looking even more difficult, but Matty and his friends let out a collective whoooaaaa and rushed past me. I took a breath and turned around.

My dad walked toward us with a confident gait, the silhouette of the Blood Revenger outlined by the blinding afternoon sunlight pouring through the propped open entrance doors behind him. His approach seemed to happen in slow-motion to match the crescendo of my own mortification. The closer he got, the clearer he became until our eyes adjusted to the backlight and he was standing right in front us.

There he stood, arms folded across his chest and head covered in the Blood Revenger's signature full-faced, featureless mask with only his eyes visible. Matty and his friends had no idea who was behind it. They didn't notice the buttons on my dad's red dress shirt straining against the tiny pudge of a middle-aged man's stomach, nor did they observe the hem of his wine-red dress pants rising just above his ankles like he was expecting a flood. The pants were also exceptionally tight and I was thankful he'd strategically placed his utility pack directly below his belt buckle. Other than those few giveaways, it was actually a fairly accurate representation of the Blood Revenger's

90

suit. His trip into the thrift store suddenly made sense and it probably cost him less than twenty bucks all told.

"I hear you travelled quite a ways to be here today," he said, winking at me through the left eye hole. "That's a long time to sit in a car. Wouldn't you agree, Matthew?"

Matty's mouth dropped open at the mention of his name. He nodded slowly with no audible response, like he was three seconds away from going catatonic. I envied him in that moment. I envied all four of the boys whose eyes were locked on the red silk scarf my dad used for a mask. They truly believed this was the Blood Revenger, their hero, and that he'd come to some random condo shopping tower just to see them. The other father played along, asking if he could take a picture of the Blood Revenger with the boys.

My dad nodded then glanced my way. "Would you like to join us, Katherine?" he asked in his refined Blood Revenger voice. I shook my head and Matty looked shocked that I'd refuse a picture with someone I'd idolized longer than he had. Seeing confusion creep into his eyes, I quickly back-pedalled as not to ruin my father's ruse. "Just kidding," I said with a forced laugh. "Where should I stand?"

We took several rounds of pictures. Some with all of us, some with just the boys and a few one-on-ones with my dad doing classic Blood Revenger poses. He must've sped-read Heropedia during lunch to do such an accurate impression. His focus on getting the voice right in the ride over paid off as well. As the camera kept flashing, others in the vicinity started taking notice. Adults and kids alike collected around us, expanding down the railing until there was such a commotion going on that it drew the attention of a nearby security guard.

He walked up to us, at first a little confused since he probably thought it was Marcen himself, but after closer scrutiny, his demeanour changed from uncertainty to macho-security-man bravado. "Sir, you can't be here," he said, his hand resting on his radio like it was a gun. "I'm going to have to ask you to leave."

My dad, bless his dorky heart, ignored the orders and took some more pictures with a few kids that'd finally pushed their way through to him from the outskirts of the crowd. The security guard repeated the order but my dad never acknowledged him until he'd shaken the hand of every last kid (as well as a couple of adults wearing Blood Revenger t-shirts).

"Sir, you need to leave. Now," the guard said, quite loud and abrupt.

My father nodded and turned to the crowd, addressing the children. "Dear friends," he said with his hands extended over a dozen awe-struck beady eyes, "my good friend here has told me I am needed elsewhere. Doctor Venison–"

"Veneesean. Veneesean," I whispered loud enough for him to

91

know he butchered the villain's name.

"Doctor Veneesean is attacking a nearby city, and I must go. It has been an honour meeting you fine people. Now I must leave with the guard and take care of the doctor." He produced the Blood Revenger's signature crimson flower from behind his back and handed it to me with a light bow. "Farewell, my dearest Katherine."

Some of the kids made that mushy, romantic ooooooooh sound that kids do and I blushed, but only because it was so damn embarrassing. It worked well with my dad's act though, and to finish it off, he (quite unexpectedly) hopped the railing and ran toward the same door Marcen had left through. The security guard chased after him like a sidekick worried about being left behind. It was perfect.

"That was awesome," Matty said to his new friends. The crowd expressed similar sentiment before dispersing toward various storefront samplings, like ants looking for the next food crumb. A few minutes later my dad appeared behind us, back in his normal clothes.

"Ready to go?" he asked as Matty ran up to him, grabbing both sides of his face. "Dad you totally missed it."

"Missed what?"

"The Blood Revenger. He was here. And he knew my name. And he took pictures with us. And, and he gave Katie a flower. He ran that way but you won't find him. He's going to fight the doctor."

My dad feigned extreme disappointment for missing such awesomeness and I felt my lips curl into a smile despite the image of Marcen walking away still burning ferociously in my mind.

"Thanks again, bud," the other father said, trying to corral his boys toward the entrance. "You're a standup guy."

My dad shook his hand and we parted ways, heading back to the car that he hadn't actually moved. Matty called shotgun and I didn't fight him on it. I flopped into the back seat and connected my earbuds to my phone. I created a playlist of sad music suitable for a crestfallen drive back home. I just wanted to be in my room so I could tear all my Marcen Weston posters off the wall and cry into my pillow.

Three hours later as I was drifting in and out of sleep, my phone died and the music stopped. Matty was passed out in the front seat and my dad was just staring straight ahead at the road with a faraway look in his eyes. I couldn't go another two hours without any distractions, so I pulled my dad's laptop out from the back of his seat and propped it up on my legs.

I flipped open the lid. The Blood Revenger's entry on Heropedia was still loaded into the browser along with another tab marked with the URL www.marcenwestonsucks.org. Curiosity got the better of me and I clicked it. It was a site dedicated to people recanting various tales of showing up to meet Marcen only to find he'd left early or never shown up at all. He'd never, not once, stayed until the end of any of his meet-and-greets. It was clear this is what prompted my dad to run into the thrift store for a backup plan should Marcen keep his streak alive.

I wouldn't have known this about Marcen because I never would have visited such a blasphemous site before today. Now I wanted to donate to it. Actually, I didn't even want to see his face. I closed the browser down, including the two popups asking if I really wanted to leave Marcen's Heropedia page. I did. I so did.

The browser disappeared revealing my dad's e-mail which he was usually very careful to keep closed. He hadn't this time (most likely due to my forcing him to take Blood Revenger 101 during lunch) and before I could shut it down, my eyes landed on the last e-mail he'd received. It'd come in at 11:37 a.m. this morning and read:

Dear Applicant,

Thank-you for taking the time to speak with us last week. We've had several meetings regarding the open position but unfortunately have decided to go with a more suitable candidate. Good luck and please feel free to apply to any future openings within our company.

Sincerely,
Soul-crushing Middle Management Dickheads.

I made that last line up of course, but it didn't mean it wasn't true. I felt my throat tighten. The e-mail had come during our stop for lunch, just shortly after I loaded Heropedia for my dad and abandoned him to sit under a tree by myself. And I thought Marcen was a spoiled ass.

"I'm so sorry, Dad. About the job."

His eyes flicked back at me through the rear view mirror and he shrugged. "They'll be other opportunities, kiddo. Better ones."

"They were stupid not to hire you," I said. "Don't they know they could've had the Blood Revenger working for them?"

"Tis true," my dad said, "but the sacrifice of one was for the sake of the many. Or at least, the sake of two," he added with a wink.

So now I was crying.

Despite a crushing job rejection, my father continued to drive five hours upstate; helped a stranger change a flat in the pouring rain and cosplayed the Blood Revenger, probably violating a dozen copyrights. And all so his bratty, teenage daughter could meet her ex-idol and for the sake of his seven-year-old's awestruck wonderment.

They say that heroes walk among us. Capeless. Unseen. They say they're unknown to the little people milling about their everyday lives and that we're blind to their heroics until they don their mask. I know that now to be true. How blind I was.

I unbuckled my seatbelt and jumped forward, throwing both arms around my dad. He startled as I squeezed him tight. I probably should've warned him it was coming, but I was a slave to the love and unbridled admiration exploding in my heart at that particular moment.

"What's this for?" he asked.

I kissed him on the cheek. "For my hero."

Bounty of the Everdark – Lilian Oake

For the dark elves of Jaydür, the shadows of the Everdark are their citadels and the closest thing they have to freedom. Their ebony skin blends with the night, making their every move naught but swaying eaves to the untrained eye.

It was behind this shield of shadow that Lorel came to know of the planned attack upon Castle d'Oruth. Two dark elf hawkers, a goblin, and a man passed through the realm of her people, loud in their scheming and senseless in their traipsing, letting the whole forest know their design.

The branch she perched upon allowed neither creak nor crackle as she crawled through the boughs and descended the trunk to better see her company. It was only in moments like these that the perpetual dark was valued. Night in the Everdark was a constant and had been likened to the shadowy side of the North moon – talked of in whispers, an undesired destination for most. It was interesting that any man that was unable to blend with the murk would be walking within that wood, but there he was, associating with some of the lowliest creatures in the realm. He was a traitor to his own kind and, judging by the pin hung upon his shoulder, to his own Queen.

"Within the fortnight Queen d'Oruth passes through the Low Road," the man explained to his companions. "She rides with a Priest from Burdsfilt, four Holy Men, and six soldiers. A party small enough to pass through unnoticed."

The goblin knifed a rat scuttling by his foot and lifted it to his mouth with a rotting grin. "Maç'g eçk norlino lorinthak," he laughed.

The man looked to one of the dänotei with a nauseated frown. "Drogan, I do not speak Lançir. What did the beast say?"

"That the woman is as stupid as you are," replied Drogan, leaning on a birch. "Essentially." He crossed his arms over his broad shoulders and scanned the trees above. He knew Lorel was there but he would not reveal her. He'd deal with her on his own time. "Tell me, Man-Levi, how did you communicate with the goblin when you fail to understand so few words in Shadowspeak?"

The man licked his teeth in an attempt to hide his contempt, but human contempt reeked almost as badly as a rotting pixie. "He found *you*, didn't he?" Levi said before spitting at the ground. "I think I got on well enough."

The second elf threw his head back and laughed. Lorel immediately recognized him as Logil, Drogan's brother. "Are we really going to involve ourselves here?" he asked with a sporting nudge in his brother's side.

"Of course you're going to," the man said. "We already made a deal. Now, listen. You keep your little friends away from the Queen. You let her pass and I will deliver your bounty at the feet of the birch dryad."

Drogan cleared his throat, bringing to mind the footless tree-maidens of the forest. They were well known to be part of the tree and therefore, rooted into the ground. "A dryad has no feet," he explained.

Lorel stifled her laugh as best she could but Drogan was no fool, and Logil quickly caught on. He sent a slow glance over his shoulder and one corner of his black lips curved into a knowing smirk.

Blood rose to the man's face; not even the shadows could hide it. "You know very well what I mean," he said, adding a bite gesture to make his point. "Will you allow the Queen safe passage through the realm?"

Drogan waved his hand dismissively. "Yes, yes, don't worry. She won't be touched."

"Swear it."

"It is sworn."

"Idiot," Lorel said, loud enough for just her fellow elves to hear.

Logil tossed Drogan a glance and shook his head.

The man looked to the goblin. "And him?"

"Thik," Logil began, catching the goblin's attention. "K'nok hifilt lont ell iç d'Oruth hem?"

Thik nodded.

Drogan laughed. "He's not happy about it but he swears."

The human departed with a bow of gratitude and headed toward the Gate. When the air no longer carried his scent, Lorel dropped to the foot of the tree among the others, startling the goblin just as he finished off his rat. He threw the remains onto the ground and let out a long string of vulgar utterances about females then went on his way into the woods.

"Lorel," Drogan began. "I'm not surprised to see you here - and I certainly am not surprised by your disapproval of my business with Dal – but rest assured, it is nothing you need to worry about."

The mud squelched beneath her boots as she levelled her weight and looked him head on. "Since when do we make secret deals with humans?" she asked.

"Since they were leading me into a hoard of treasure," he snapped in reply. "No one will be hurt. I will simply allow Queen d'Oruth to pass through."

Drogan's eyes were dark and cautious. Something told Lorel he was still hiding something and she was going to find out.

"What is Dal doing with the Queen?" she insisted.

Logil looked on his brother with uncertainty and a level of discomfort that only fuelled her desire for knowledge.

"If that human is planning to hurt the Queen and you two are involved, all our years of collaborating with the humans will be for naught. Our people are too few to be causing any more problems with the humans. It will only bring us closer to extinction."

Drogan threw his hands into the air with an "ach" and passed Lorel by. "The man only intends on her capture for leverage," he said. "When he gets what he wants from her, she'll be released and we'll be rich."

Lorel turned and followed him, keeping in step with him. "And then when you are discovered with the crown jewels, we will be hunted, impaled and used for decoration in the mad-king's throne room! Since when were you so foolish! You know I cannot let you to go through with this."

Drogan stopped and looked darkly at Lorel. He was not the kind to take threats lightly, she knew.

That was the end of the conversation as Drogan and his brother Logil dismissed her silently and left her to ferment in her anger and disappointment.

⌒∞⌒

The North Moon waxed and waned when the first sound of wood and metal creaked through the Everdark, not a hundred yards below Lorel. It was the first day of a new month and little light was given from above. Excitement was the first reaction to the uncommon sight but when the horse sigil of the Crown d'Oruth tipped and teetered over the unlevel earth, her stomach soured and her jaw ached in tension. Queen d'Oruth knew what she risked and yet, there she was.

"Stupid woman," Lorel murmured to herself, thinking back on the goblin's words. She scanned the trees around them and found no sign of any creature in their midst. Drogan and Logil must have drawn everyone away from the path through the Everdark to make sure none would harm her.

She clutched a thick branch above her and swung, silent as the night, to the boughs below. Her movements were quick and fluid as she slipped through the trees with speed only the dark elves could achieve and made her way to the edge of the wood. There the path was near its end and there she waited for the Queen's carriage.

It wasn't five minutes before the squeaking presence of the

Queen reached Lorel. She stood in the road, about ten yards from the Everdark's exit – still deep enough to be hidden in the forest from anyone waiting to capture the Queen on the outskirts. The anticipated six soldiers were in clear view but the holy men must have been seated inside the carriage with the queen. Lorel stood tall and confident.

"Halt!" the soldier on horseback, who rode a few yards ahead, cried. The ring of blades leaving their scabbards sang unanimously. "Stay where you are, dark elf!" the lead commanded.

"I am unarmed," Lorel called in return with her arms outstretched. "Though the men waiting for you beyond this forest seem prepared for a fight."

The front soldier's eyes flickered to the pathway leading out of this place. "Why should we trust a creature of the Everdark?"

Lorel took a step forward, biting her cheek and holding back a snappy retort. The stories of old were hard-pressed into the minds of people, such that convincing the man of the truth in her words seemed like an impossible task – but she had to try. If anyone discovered the involvement of the dark elves in the Queen's kidnapping, it would surely mean the death of any possible alliance between the races.

"Sir," she called back, remaining where she was. He was so on edge, she could see his temple twitch with every beat of his heart. A white-gloved hand tugged slightly on a curtain in the carriage. Lorel made sure to speak louder and more clearly. "I swear on my own people that there is a conspiracy against the Queen underway. I am aware of a plan by a man named Dal to kidnap and use her for ransom to gain riches."

The other soldiers stood in a line before the carriage but for two who kept a keen eye on the trees and distance from the back and sides of the carriage. A quiet hum of conversation or arguing came from within.

"Deception!" another soldier claimed with a scoff. He turned to the other soldiers and added, "Her words are as poisonous as the blood that keeps her alive."

"I assure you, your blood is no better than mine – nor is it a better shade of scarlet," she replied, pointing an accusing finger at the man. "I speak the truth. Dal is just down the road, waiting for Queen d'Oruth and I intend on stopping his plans."

A voice called from the carriage, clearly old but well enunciated in the common tongue of man. "And why would a lady of the Everdark be willing to stand up for me?"

Perfect. The Queen was involving herself now; maybe she would have more sense than the sword-happy soldiers. "Your Highness," Lorel began. "I grew up with tales of the hatred between human and dark elf. Since I was a child, I have dreamed of an alliance – or at the very least, acceptance – between our peoples. This dream is something I desire to see fulfilled in my lifetime."

"This conspirator – the man you call Dal – he awaits my arrival beyond the forest?" the Queen asked, though she remained hidden within the carriage.

"He does," Lorel replied.

"And you think me foolish and my men too weak to protect me?"

Lorel looked up to the heavens with an inner groan. "Your Highness, I claimed no such thing. I am simply trying to do a good deed here. When you see that, I am convinced that you will be more willing to sit with my people and hear us. If we work together, we can do extraordinary things – for all of Jaydür."

The white glove gestured out of the window for the men to continue their journey. Lorel's words were being disregarded. With the soldier's swords still unsheathed and raised to her, the carriage moved forward and Lorel stepped back. A single, blue eye peered at her from behind the curtain, which closed after meeting the dark elf's gaze.

Lorel clenched her fists. In an instant, she was in the canopy of the woods, climbing higher and higher to catch a glimpse of Dal on the outskirts. Unseen from ground level, a small troop of men hid on the downward path that led to the High Kingdom of Men – enough to be victorious over the Queen and her chosen few, that was for sure. They'd be caught by surprise just as they'd crest the hill and Dal's plans would ruin the chance of any ounce of freedom for the dark elves. Lorel couldn't let that happen. She deserved a chance; she didn't choose this life. Why should her kind be looked down on with contempt when she'd done nothing deserving of it? She hadn't even finished the thought before she was on the heads of the Queen's soldiers, a shadow within the shadows like a bat in the night.

"Arms!" A soldier cried as the man before him rose off his horse and disappeared into the cloak of darkness above. The horses beneath the three remaining soldiers nervously paced in place, unable to comply with their master's orders.

Another man was snatched from above, leaving only two who cried aloud when realization hit them that they could not fight the unseen. With no word and eyes bright with terror, they fled, abandoning Queen d'Oruth.

"Cowards," Lorel muttered as she finished fastening a ribbon of weaved leaves and vines around the mouth of a soldier, before dropping onto the carriage.

"By the Highest!" the Queen gasped.

Lorel jerked the door open and offered her hand to the jewel-embellished Queen and her Holy men. "On my life, I swear what I caution is true. You cannot remain here, nor continue your way to the kingdom – not until Dal is gone, and he will be soon, I assure you."

The Holy men gripped what they could in fear and Queen d'Oruth's hand trembled at her red-painted lips. The dark elf woman who'd done away with her royal guards was black as night with lips as grey as the mountain peaks in summer. Her eyes were as the stars, clear and bright in the murk but distant and full of mystery.

"Come with me!" Lorel hissed. "Now!"

Hesitantly, the Queen took the dark elf's hand and stepped out of the carriage, her boots squelching in mud beneath her weight.

"Your Majesty," one of the Holy men began. His hand waved in the air in a motion unfamiliar to Lorel. "May the Highest bless and protect you. This woman has sworn on her life – may her words be true or..." his eyes set upon Lorel and stole her gaze. "Or may she die a most terrible death for any lie on her lips."

Lorel frowned at the Holy Man's words. "You worship the Highest? Then it may be of comfort to know that I know Him well enough myself."

The Queen and Holy men exchanged glances, astonished at the words coming from the woman.

"Listen, Dal is sure to come looking this far when he realizes your carriage is nowhere to be seen. The sooner we move out of sight, the sooner you will be safe. I will help you reach the safety of your castle walls but to do that, you must trust me."

Something moved in the shadow not three meters from her right and before Lorel could lead the Queen away, Dal stepped out into the grey light. His men – the men huddling beyond the hills – stepped out from all directions, encircling Lorel, the Queen and her carriage.

"You're right," Dal said, wielding his sword. "Though it's a pity you didn't get out of sight in time. Hand the Queen over to me."

The Queen placed her hand over her heart. "It is true! A traitor to his own Queen!" The men laughed as they took a step forward, closing in the circle just a little tighter.

The Priest and his Holy Men were still in the carriage. Don't say a word, Lorel prayed to herself. She stepped up and the side of her lips rose into a caustic grin. "Don't be foolish. As a resident of the Everdark, the creatures here will come to my aid. Are you willing to risk it, Dal?"

With that, Dal's eyes flickered left and right. His hand gripped the hilt of his sword and his throat dropped and rose with his skittish gulp. "This part of the forest is empty until the moon rises – at the very least," he said, more in an effort to calm his own nerves. Dal's stomach soured as the dark elf's expression was unchanged at his attempt to frighten her.

"Treachery earns the gallows," the Queen interrupted. "All of you will be brought to justice!"

Dal laughed, a loud, boisterous guffaw. "You don't serve justice," he said, and then spit at her feet. "I don't need to answer to an old bag like you. You, who sits on her throne of jewels and points your gold-plated staff at the poor." He stepped closer, pointing his sword at the Queen. "What did you do to deserve all your treasures?"

"Again I ask," Lorel cut in. "Are you willing to risk it? The smell of blood alone will attract the pixies of these woods and they won't hurt those of the Everdark. That means they'll focus on you. Can your men handle those wicked, little nightmares?"

"Pixies?" one of the soldiers said. His blade trembled in his hands and lowered. "I never agreed to this!"

Dal raised a shushing hand at the man but he trembled more violently with every second. "No, Sir! I 'been plagued by them damnable creatures when I was a child. I won't tempt them after my family."

"Then get out, before I cut you open and leave them a hodgepodge for lunch," Dal hissed.

The man's sword dropped into the mud and he turned and rushed out of the wood.

"So there was only one so wise among you?" Lorel asked with a laugh, flickering her attention to the dropped sword. She hoped the rest would follow suit, as she was still unarmed. It would be wiser to call for help, she knew, but she would likely have a blade in her gut before anyone actually showed. Still, she cut into her fingertips with her knife-like nails until she broke the skin and warm blood dripped from her fingers. "Dal, you still have a chance to turn and walk out of my realm. If I were you, I would not hesitate on a thought."

The man's face turned red in his seething anger. "We had a plan, Elf," he said.

"No, you and that fool, Drogan, had a plan, but such a plan would poison any hope of peace between human and dark elf. I am not going to risk the future of my people for your foolish attempt at wealth. Put your hand to an axe and work for wages like a man."

Dal lunged forward and pressed the cold metal of his sword against the ebony flesh of Lorel's throat. "Why should I work when others have more than enough to share?"

A deep humming came from the depths of the Everdark, drawing Dal's attention. The smell of her blood travelled on the wind as she'd hoped. Leaves rustled in a rush of air and the leather of Dal's hilt cracked under the stress of his grip.

"What've you done?" he asked, looking down at her bleeding hand.

Lorel's eyes, silver as the moon, pierced Dal's surety. Her lips curved into a grin that flashed her sharp, ivory teeth. "Men like you are parasites in this world," she whispered just loud enough for him to hear above the rising buzz. "And so you must be exterminated if there is to be any hope."

"Pixies!" One of the men cried.

"Call them off!" Dal demanded.

"I cannot. The bloodfever has taken hold." Dal's eyes widened as a grey billow came rushing toward them. With a breath held in her lungs, she bashed her head into Dal's, knocking him onto the ground. Just as the swarm came upon them all, Lorel turned and grabbed the Queen who swatted at the pixies droning all around them, biting at whatever flesh they could reach. Lorel tore off a piece of cloth from her tunic and soaked it in the blood from her palms then tossed it behind her. Taking hold of Queen d'Oruth, she lifted her onto one of the horses then mounted and rode out of the Everdark.

◦✍◦

Sunlight was a curious thing. As dwarves would look upon the mountains' size and splendour, so was the reverence the elves of the night held for the sun. An orb hovering in the sky with nothing to hold it in its place, giving out warmth known only by the fires of a hearth — dark elves were drawn in a dreamy daze at the sensation.

Lorel squinted, estimating their arrival to the castle. It looked close but as her eyes were not accustomed to such light, she couldn't tell if it was really farther than it seemed. To her delight, they reached the gates just moments later. Dropping from the horse, Lorel helped the Queen down. The poor woman looked battered with bruises and bites on her cheeks and neck. Dried blood crusted the top of her left ear, all the way down to her chin.

"I am sorry," Lorel said when the Queen regained her footing.

The Queen pursed her lips with a frown. "For what? You saved me, young lady. It is I who should be apologizing for not listening to you — for giving in to the rumours and legends of your kind."

Lorel tucked a few stray white hairs behind her ear. "It's understandable," she said. "I suppose it would be a surprise to anyone with a childhood in Jaydür. We all hear the tales."

The Queen held out her pale, frail hand and took Lorel's. "My dear girl, it will be a most welcome surprise to children all over the world when they find that their tales of dread are not true — that all of the Everdark is not so terrible." She paused. "Well, except for the pixies."

Lorel smiled, closed her eyes and faced up to the sun as a renewing hope filled her. She'd done her part for her people. The future had room now for change.

"Come," the Queen went on. "Let us mend our history and forge a new future — together."

102

The Prince's Parish — Joshua Robertson

I

The dice dropped from Edgar's wobbly hand. His fingers trembled as if buried in midwinter snow. He swallowed a mouthful of stale air and paused. Gambling in a church was going to send the lot of them straight to perdition. His eyes widened as the dotted cubes smacked against the shoddy tabletop, recoiled, and settled.

"Ginger! Three fives and a four," Morgain exclaimed. "You won. I cannot believe you actually won, Edgar." He shook his shaggy head, grinning as wide as his cheeks would allow. "I guess that's game. Ten pence apiece. Pay out, boys." Morgain slapped down his coins as an example to the rest.

"B-b-beginner's luck," Pip remarked, mirroring Morgain's smile. The bright-faced chap pulled the pence from the pouch at his waist. The lad seemed to be in good spirits most of the time, despite his stutter.

Thomas, on the other hand, pouted from across the table. His curly, black hair hung over him like a nasty storm cloud. Thomas's face reddened all the way to his ears; Edgar did not think the table between them was strong enough to hold the lad back.

Thomas's voice cracked, marking his transition to manhood. "The whelp cheated. No one rolls three fives on their first game. Say, I have been playing Hammy for two years and never rolled three fives."

Pip clutched onto his pouch, pulling his lanky arms back to his sides like his money might be snagged from him at any moment. He nodded his head at Thomas, his white teeth disappearing behind his oversized lips. "Um, yeah, ch-ch-cheated. He must've."

Their bellyaching parroted back and forth in hushed whispers over the tattered table. Edgar was speechless, unsure of how to respond to the accusations. He felt his legs start shaking under the table. He did his best to hold them still before they started bouncing.

Morgain picked up on his discomfort and shushed the cacophony of the two disgruntled boys. "C'mon, don't be sore. You boys haven't

103

even been here a day and you're at each other's throats. Listen, Edgar didn't cheat. He came here to be a curate of the parish like you. Only sinners cheat. Tell them, Edgar."

Edgar blinked. He had not let his eyes close since the dice hit the table. He was too afraid to say it out loud, but he was certain lightning would strike him dead for playing Hammy. The boys back home use to play it down by the watering hole when the adults were away, but he never ventured too close. His grandfather would have had his hide for risking hard-earned coins at the fate of dice.

He noticed that Morgain was nodding his head with encouragement. The older chap was almost a man, looking at him much like an older brother might. Edgar wanted to say something slick or wise, but he was not quick like the others. He was the grandson of a sheepherder sent to become a curate. His childhood was spent roaming green fields and watching for wolves, not exchanging words with boisterous boys in a basement.

His mouth was dry. Footsteps resounded from the parish above them, giving Edgar a few more seconds. Minister Brus was moving around in the church, likely thinking that they were all asleep.

"Go ahead," Thomas poked. "Tell me you weren't cheating. I dare you."

"Yeah," Pip echoed, "g-g-go ahead."

His grandfather had told him it would be a good thing to serve at The Prince's Parish. This place was supposed to be safe from evil men, honouring Prince Arterbury, who ruled while the King was away at war in the Midlands. Yet, after only half a day, Edgar was gambling and picking fights with the other boys.

Edgar meekly grunted in the sound of a single word. It sounded more like a squeal. "Yeah."

"Ginger! What's wrong with you, Edgar?" Morgain asked. "You just won a month wages fair and square. Tell em you weren't cheating and be done with it."

Edgar rubbed his hands against the wool wrap that itched against his bare skin. It was not made as finely as it should have been. He was not sure why he had to trade his old clothes for this scratchy robe. "You guys can keep your pence. I didn't mean to win. Really."

"What?" Thomas snorted. "You expect us to believe you weren't trying to --" Thomas lifted his hand, palm facing the ceiling at a loss for words. When no one else spoke, he said, "The boy is a lout. He must be plumb out of his mind. A dummy, this one."

Pip wrinkled his nose with amusement. "A d-d-dummy."

"I am not!" Edgar gushed, cheeks warming. He was certain that his ears were bright red, too, even in the dim light of the burning wax. His grandfather always said that he blushed like a girl when he was angry.

104

"C'mon, you two. Let him alone and pay out already. Never seen such ruckus over a boy winning fair and square in all my life," Morgain sniggered.

The throaty voice behind them just about made Edgar jump straight from his chair. "Winning at what, did you say?"

"Minister Brus!" Thomas shouted, dark curls bobbing. He scooted back from the table as though it were a roaring fire about to burn his hands.

"M-m-minster Brus, he was just--"

"Pip, lying is as equal an abomination as any other sin. The common man may ask forgiveness, but a man of the church would have his tongue cut out. It would be my duty to see it done under the law. Prince Arterbury is quite particular about these matters." Minister Brus looked on Pip with sorrow, his eyes pleading to keep him from seeing the task done. His ruffled eyebrows were fuddled, arched and quivering upon his wrinkled forehead. His old lips smacked, pressing his greying stubble to his shaggy moustache.

Minister Brus could have been as old as the church. Edgar had met him when arriving that morning, but it was only now that he truly noticed the age of the old man.

Pip second guessed himself, sitting straighter, mouth gawking. "H-h-he was gambling. We all was gambling."

Thomas socked Pip in the shoulder. "Say, we didn't mean nothing by it, Minister Brus."

"I see," the Minister said, folding his hands in front of him. "Gambling is punishable in the same way as stealing, I'm afraid."

Edgar gulped, nearly afraid to ask, "And, how is that, Minister Brus?"

"Lashings and severed limbs." He replied. His voice was desolate, heart-breaking.

"L-l-lashings?"

"Yes, Pip. With the cat-o-nine-tails – in the courtyard – for all to bear witness." Minister Brus was as solemn as any priest would be when giving his sermon from the pulpit. "The Prince," he paused to look to the distance, as though he could see the castle through the parish walls, a short distance away, "will frequently deliver the thrashing himself. The man is a warlord, you know, like his brother. Strong and steadfast. One lashing will tear through to the spine."

Pip squeaked, "How many?"

"Ten." Minister Brus was quick to answer. "More if you flinch."

Edgar's heart sank, caring little about the lashings, but worrying more about the latter punishment. "You will really cut off our hands?"

Minister Brus guffawed, unable to keep the joke going any longer, spraying droplets of saliva from between the edges of his sagging mouth. He gripped his belly and threw his head back with such force he could have snapped his own neck.

Morgain, who had been quietly stifling his own laughter, chortled, "You will have these younglings wetting the bed like infants talking like that, Minister. You are supposed to be the parish priest, not a trickster."

Edgar heaved a sigh.

The minister swatted his hand in the air good-naturedly. "I am a lot of things, timeworn being the topmost. I, too, need moments of jollity when serving in this monstrosity – erm – monastery. Now, place your bets and fetch me a chair. The night is still young."

II

Edgar shielded his eyes from the morning sun. The golden ball hovered just above the easternmost tower of Arterbury Castle. The fire that burned nearby in the courtyard was stifling with white smoke churning towards the sky. Sweat dripped from his brow already and the rooster had barely crowed.

"Let's hurry it up," Thomas snorted, trekking by him with a hacked limb thrown over his shoulder. The boy seemed to be as strong as a grown man. "Morgain will be back in a bit to check on our work and we aren't even halfway done."

Pip sniffed. His arms were as tense as barbwire, dragging a smaller branch at a snail's pace toward the burn pit. "I-I-I'm trying."

"I don't think anyone has picked up this yard in half a century." Edgar gulped a mouthful of the spring morning, clutching a log under his arms awkwardly. He waddled towards the pile of burning brush where Thomas had already dropped his load. He was turning back to find more wood.

"You fell asleep a good three hours before the rest of us, Edgar, and you are moving the slowest. Even Minister Brus was up before you. Better pick it up, or I am going to think those stories about sheep farmers sleeping all day are true."

"This is a lot heavier," Edgar huffed, "than what you were carrying."

"That's a laugh!" Thomas hooted, raising his arms and flexing for show. "My branch was twice as long."

"And needle thin," Edgar muttered.

Thomas threw down his arms and marched over to block Edgar, "What was that, boy?"

Edgar lifted his eyes, unable to stand straight because of the weight of the log. Thomas's face was nearly as red as it had been the night before. The lad was maybe a smidgeon older that Edgar, but even when stooping, Edgar could look straight into his enraged eyes. Thomas was about as livid as cat in gunnysack.

"N-n-needle thin," Pip repeated. He froze when Thomas cranked his head around and glowered. "Ah, b-b-but it was a b-b-bit b-b-bigger than a needle." He shuffled his feet to try to get his branch closer to the flames.

"Damn straight." Thomas puffed up his chest, face as red as the cherries Edgar used to pick from the tree outside his grandfather's house.

Edgar swallowed. The boy was swearing! Edgar was not sure how to respond or if he should respond at all. The hefty kid did not budge, squinting back like a half-deranged hog searching for its slop. Edgar tried to ease the tension, "Why--"

"You don't think I can lift that?" he interrupted, challenging.

Edgar had never met a kid so bent on causing conflict. Already, his muscles were starting to shake from the weight of the log. "Let's just get done, like you said," Edgar finally managed to blurt out.

"Say, you think I'm weak!"

Edgar knew Thomas was not really asking him a question. The lad's eyes were glassed over with emotion. Edgar had seen the same look and heard the same tone from his grandfather when he had forgotten to latch the gate and half a dozen sheep had gone missing. The difference was that his grandfather had a switch to act out his anger; Thomas only had his bouncing, black curls.

"Give me that," Thomas scoffed, yanking the wood from his fingers. Edgar flinched as small splinters pierced his hands. "This is not that heavy, you dummy." With a grunt, Thomas reeled sideways, throwing the log towards the red-hot flames.

Edgar yelled in dismay, dread filling his chest. In horror, he ogled at the log that wheeled towards the pit – and Pip. Next to him, Thomas's face transformed from smug, to shock, to panic, while he gagged on his own half-hearted bawl.

Unaware, Pip let loose his branch into the licking flames as the log smashed into the middle of his back. The boy flailed his gangly arms and lurched forward, rocking on his toes only to plunge forward into the piping hot fire.

Pip's squeal started before he landed in the embers and twisted into a blood-curdled shriek as the inferno splashed around his raggedy robes and youthful flesh. The wool of his clothing caught to flame straightaway. The cries intensified, mixed with whimpers and wails, as Pip writhed about, flailing and rolling, looking for something to grab that was not burning.

His skin was melting from muscle. Black and bloodied.

"No!" Edgar cried, rushing for Pip.

"Goddammit!" Thomas screeched, sprawling to the edge of the

pit. "I am going to be in trouble now."

Edgar rotated to Thomas, having to look away from the burning boy. There was no way to pull him free without getting burnt himself.

"Water." Edgar said. "We need to find water."

No more had he said the words that a bucket full of water splashed into the pit behind him, sending up ash and smoke, eliciting a strained outcry from Pip as it hit his flesh. Another wave of water crashed into the woodpile causing a similar effect.

The fire still burned.

"Get more water!" Morgain slammed the bucket into Edgar's chest, pushing him towards the parish. Edgar grunted, stumbling back to do as he was asked. Minister Brus was waving his arms and shouting frantically at Thomas.

The boy only gaped at Pip.

Edgar reached out to take the bucket from Minister Brus and pulled at Thomas. His eyes were locked on Pip, unmoving.

"Come on!" Edgar shouted at Thomas.

"Let it be," Minister Brus blubbered, giving up and falling to his knees. "The boy is dead."

∞

III

"I have sent a pigeon to the Prince to inform him of the situation," Minister Brus whispered, walking with difficulty toward the chair behind his desk. His eyes were still irritated, swollen from crying. "I have sent another to Pip's family. I expect they will be here within a couple days to collect his remains."

The quarters of the priest were silent in response. Morgain stood hunched near the window, staring out at the fuming smoke that had begun to thin out. One hand was glued to his hip, and the other raking through his hair as though it were a comb. The older boy did not seem to have the strength to look at Edgar or Thomas.

Edgar's jaw quivered. He was certain that he was the worst boy to ever walk into the Prince's Parish. He had gambled, squabbled, and watched a boy die, all within a day's time.

Thomas, sitting next to him in an identical wooden chair, had his arms crossed. The boy's eyebrows were angled in such a way that they could nearly fill the space between his eyes. His lips were pressed outward, nostril's flaring. His gaze was fixed on Minister Brus like the holy man were the devil himself.

Edgar looked away as chills started creeping up his arms and neck. He knew that he had done terrible things, but Thomas had bad blood.

"Pip was stupid." Thomas groused between clenched teeth. "The stuttering dummy knew we were working and hovered over the fire like a ... a half-brained lout!"

"Thomas!" Minister Brus rocked back in his chair, hands pressed to the table. "That is no way to speak. Where is your compassion? The boy was barely here a day and has died..." The Minister turned his head away, shaking it as though he were trying to make sense of what had happened. He noticeably swallowed, and folded his shaking hands. "It was an unfortunate incident but we should not be placing blame."

Thomas squirmed under the harsh tone of the priest.

"It was an accident," Edgar uttered.

"Of course," Minister Brus dipped his head. "The Prince will come and see that the parish is exonerated and that the family's heartache is lessened...whatever can be done."

Thomas balled his fists in his lap, face enflamed as ever. "Say, it was an accident. I don't see why you had to go and tell the Prince. You are trying to get me in trouble. He may hang me, or worse."

Minister Brus inhaled, blinking several times before blowing out. "No, no. I am not trying to do anything, especially have any of you hanged. You are but a boy, Thomas. I am certain that the Prince will forgive this mishap. After all, it was an accident."

His gentle, widened eyes searched Thomas and Edgar.

"It truly was," Edgar said.

"We best be sure before the Prince comes," Morgain rattled from the window. It was likely the first time he had said a word since they had come inside. "We need to know what happened exactly. Have em tell us their story, word for word."

Edgar opened his mouth to explain, but was cut off by Morgain.

"Separately."

Minister Brus looked to Morgain, and after a moment, nodded. "Indeed. It would be wise to have the details before the Prince arrives. I will take Thomas to the basement and you can speak to Edgar up here in my office. When we are done, we can reconvene to look for any inconsistencies in the story."

Edgar could feel Thomas's eyes burning into him. He kept his eyes straight forward, refusing to look at the boy and his dark curls.

"Come with me, Thomas." The Minister stood up from his chair, the wood scraping against the flooring, and headed for the door. The boy stood nonchalantly and made his way toward the door, but not before whispering in Edgar's ear.

"Say this is my fault and you're next."

Edgar trembled. His eyes darted to Morgain, gazing out the

window, and Minister Brus, halfway out the door. Neither had heard the threat.

Would Thomas really kill him, too?

The door clicked shut, leaving Edgar alone with Morgain. The older boy, who had acted like a brother yesterday, had lost the tenderness shown the night before.

His voice was broken, distorted with agony, "Geez, Edgar. Just start from the beginning."

"I..." Edgar listened for footsteps, turning to face the door and then twisting back toward Morgain. He could not figure out why Thomas thought he would try to blame him, or anyone. It was an accident. "There is not much to say. We were moving wood like we were told, cleaning up the yard and all."

"C'mon. Keep going." A twinge of kindness surfaced on Morgain's face, his cheekbones relaxing.

Edgar settled into his chair a bit, trying to calm down. Morgain was not blaming him for Pip's death. "Is the Prince going to question us, too?"

"I don't know." Morgain cracked his knuckles. "Please, tell me what happened."

"Okay." Edgar gulped. He had to tell the truth, no matter what Thomas threatened. He would not be adding lying to his list of unforgivable sins. "I was carrying a piece of wood to put in the fire pit. Thomas came and took it out of my hands and threw it, without looking, and accidentally knocked him in."

"Who?"

Edgar shifted in his chair, "Pip. He accidentally knocked Pip in the fire." The study blurred as tears started to fill his eyes and stream down his cheeks. It was instant, like water from a natural spring, choking him up. "I mean we ran to the fire as soon as it happened, but there was no way to pull him – to pull Pip – out, you see? It was too hot. The flames were too high! And, Pip couldn't get out either. He was screaming and crying..."

"Ginger!" Morgain stood up, suddenly regretting his suggestion. He, too, had water dripping down his face. "I'm sorry, Edgar. It might be too soon to talk about this. It's okay."

"It's really not." Edgar shook his head, burying his face into his hands. "It's terrible!"

Morgain's hand touched his shoulder.

Before the older boy could say something comforting, a crash and bang sounded from beyond the door.

"What?" Morgain jerked towards the door, rushing out. Edgar strained to follow, his legs feeling as heavy as the logs he had been carrying. Morgain pulled ahead, rushing toward the basement at the opposite end of the church.

110

"Ginger! What happened?" He could hear Morgain shouting.

Thomas's voice was waterless. "Minister Brus slipped and fell down the stairs. I think the old cod broke his neck."

∽∾∿

IV

Morgain and Prince Arterbury had been within Minister Brus's quarters for the past two hours. The two had not come out for drinks or even a stretch since they had entered the study. The Prince had arrived with a carriage, defended by more men with swords and crossbows than Edgar had ever seen in his life. The guards had stayed outside the parish, disallowed from bringing weapons inside the holy church.

Edgar twiddled his thumbs, his legs shaking as he sat in the pew in front of the pulpit. The parish priest's office was only a handful of feet away. Edgar strained, as he had for the last couple hours, trying to hear what was being said. Nothing.

"What did you tell Morgain?" Thomas scooted closer to him on the long seat, hissing between his pursed lips. "You didn't say it was my fault, did you?"

"No," Edgar whispered. Even with a single word, his voice was clearly shaky. He glanced at the sturdy kid in his peripheral vision, unsure of what to expect. He had threatened him right before Minister Brus had died, but why?

Thomas was calm, with the composure of sheep sleeping in the pasture.

Edgar asked, "Aren't you upset?"

"About what?" he asked, clearing his throat.

Edgar wiped his eyes, focusing on the layered wool that hung over his knees. "Pip. Minister Brus. They are dead, Thomas."

"So?"

Edgar could not believe his ears. "What does that mean? Don't you think it is horrible that there have been two deaths since we arrived here? Doesn't that seem odd? I cannot help but wonder if we are being punished for something." Edgar kept his eyes off of the dais where the priest would usually give his sermons. He was sure there was a religious idol or statue somewhere that would be overlooking him, judging him.

"Are you a dummy, really?" Thomas said wryly from the corner of his mouth. "Say, you think that a god is trying to chastise us for wanting to be curates?" He chortled in his throat. "You act like you have never lost anyone before or ever seen anyone die."

111

Edgar swallowed. "I have, too. My parents both died when I was around five. They had the sickness and I was sent to live with my grandfather. But, it isn't natural –"

"Ha! It's about as natural as it gets. We all die. It's really the whole point of life."

"I was saying it isn't natural for so many to happen at once." Edgar said, scowling from being interrupted. "I wonder what is going to happen now. The Prince's Parish doesn't have a parish priest."

"Who cares?" Thomas snorted. "I didn't want to come here anyway. My pa said it was better to serve the church then be strung up in the stockades."

"The stockades? For what?"

Thomas ignored the question. "Besides, I don't think it will be the last one."

"What?" Edgar spun on his haunches. The boy had his eyebrows angled once more with the dark curls casting a shadow over his eyes. "What do you mean by that?"

Thomas shrugged, facing the door to the study. "Just saying that Morgain isn't the most pleasant fellow. I wouldn't be surprised if he fell down a flight of stairs, too, shouting *Ginger* the whole way down."

"That isn't funny! That isn't something to be joked about."

"I am guessing there is a better chance of breaking your neck if you are given a little push is all." Thomas winked.

He tried to keep his hands steady, "You pushed Minister Brus down the stairs?"

Thomas scooted closer. Edgar shifted, moving further away from the boy. His heart was racing. Thomas continued to advance across the wood bench with a strange expression on his face, contorted with delight. When Edgar smacked into the railing at the edge of the pew, he tried to move further but was trapped by Thomas, who had his eyes locked onto him with a haunting glimmer of excitement.

His voice was raspy, still at a murmur, "Did you see Pip's eyes fade out when he died? It was hard to see with the flames and the bastard thrashing about, but it was...like magic. Yes, so unbelievably magical! Say, if you looked close enough, you could see the light flee from his body with his last breath. It was like it had somewhere else to go." Thomas grinned. "I wonder where it went."

Edgar held his breath. He had never been so afraid. He struggled to hold back tears.

"Minister Brus died so much quicker. I mean, don't get me wrong. I rushed down the stairs as fast as I could. I grabbed his head and lopped it sideways to catch sight of the same thing. But, I was too late. His neck snapped and – well, that was it. No breathing. No heartbeat. No light. I wonder if folks have to die really slow to catch the light disappearing."

112

"You killed...him."

Thomas ignored Edgar, "I bet if we kill Morgain slow, we could learn more about what happens to that light behind the eyes. Say, we could tie him up. Cut him and watch the blood drain away drop by drop. We would really have to take our time. Be deliberate. We cannot be hurried, not like with Pip or the Minister."

Edgar's breath funnelled out through his lips. He wanted to cry, to puke, to scream. He could barely speak, "You really killed them."

"Mm," Thomas shifted his eyes toward the study. "Don't worry. I'll let you play with me next time. Just don't spoil the surprise." He tapped Edgar on the knee. "I would hate to kill you, too; though, that would be something, wouldn't it? Say, it is really something! Nothing like with mice and kittens."

Edgar's stomach bubbled. He pressed his lips together to keep himself from puking.

The study door creaked open and Morgain walked out. His shaggy hair clung to his ears, nearly to his sagging shoulders. There was no smile on his face, not like there had been yesterday when they were gambling in the basement. The man was shattered. Edgar could only picture him with blood dripping slowly from his body.

Thomas scooted to the side, squaring off on the seat as though nothing had happened. Edgar gripped his knees; they were shaking beyond his control.

"The Prince has declared both deaths an unfortunate accident. He has," Morgain cleared his throat, "appointed me as the Parish Priest in the absence of the Minister."

"What should we do?" Thomas said, holding back a grimace. "Can we go home?"

Morgain shook his head, caught up in his own misery. "No, we have our duty as the holy men of this church. We will continue to care for the estate. Though, I think it is best we take the day for mourning and rest. We will speak again in the morning."

V

Edgar's eyes burned, bloodshot and dry. He closed his eyelids, a wave of sleepiness washing over him, coaxing him to lie down on the cot.

He jerked, almost falling out of the bed. His head was heavy and his body was still sore from lifting the logs, but he could not sleep. Edgar was certain that the moment that his eyes shut, Thomas would wake up and gut him. He bit his inner lip until he tasted blood.

"Ow." He mumbled, holding the side of his face.

A stammering grunt bounced off of the basement's stone wall on the other side of the room; he froze in his cross-legged position. It reminded him of Pip stuttering.

Edgar peered through the darkness that engulfed the basement. He could not see past his nose. Nothing stirred. He could only hear the reverberation of the boy across the room. It seemed that Thomas was still sleeping, snoring.

At snail's pace, Edgar inched out of the cot, balancing his weight to reduce any creaking or squeaking. His feet pressed against the chilled, gritty stone floor. Lifting his hands, he steadied his footing and stepped forward into the pitch. After two steps, his knee hit something hard.

A chair. He was near the table in the centre of the room, where he had sat and gambled only yesterday evening. That meant he was only a few feet from the staircase that led upstairs. The plan was simple. If he could make it up the stairs and find a way to block the door, then he could tell Morgain about Thomas. Morgain was nearly a man and was now the parish priest. He would know what to do.

Edgar took another step, his foot banging into the table. The sound echoed and the snoring stopped. He held his breath.

"What are you doing, you dummy?" Thomas's voice was clear. He did not sound as though he had been sleeping at all.

Edgar suppressed a whimper. "Going to the bathroom."

A light flashed as Thomas lit a candle near his cot. A small glow flooded the basement, illuminating the boy's dark curls and cold gaze. "In the dark?"

"Y-y-yes." Edgar's chin trembled. He could not stand to look at Thomas. His eyes fell to the tabletop where the dice were still lying from the previous night. The dark dots were reflected by the pale glow of the candlelight.

"Say," Thomas stood up, "why don't I go with you?" He held the candle outright in front of him, swishing it back and forth in the air impishly. "It can be dangerous walking about in the dark all by yourself."

Edgar said, "Thanks, Thomas. I don't have to go anymore. I am just going to go back to bed. Goodnight."

Thomas tilted his chin, "Oh, c'mon, you dummy. You have me out of bed. We might as well have some fun while we are awake. You think Morgain is awake?"

"I...I don't know." Edgar said, settling back on his heels. He tried to be brave, but his nerves were rattled. "I'll see you in the morning."

"I see." Thomas clicked his tongue on the roof of his mouth a few times, his hands shifting against his body, a silhouette against the light. "Say, I don't think you were going to the bathroom at all. In fact, I wonder if you were aiming to go tell Morgain what we talked about earlier."

Edgar shuddered, his breath rushing from his nostrils.

"You was!" Thomas inferred angrily, eyebrows slanting. Even in the dark, Edgar could see the redness in his cheeks. "I cannot have that." The dark-curled boy moved towards Edgar and put the candle down on the table.

"What are you doing?"

Thomas did not say a word. He balled up his fist and took another step.

"Stay back!" Edgar shouted.

"None of that now," Thomas shushed.

Edgar did not know how the chair had come into his hands, but he swooped it upwards and clocked Thomas in the upper body. Blood oozed from the shorter boy's lip on impact, causing him to grab his mouth and stumble back. He sneered, seeing his own blood.

"You half-brained lout! Look at what you did," Thomas bellowed.

Edgar rested the chair on the ground.

"I'll get you for this!" Thomas rumbled with fury and stormed forward again. His eyes were dusky, shadowed by his curls. He reached to pull the chair from Edgar's grasp.

Edgar cried out, as he imagined a fighter might on a distant battlefield, and yanked the chair back toward him before swinging it forward with all his strength. Over and over again. It struck Thomas in the nose, chin, and chest. Thomas's high-pitched scream rebounded off the walls. It sounded like a sheep bleating while being ripped apart by a pack of wolves. Edgar did not stop.

This was life or death.

Thomas fell to the ground, his legs crumpling underneath him with his arms raised to protect himself. Edgar's guttural roar was unlike any sound he had ever heard come from his own throat. He brought the chair down time after time, again and again, against the devilish child.

The boy was a murderer.

At some point, Thomas brought his head up to crawl away, and the chair broke when hitting his skull. Thomas collapsed into a motionless heap. His screams were reduced to whimpers, then silence.

Edgar did not stop.

Crimson liquid gushed and flooded across the floor. Blood oozed. He ignored the warmness against his bare toes.

"Stop! Edgar!" Morgain's voice pleaded from the darkness. "Ginger!" Strong hands wrapped around him, pulling him away. He swung the chair mercilessly, assuring that the murderer was dead.

In the feeble ruddiness of the flame, Edgar clung to Morgain. "I had to stop him. He killed Pip. He killed Minister Brus. He was going to kill you, too!" He affixed his gaze to Thomas's dastardly eyes, emptily staring back at him. The light within faded away...like magic.

Lineage –
Shannon Hawthorne

I

Captain Inga Lincoln endured, standing sentinel before a closed door. She had stayed up the night prior to shift the buttons of her dress blues to the edge of her jacket, but they still strained over a stomach that was soft and generous from her recent labour. Her breasts ached, her back ached and the grey and blue loop carpet appealed to her exhaustion.

The vaulted chamber she stood in was the heart of the Prime Building, and a museum in miniature. Pieces of gleaming gear, some still active, hung suspended as an homage to ancient time-travel tech. The crown jewel of the collection was what looked to Inga like a metal coffin with running lights, but it bore the char marks of the very first manned mission through time. Just looking at it set off Inga's claustrophobia.

Behind the door, the governing body called the Prime Synod processed the command requests for upcoming missions. Inga had built up a strong case for her desired assignment, but now kept her expectations low by listing all the reasons why she wouldn't get it. There were several.

First, she had just given birth. She was cleared for duty, but an active command was athletic. A good captain walks her ship and squats in the trenches with everyone else. Squatting of any sort was out, currently. Second, in recent months, she had become a quasi-celebrity. Her limelight pinwheeled around Charlie Fisk, the true celebrity and long-dead genetic father of her infant daughter, Gianna. Inga revered and resented the role of "Holy Mother" to Gianna Fisk; it followed her with an omnipresent hush that she found frustrating. They might not send her sacred person on a mission perceived as dangerous.

She hoped they could still see her as Inga Lincoln, the genetic daughter of Abraham Lincoln and a surrogate. There were now enough Lincoln children that the reverence took on a casual patina and she was able to pass unhindered through public spaces, until her own surrogacy with Gianna. However, she was a good captain with a blemish-free record, an excellent example of the Lincoln poise in her

117

breeding. She was ready to command a ship again, even against the protest of her recovering body.

The mission she requested was historical in nature. The captain would take a ship back over a thousand years to their ancestors' settlement. There, they would gather information on how they defeated Earth's pernicious enemy, the Verlex. The records held gaping holes of mis-information and conflicting opinions. None of that mattered, until in recent months, one Verlex washed up on a white beach in the Caribbean, and another was found in a sawgrass marsh in the Everglades.

She was patriotic. She wanted to serve her country and planet by providing the best information on these monsters. The fact that Charlie Fisk would be there was a small benefit. She would like to meet him, yes, but there were many other elements at play here. She enjoyed informational reconnaissance and offered specialization in Fisk himself. She had studied him for years. His portrait was in her room so she would know him on sight. She carried his child, which could be positive or negative depending on perspective. No, the fact that the captain of this mission would interact with Charlie Fisk didn't affect her at all. The mission appealed due to historical significance, she told herself.

She jolted when the door slid open, but smoothed her face back into military comportment. The white-haired Synod consul, Patrick Murdock, looked up at her and raised one eyebrow. "Captain Lincoln, I'm surprised to see you at this hour. Is everything alright?"

"Everything is fine, sir. I was hoping to get my assignments so that I could begin preparations."

"Ever on the ball," he tapped his temples to activate his retinal reading lenses and flipped through the paperwork he held, "An electronic copy will be available in a few hours."

"Please sir, I won't be able to sleep until I know."

"Ah yes, the Settlement mission. You were very passionate in your proposal," he said. She tried to gauge his tone, wondering if she came off too emotional at the Synod presentation. "Ah, here it is." He separated out a sheet of paper in a fluid movement and handed it to her.

She read: *Captain Inga Lincoln, with greatest consideration,* so on and so forth, she scanned down the page until she found the sentence that she searched for. *You have been chosen to lead the Dauntless to the year 1 A.L. (after launch) for an informational reconnaissance on the Verlex invasion.* She looked up to Commander Murdock watching her with an amused look on his round face.

"Oh dear, I have ruined any chance of sleep for you now, I suppose," he said.

"Yes, sir. Thank you, sir." She took his outstretched hand and pumped it up and down.

"Try and get some rest, Captain Lincoln. You have two weeks to prepare and your best work is not done in the haze of exhaustion."

"I'll try, sir."

"Dismissed."

She put her heels together and saluted before turning away. She refrained from running down the hallway, but already packed her ship and picked her crew in her mind.

II

She raised a hand to the gathered crowd, and then marched with precision down the royal blue carpet laid before the gangplank. Following her was Gianna, swaddled and held by her nurse and surrounded by an honour guard of six. They would remain with her on the ship at all times. The procession was tedious and Inga burned to break atmosphere, but the pomp was necessary to her on a superstitious level.

After her assignment, the details on the decision had trickled down. The Synod wanted to encourage more surrogacy, which many women chose to forgo in order to maintain strong careers. As the premiere surrogate to the new Fisk line, Inga was visible and important. She bristled at being used for political reasons, but the mission held so much value to her that she held her tongue. Gianna's presence was a balm, both to show her as a working mother and to quell any complaints that the mission was dangerous. It was a simple, straightforward task.

Lastly, there had been some kerfuffle about a surrogate's right to meet the genetic father in life. When time travel was new, the surrogates went back and collected the samples in ways that are now considered immoral. Progress allowed for the genetics to be collected through residual samples left on objects handled by the person, so there was no need for the surrogate to get close to the hero in question. Many advocates felt that the first surrogate of a new line should be able to meet the father or mother, to further educate the children in the ways of the hero and serve as a teacher for the world at large.

She walked up the gangplank, the clanging of her footsteps heralding a new errand to be done for Prime and planet. Missions like this gratified watchers and drew large crowds. Neon pennant flags fluttered to mark the safe zones for the huge crowds filling the hillsides. The time stream would appear in front of her ship and they would see the Dauntless cross into it, and then come out of a second timestream an hour later. The timestreams were controlled by Prime command; she would have to catch the return tunnel that they would send her. She had one week in her timeline to complete the mission.

In front of the main hatch of the ship, a small amplifi-drone hovered. She stepped aside and allowed the honour guard to bring Gianna into the ship before taking her place before it.

She took a breath and began, "My father once said, 'If I had eight hours to chop down a tree, I would spend six of them sharpening my axe.'" Light laughter and applause reached her from the fields. "I believe today is a mission in sharpening our axe. We know the Verlex. We've looked them in the face before and held our own.

"Humanity is here because one man said, 'Enough.' I am proud to call that man the father of my child, and I am proud to travel with the fruit of his hard work, the apple of my eye." She paused as the crowd cheered and whistled. "But Gianna is not the only child of Charlie Fisk. Because of his bravery in saving a remnant from the Verlex, protecting them and building a colony, we are here today. We are all children of Charlie Fisk."

She waited until they quieted, "Now you have all seen the news. We know that the Verlex have made a few appearances. But we are in possession of a line to the past, and we know that the Charlie Fisk who laboured us into existence will help protect that existence before it ever becomes threatened."

"Today we sharpen the axe. We sharpen it through preparation and clarity of action. We are wise to reach out to our allies, past and present. And thus, 'Having chosen our course with pure purpose, let us go forward without fear and with strong hearts.'"

She stepped back and took in the applause. Smiling, Inga waved to the crowds before ducking through the door and letting it seal off the noise behind her.

A great bear tackled her from the side, "Oi, you. Thought it would be another year before I got to see your face on a starship again."

She slapped the back of her executive officer, a broad, beaming Isaiah Lincoln, whom she had grown up with. Isaiah's mother had imbued him with zest for life and any memory Inga had of getting in trouble had Isaiah at its centre. "Isaiah!" she coughed, "Let me change modes for a second before you strangle me."

"Sorry, kid. Presentational mode off, if you please, m'lady."

"Done," she grinned and slugged his arm as they walked towards the command station, "How're your girls?"

"Reading and doing all sorts of horrifying stuff like that. I'm terribly old." He clutched his chest, "But Gianna, Gianna! What a heartbreaker that kid is."

"You've seen her already?"

"On the news, on the net. That nurse almost beat me to death when I tried to steal a snuggle as she passed by, though. She's worse than the guards."

"Good! She's supposed to be." Inga chuckled. "I'll make the formal introductions between you and G tonight over dinner in my cabin. We'll pretend we're working and you can do all your Uncle cooing without ruining your intimidating reputation."

He stopped her and put large hands on her shoulders, "I love babies. Babies are amazing. You put them down and when you come back – get this--they are in the same place. They aren't destroying things, they aren't talking about the Kennedy boys at school, they are just there. In the same place. It's a beautiful thing." She laughed and then looked at the closed port in front of them.

"Presentational mode on?" he said.

"Presentational mode on," she replied. They both calmed their expressions and drew up to full Lincoln height. Inga entered first, and he followed at her right shoulder. She heard someone call out "Captain on deck," and everyone rose, standing at attention.

"Good morning," she said, "welcome to the Dauntless." She gave her customary welcome speech and then gave permission to begin the last checks before take-off. She sat down while Isaiah made the rounds and fussed over details. Finally, all checks were in. He moved to stand behind the control station and Inga gave the go code to Prime Command.

"Timestream forming." An ensign moved his hands across the controls. Inga watched as the ground fell away beneath them through the forward window. Her stomach flipped as they rose through the clouds, then the upper layers of atmosphere. The horizon took on a gentle curve as the sky darkened to space. The Dauntless rotated and Inga complimented the level turn and smoothness of their rise.

Before them, an anomaly formed. It started as a red glow, then ribbons of yellow broke out from it and got pulled back in. It was a dance, the struggle to build a bridge between places in time. As the bridge grew stronger, the red glow grew brighter and bigger until it had formed a sort of strange depth that sometimes looked flat and sometimes looked like a hole down which you could fall forever.

"Perfect," Inga said, "Check date. Year One past Ark Launch."

"Confirmed, Year One."

"You may proceed." The ship shifted a few feet downward in a jolt, and the crew looked around to each other, uneasy.

"Sorry, adjustment made," muttered the Ensign, "entering timestream."

As the nose of the Dauntless passed no return, a sharp ping sounded off the port side surface, followed by what sounded like the ship passing through a shower of sand. Inga stood, but Isaiah touched

121

her arm, already moving toward the sound, "Buckle in, Holy Mother. I've got this."

A huge metallic crash rang out. A portion of the ceiling went from concave to convex with the screech of crushed metal. Something hit the side of the ship and knocked it sideways, where it crashed and skidded along the inside of the timestream tube. As they ran against the wall of the stream, a piece of the Dauntless seemed to enter the wall itself, yellow flares thrown up from their side, burning across the front windows and then the whole ship crossed through the wall with an ominous ripping sound.

"Report!" Inga barked, "What the hell just happened?" Half of the deck had gone dark, and several seats had been crushed under the ceiling. Every alarm notification was blaring across her screen. She wiped several of them away; she could see her ship had been half crushed, thank you.

"A meteor, Captain, or something like it. It hit us in the timestream," the science officer looked shaken, "We didn't even know something like that was possible."

"Get a med team up here, now." Reports were coming into her station from all across the ship. 10 dead in this department. 2 in another. Main engines down. Flying blind. "And get me a report from the nursery, I don't care if you have to run there personally!" She saw someone exit out of the corner of her eye.

"Surface approaching!" The Earth appeared before them, though they had just left it behind them. Its sapphire surface belled out before their forward window, flattening with distressing speed.

"What year are we in?" she snapped. "Does anyone have a lock on our timeline right now?"

Ten seconds of silence passed, then, "Year 0, Captain." Her crew stopped as one and looked to her.

"It'll be alright. We're not that far off from intended date." Inga gripped the shoulder of the pilot at the helm and said in his ear, "Aim for blue, Ensign."

The young pilot's face was grey, but he nodded. She fought the desire to shove him aside and take the controls, but a Lincoln trusted others to do the job they were given. She allowed herself one piece of advice, "Into the skid, son," she said, and crossed to her command chair and buckled in, issuing a ship-wide command for her crew to do the same.

"Commander Lincoln, report!" She commed him. No response. "Isaiah, I need eyes on nursery damage!"

"Captain," a young skyman said, hesitant, "Commander Lincoln is..." he trailed off, and gestured to the wreckage on the side of the deck. She looked and then turned her face away, squeezing her eyes shut.

When she opened them, she focused on the ensign with hands flying over the controls, "We're diverting all extra power into the secondary engines, ensign. Bring us in clean."

The Dauntless shook and bucked when it hit Earth's atmosphere, and heat trails burned against the forward window. Inga eyed the crushed hull as the deck rattled and grew swelteringly hot, but it held. The descent was a matter of seconds, but each second crawled for an infinity. As the ship fell, it angled nose first toward the line between continent and ocean. At the last two seconds, the ensign, in a force of sheer will and flying brilliance raked the Dauntless out of her free-fall. They skipped like a flat Michigan stone across the ocean's surface before coming to a rest about a mile from shore.

Inga squeezed the shoulder of the pilot as the crew broke out in weak cheers. She walked off deck, presumably to check the rest of the ship, but once into the hallway, she ran until she found herself outside of the nursery door. It opened half way, but she squeezed through it to find the nurse extricating Gianna from the emergency webbing of the bassinet

"She slept through it, can you imagine?" the nurse said.

Inga took Gianna into her arms and dismissed the nurse and the guard without ceremony. Once the doors shuddered closed behind them, she allowed herself to cry into the downy head of her child.

∞

III

It was day four of floating in the waves. Inga and her senior staff had gone in circles. Did Prime know what happened to them? Would the timestream come to them immediately, in a week, maybe a year and a week, or not at all? The mission was aborted. The main focus was getting Gianna, Inga and the rest of the crew back home and that meant engines that worked and a ship that could fly. They had neither. Prime could relaunch the mission after their return.

On day four, a knocking came on the anterior window of the ship. Inga had just entered the deck when she saw several men peering through cupped hands down at them. They gestured, and their movements seemed like they were requesting to meet. Inga motioned them to the back of the ship, and commed security to send a team to the bay doors.

Backed by ten men and women with weapons out, Inga unlocked the bay doors and the compression hinges lifted the door high, letting a barrage of saltwater rain down into the bay. The men from outside arrived in seconds, crawling over the wall like spiders and dropping into the hanger.

Inga took a step forward, her hands out and empty when one man yanked a strange globular object out of his bag. The thing was a greyish ovular grub with ridges and it moved in his hands with a sort of juvenile sentience. Inga saw it for a second before he threw it on the floor and crushed it beneath his boot.

It screeched and writhed before it popped under the pressure, expelling its innards all over the bay floor. Inga gagged, and many others turned away. The smell was rank, like a sulphuric skunk had emptied its glands in the room.

Then something huge was in the bay. It had come through a tunnel in the air, red and yellow like a timestream that opened and shut in a second. It happened so fast that Inga's mind struggled to follow, but she and her crew fell towards the monster as the ship bowed underneath its weight. She caught herself and scuttled backwards, away from what could only be described as an insectoid beast. A few were not as lucky, and with a speed that defied comprehension, the beast devoured two guards mid-tumble. Its skin was gelatinous and translucent, and she could see things inside of it. Horrified, she realized that one of those things was moving, a hand beating against the inside of the creature, but the thing shifted and she couldn't see it anymore. It was full of similar looking shadows. She jerked away from the fringe of short, jointed legs, clacking as it swivelled.

"Damn," A man spoke, astride the horrific monster, " It's smaller in here that I thought." He swung a leg over the side and slid down to the floor.

"Stand back," Inga said, getting to her feet, and she heard the distinct power-up from the few guns behind her.

"Ah," was all the man said, and he fiddled with a strange remote-like object in his hand and then ran directly at her. The strange creature went berserk, behind him. It bucked and thrashed and all of the legs went scrabbling faster than Inga imagined possible. The man tackled her to the wall and wrapped her in a sort of rope contraption and she was jerked high off the ground, with him holding onto the outside of the rope cocoon. The other men picked up on the invisible signal as well, and they used grappling hooks to get up out of the way of the monster.

It was over in moments – her whole team trampled, not even able to get one shot off. They lay below her in a grisly display. The man next to her touched the remote and the creature calmed.

"Take her," he said, jumping down and motioning the other men towards her, "She's nursing. We've got some babies you can help." She looked and realized that her milk had let down and the front of her was wet. She tried to turn away, but the elastic ropes held her still and exposed. "Kill the rest, strip what we can use."

"Wait, we can help you!" Inga cried out, desperate, "We have resources that you have never dreamed of."

"No, you have infestation that we never dreamed of. You and your kind brought these things into our world," he jerked a thumb toward the newly docile creature behind him. "I need your milk, and that's it. You can leave your future and your knowledge and your starship, they won't help you now."

For the first time in her life, Inga was speechless.

"Get her down," he said, and men swarmed her, grabbing and yanking at the ropes. "Take their weapons and search the ship. We have fifteen minutes."

"My baby!" she yelled, as they lowered her, feet first, to the floor, "I need my child."

"Find the kid." He didn't look at her. He tossed the remote to one of the men, and the giant creature followed them through the tunnel and disappeared with the click of a thousand legs.

"We're here seeking to speak to Charlie Fisk about the Verlex invasion," she said, trying to shift her weight so she could look up at the man, "We crashed and now we're just trying to get back home."

The man stared at her for a moment, and then doubled over with laughter, "You want to speak to Fisk about the time tick invasion? That's just rich."

"Please, I know it's difficult to understand, but we're from the future--"

"Oh, I know you are." His face twisted in sarcasm. "The whole world knows that you're from the blessed future, and we're dying because of it."

A thin foot soldier walking in with a bundle held in his arms interrupted them. He bounced it a little, and Inga was chagrined that it had taken such little time to get her away from the nurse and the guards. She held out the arm that had not been bound, "Please just give her to me."

The lead man took Gianna into his arms, and turned away from Inga. The soldier muttered in his ear, but Inga overheard what was said. "Most of the crew jumped ship. Want us to pursue?"

"No," the man said, "They don't have long out there." He walked with Gianna in arms to the open bay doors and dangled her over the edge without ceremony.

Inga screamed and writhed and fell, hauling herself towards the two of them in desperation.

He looked at her, and she saw a trace of sorrow on his face, "She will die a terrible, terrible death. By time tick or by Fisk himself. He doesn't take in babies now. This way is kindest."

"She's his daughter!" Inga screamed. She heard Gianna wake and begin screaming with her. Over and over she screamed, "She's

125

Charlie Fisk's daughter!"

Gianna's screams stopped.

Inga thrashed herself to the bay opening. She was ready to throw herself into the waves to save her daughter or die with her, but when she looked up, the man was shushing Gianna and holding her to his chest. He held her until the other men came back, then he showed her to them and they whispered back and forth. Inga was afraid to breathe lest he hoist her over the edge again, and only exhaled when he walked away from the bay doors.

The enormous millipede-like monster returned with the rest of the men. All in the bay gathered and held their hands out towards it, fingers hovering over its legs as though they were warming them over a fire. A few of the men reached out and grabbed Inga's ankle and wrist, keeping one hand outstretched towards the beast.

Without warning, the metal floor was gone and she found herself with her cheek pressed into dried brown grass and dirt. The men yanked her up and cut the ropes binding her legs. Inga felt nauseated. How did they move from the sea to the land so quickly? Where were they? She looked toward the sun, which was now far west of her. They must have travelled hundreds of miles in an instant.

There was a man waiting to meet them, and another of those sickening ovals lay smashed on the forest floor. He turned and began marching, and all of the soldiers around her fell into place.

They marched for a few miles due north. Inga kept her eyes on the yellow nursery blanket that wrapped Gianna, her black eyes peeking out over the man's shoulder.

They entered an encampment fortified by thick mud-brick walls. There were hundreds of people outside, and the guards lowered weapons and the crowds skittered back. All around the walls were spikes that glowed with a blue light. Some in the crowd tried to scale the wall, but the blue glow intensified and sent out a shockwave that knocked them down and left one man limp and hanging over the wall. They approached a wicked looking gate, crude metal soldered together with barbed wire and spikes along the surface. The glowing spikes on either side of the gate went dark, and they approached. The creature lead the way into the encampment with the smooth glide of a millipede, drawing a deep undulating line in the mud. Once they made it inside, Inga looked back to see the spikes light up again as the gate was lowered.

He told the men to cut Inga loose, put her in a tent, and make sure that she stayed there. The structure they brought her to was a yurt of sorts, bare, no more than a mat on the floor. No weapons, no blunt objects of any kind. She eyed the tent poles themselves; they were slim and flexible, but it would be noticeable if the tent collapsed on its side. A thought for later, but for now she would wait. She stayed there for an hour without contact.

She heard Gianna crying, and leaned out of the tent. "She's hungry. Can I feed her?" They ignored her. She asked the question over and over every few minutes. Stay humble, Inga. Squeak, but don't squeak loud. She went back inside when they told her. Eventually, she didn't hear her anymore and her heart lodged in her throat and stayed there.

Finally, someone came for her and she followed him through a maze of tents and small dwellings of scrap cardboard and metal. Things were clean, there was no garbage in the path, and Inga could smell food cooking on the glowing fires outside every third living quarters.

She was brought to a squat building of corrugated metal with wide windows cut into the sides, but with no glass or paper to protect from the elements. Her silent guide motioned her inside but left before she crossed the threshold. She pulled herself up to full height and entered the slim doorway cut in the metal.

As her eyes adjusted, they fell upon Gianna, curled in the lap of a woman near a far window, and sucking her fist in sleep. She had to bite her lip to keep from crying. There were several men and women in chairs alongside the far wall, and a strange cylindrical piece of technology that hulked against the opposite wall. Other than that, the room was full of empty benches.

Inga approached them and a man stood. She had gazed at the portrait of this man for years. It had sustained her through the lab tests and the failures and her tears as the doctors worked to create a tiny baby from their genetics.

Her gaze faltered under the contained anger in his eyes. "Your name," he said in a curt voice.

"Inga Lincoln. And you're Charlie Fisk." Presentational mode on, she said in her mind and thought of Isaiah for strength, then she muted all her emotions and focused on the man before her. "That is Gianna Fisk, that you are holding," she directed her voice toward the woman. "She is very important to my timeline, and so are you, Mr. Fisk."

He brushed past her words, and the woman shifted so that Gianna was hidden from sight. He said, "Something hit your ship on the way through the timestream, what was it?"

Her eyes narrowed, "How would you know that?"

"Since you don't know, I'll tell you." He circled around the table and came toward her. She met his eyes, but it was difficult not to marvel at the image come to life in front of her. He continued, "It was a Time Tick, whom you met today with my men, or what you would call a Verlex."

She fumbled, "Yes, I am here to speak to you about the Verlex infestation."

"They are not the infestation. You are."

"Excuse me?"

He jabbed a finger in her direction, "You are the infestation. The Verlex are just a by-product. You rip open the fabric of time and space every time you make a little trek to the past, for the genetics of a Churchill or a Christ, or some poor sod just trying to do his job. When you rip it open, what's inside comes out."

"The Verlex come from inside of time?"

"They hitch a ride on whatever is big enough to carry them through. And they arrive hungry," his mouth twisted wryly, "Apparently, there's not much to eat in space." He leaned back on the table and sat on the edge of it, backed by the solemn men and women weighing her with their eyes. "Now, this...child. You say she is mine, and we have tested the genetics. You're not a liar. You get that from what, your father, George Washington, I suppose."

She frowned, and his mouth twisted in a sardonic smile.

"Oh, I know about your lineages. Can't throw a stone at you all without hitting a second coming of Genghis Khan."

"We don't use the genetics of murderers."

"Then how is she in existence?" He pointed a finger at Gianna, "My hands aren't clean, but I suppose history has whitewashed the blood away. What am I, a hero where you come from? I can't even save my own people." He walked back to his chair, shaking his head, "I'm not sentimental but I won't kill my own child. However, I do have a use for you."

Inga looked to the woman holding Gianna, her eyes adjusted enough to see her in detail. She was meek-looking with dirty blonde hair, but her arms were banded with muscles and her hands were rough from work, just like the others in the rom. Inga noticed the plain band on her fourth finger and that her eyes kept flicking to Fisk. His wife, she assumed. How foolish she had been all these years, pretending she would mean something to a man who was born a thousand years before her. She meant to ask what she was needed for, but the sentence that came out was "I want the child."

She watched Fisk and the woman share a look, and that confirmed it in her mind that they were married. "You can't have her," he said, simply.

Something dawned on Inga, "You never had children in life..." she said, "You can't, can you?"

He stood, "How dare you--"

"Your base is fragile," she said, picking up momentum, "You can't handle another influx of Verlex. You can barely handle what you have now. Listen, if my mission fails and I don't come back with Gianna, the government I work for is going to rip open all of time and space to find us." He crossed his arms and raised one eyebrow, and she continued,

"I can stop them. I can advocate for you and close the time jumps. Hurting you hurts us, if you die...we die."

She looked to him for his reaction, and he didn't speak for a moment. He turned away from her to the men and women beside him and they conversed in low whispers. Fisk's wife took Gianna to the window and began a gentle sway with the infant in her arms. The discussion became heated, Inga could sense it in the percussiveness of the voices, but she couldn't make out what they were saying. Finally, Charlie straightened and turned back to her, "I have a way to get you back to your timeline."

"With Gianna."

"No, you'll have to leave her here."

"Then we have a problem."

A muscle in his cheek twitched, and a few of the men and women behind him muttered, but he continued, "Listen first, agree second. The Verlex. The one we captured is a mother, and it took almost all our resources and the lives of dozens of men to catch the one. If the eggs or larvae are threatened or hurt, no matter where the Verlex is, she is drawn back to them. They use time to move, it's why they are so devastating. Imagine an enemy that can travel instantaneously, and you never know from which direction it will attack. If a larvae or an egg is hurt, it instinctually creates a tunnel directly to its young."

"That's how you got on my ship. You crushed its larvae."

"And how we got back."

"So what, we get one of these eggs to the future, and I ride a Verlex back to my own time?"

"The ride would be inside a Verlex, but yes."

"Inside a--?" she clamped her mouth shut.

"Of course," he said, "There's no atmosphere in time and you'll be travelling a lot farther. Can't have you die en route. Once you are there, you do what you say you're going to do; you advocate for us, you make travelling to our timeline illegal, you work with your government, then we work out a way to get you the child."

He waved a hand to the hulking contraption on the far wall, "That is a teleporter, gleaned from a ship before you. We were not so kind to their inhabitants. It's not enough to send a person through, unfortunately, but--"

"An egg. You could send an egg."

"Yes." He pushed up from the table, and she could see that his fingers made sweat trails. Nerves, she thought, common mistake to put your hands down on a surface that marks.

"Who was going to go?" she said.

"Excuse me?"

She shot a glance at the technology on the other side of the room, "This isn't a new plan. Who were you going to send?"

Fisk folded his hands in front of him, "Myself, actually. The hope was always to convince the future civilization to cease time travel. That plan hasn't changed. Only now, I'm taking you with me." He signalled and four men stepped from the shadows and held her still, as she yanked against their rough hands. Inga watched as Charlie walked to the woman by the window, dropped a kiss on her forehead and touched Gianna's cheek. Her stomach clenched and she fought the men holding her to no avail. "Bring in the time tick," he said.

The men and women behind the long table stood as one, and fell into a rhythmic pattern of doing things that Inga didn't understand, to the machine that was pushed forward into the centre of the room. Levers were flipped, gear teeth engaged and turned and a man with a cream coloured egg stood to the side. A door opened in the side of the cylinder and the man slid the egg through and then closed the door. There was a bright flash from inside the cylinder and the light bled through the seams of the door and seared an after-image on Inga's vision. She blinked away the neon square in her vision in time to see Fisk open the door and confirm that the egg was gone.

"We don't have much time," Fisk said, and the men holding her pushed her toward him. They let her go as Fisk himself took her arm.

"Mark my words, Fisk," Inga hissed, "if even one hair on my daughter's head is hurt, I will rend your sky with ships and bring in a destruction like you have never known."

"You'll only be killing yourself."

"I'll already be dead."

Charlie looked at her, and she shivered as his familiar grey eyes met hers, "I promise, she is in the best hands I could choose for her. And you will return to her. Maybe even to this very moment."

The clack of a thousand feet approached as the Verlex slithered into the room. Inga stared in horror. Fisk gripped her arm and said, "You must not move. If you move, she will thrash and we'll be trampled. Stay still and she'll swallow us whole."

Inga screamed as the Verlex dove toward them.

∞

IV

She and thousands of litres of slime spilled out onto the metal floor, and she heard gasps above her.

She moaned and coughed out digestive juices. Her face and arms burned as she clawed at her eyes to clear them. Her hand caught

130

her hair and long strands came away between her fingers. She felt the body of Fisk lying still next to her, her fingers slipping on the slime as she shook him.

Dimly aware of the medic team working over her, she felt the blissful relief of water being poured over her face as she was pulled away and rushed to the medical bay. She lost consciousness as they submerged her into an antacid bath and didn't wake for several weeks.

Upon awakening, Inga tried to open her eyes, but managed only a brief flutter, and a gasp of "Gia-". She caught a glimpse of Murdock sitting beside her who rose to attention, and then she fell back into darkness.

It was dim in the room when she surfaced again, faint whirring of instruments somewhere unseen behind her. An ache in her esophagus informed her that a tube would prevent her from speaking, but she heard the chime that indicated her movements to the medical staff. Soon, nurses surrounded her, their voices a dull comforting murmur. It was several days before they removed the tubes keeping her mute and tied to the bed.

"Where is Fisk?" she asked, the moment Murdock walked in the door. He looked tired, and she supposed it must be late. There were no windows in her room.

"Dead." He avoided her gaze.

"What?"

His face composed itself into a picture of empathy, but it didn't seem to reach his eyes. "He didn't make the journey back through. You barely did yourself, Captain." She felt the information hit her chest and slice down to her stomach. Her vision darkened, and she fought to keep it clear. Murdock watched her with polite discomfort before he probed into what happened aboard the Dauntless. She relayed the accident, Gianna's hostage situation, and Fisk's reason for the jump forward. When she had finished, he filled her in on what he had seen on their end. "Seeing you slide out of that monster after that egg was smashed," he shuddered, "well, it was like a terrible magic trick, frankly."

She grimaced, then asked, "Will the Synod listen? We're destroying their timeline with our jumps."

He shifted, "Ah yes, well. We already know that. I mean, we understood that the Verlex seemed to be coming through on the ships, but we weren't sure how. Parasitic, you say, which confirms our suspicious, and well done on the information reconnaissance, there. I hate to say it, Captain, but I'm afraid you put yourself in danger for nothing. We obviously do not destroy their society, because ours is still in existence today. There's no danger. We're perfectly safe."

"Yes, but they aren't. The conditions there are miserable. Fisk has a remnant safe, but there are hundreds of others outside his walls." She winced to say his name.

"But what about Gianna? To get her back, we'd have to make a jump."

"But that's only one, if we take a small ship--"

"And the rest of your crew? Listen, Captain Lincoln, I understand. Truly, I do. We never want to be the cause of another's discomfort, but time jumps are necessary for our way of life. You wouldn't exist without them, lest we forget?" He leaned back in his chair and steepled his fingers over the rise of his belly. "Most unfortunately, we shall not be making another jump to 0 A.L. The disaster of how your mission played out, and the loss of you, Gianna and your crew, well...the people will need a break before they are willing to trust the safety of jumps for awhile."

Inga sat up, wary, "The loss of me?"

Murdock nodded, "Inga, dear, I know Lincolns like I know the back of my own hand, and once one has a 'cause' in mind, it is impossible to derail them from it. I am truly sorry for what is about to happen. We had to quiet Fisk and now we shall keep you quiet as well."

His hand reached toward the call button, but Inga got their first. She swiped his hand away and cracked a fist into his temple. He went down to the floor, his girth rolling him over, and Inga yanked off the wires and found a change of loose fitting black garments in the closet. His body was quiet on the floor.

No one was in the sick bay hall, and she walked with purpose, not knowing where to go but knowing better than to attract attention by running. She wove through quiet serpentine halls until she crossed the threshold of the Synod's atrium. The lights above her flickered to life, illuminating the metallic tech, each exhibition a piece of tech that showed Prime's control over time. Her eyes fell upon the one-person-transport. It was solar powered, and the lights were full spectrum. It was possible...

She hacked the security lock easily, using the general maintenance code for the building. Sliding the door clasp open, the metal door pulled open with a loud groan. She reached inside and keyed in a few coordinates. The old computer chewed on them for a few minutes, but the ripples underneath the ship meant that it was starting to bend the time line it was in. Originally, time travel didn't require space, it was just extremely risky to do it where you could show up inside of something that didn't exist in your own time. Space was the easiest to ensure that your landing would be clear.

Two shots lasered over her head, and she heard shouts of men coming toward her. She backed into the transport and pulled the heavy door closed. Her breath fogged up the glass over her face, and she lost sight of the soldiers. The pod began to rumble and shake. She felt a mist-like vapour run over her arms and legs, but when she looked down, it was her body that had dissolved. Abruptly, she was thrown against the glass as the whole capsule dropped and hit the ground, the window showing the roll from grass to sky. It came to rest on its side, so she managed to push the door open and escape, just as the tail of the Verlex went into the building made of corrugated metal. She heard herself scream.

Presents for Francisco (A Fade Tale) - Jasmine Brennan

Ilusion Zamora walked down the side of the dusty street facing the heavy weekend traffic. It had been a long and tiring trip by foot from the open-air folklorico market where she sold ceramics to make a little money to get by each week. Her grandson, Felix, trudged along behind her, holding a large box covered in festive birthday paper that he was trying to keep clean. At the busy intersection of Calle Verde and Rio Internacional, she stopped to fan herself and catch her breath. On Saturdays, the open-air market filled with tourist crowds. Ilusion was wearing her traditional outfit of embroidered huipil, rebozo and apron over a thick, black polyester skirt. The outfit was perfect for selling the small sculptures that she and Felix worked on during the week, but not so wonderful for walking seven kilometres from the market to the posh side of the city to Francisco Paz Marcelo's birthday party.

"Almost there," she told Felix as he stood juggling the box a bit to get a better grip on it. Even though it was nearly half his size, he'd insisted on carrying it himself.

"My present will be the biggest and best one today," Felix said. He'd been so proud to buy the gift with the money that came from the little diablitos sculptures that he'd molded and painted by himself. Ilusion didn't have the heart to tell him that someone like Francisco Marcelo would receive many wonderful presents for his seventh birthday and whatever Felix had picked out for him would likely not be among the his favourites.

The light at the intersection changed and together they crossed Rio Internacional. Once again, Ilusion pulled the crumpled and somewhat soggy envelope from her cloth backpack. Felix had been so excited the day he'd come home from school with the birthday invitation. Ever since, he'd spoken of nothing but the upcoming party. Like most second graders, Felix wanted nothing more than to be liked by his classmates, but for many reasons – most of them having to do with them not having enough money for many of the things that Francisco and the other privileged school children were able to buy

134

-- he was often not included in their games and festivities.

Ilusion checked the address on the much handled invitation one more time before stuffing it back into her pack with a few of the ceramics that she had not been able to sell that morning. Leaving the folklorico market early would mean that money would be tight for the rest of the week, but the joy on Felix's face as they set out across town made any and all sacrifices seem worth it. "Just a few more blocks," she told him. "We're nearly there."

Soon, they made the turn onto Avenida Vicente where the Marcelos lived. The birthday party was in a small park next to their home, where the mighty Cupatitzio River ran through the wealthy Uruapan neighbourhood. Unlike the streets on the other side of town, these were lined with beautiful shade trees and the air itself seemed ten degrees cooler so close to the river. Ilusion wiped the sweat from her forehead with the corner of her *robozo* and wished for the hundredth time since setting out from the market that she'd had time to change out of her traditional clothing. It would be hard enough to be an old lady among the young and wealthy Uruapan mothers without looking like she'd stepped from the Purépecha Highlands.

Felix had fallen behind again and when Ilusion turned to urge him to catch up, she noticed he was gazing into the leaves of the shade trees as he passed beneath them. His lips were moving, as if he was having a conversation with some unseen friend keeping pace above him. She sighed. Only some of his isolation in the schoolyard had to do with their economic state. "Felix!" she called. "Look! Here is the party. Can you see the balloons showing us the way to the picnic?"

Felix startled a bit at the sound of his name, but followed Ilusion's pointing finger to a riotous bunch of Mylar balloons that had been tied to a gatepost at the entrance to the park. Underneath the balloons was a fancy, professionally printed sign that read "Francisco Paz Marcelo. Birthday Party. Enter."

"We're there!" Felix said with delight. He ran ahead and, despite carrying the large box, quickly outpaced Ilusion's tired footsteps as she made her way down the path to the birthday party.

She attempted to pick up her pace, but nearly turned her ankle on a loose stone. An alarming clank sounded from her cloth backpack. If one of the sculptures had been broken the birthday party would become even more costly. Broken sculptures had to be glued; glued sculptures sold at half price to the eagle-eyed tourists at the folklorico market. She would have to check her pack as soon as she found a spot to sit down.

"Senora Zamora!" With a jangle of bracelets and the overwhelming scent of expensive perfume, Elvia Constelacion Marcelo emerged from a gaggle of similarly dressed Uruapan mothers. She held her arms out as if ready to embrace an old flame rather than someone she barely knew from Sunday mass. "Ilusion," she said, coming up and blowing air kisses at either side of Ilusion's face. "I'm so glad you and little Felix could make it. We were worried you wouldn't come!" She took a step back, and her high heels wobbled a bit in the uneven, sun-burnt grass as she looked Ilusion up and down.

The other mothers came over and Illusion recognized a few from church. The beautiful Caritina Reyes and the feisty Maria Fabiola Corte de Avila, whose son Juan Carlos was considered the most popular second grader to ever grace the Jardin de los Ninos school.

"And, you are dressed so beautifully!" Elvia exclaimed. She threw her hands up in the air and her many bracelets tinkled. "The perfect clothes for a party."

Ilusion sighed inwardly. "Is there a place to sit?" she asked. At fifty-nine, she was young to be a grandmother, but too old to be a mother again. She needed a rest.

"Of course, what am I thinking?" Elvia said. "Come and sit down at the picnic table. We have nice cold agua frescas, unless..." She gave a laugh and a wink. "You'd like something a little stronger."

Ilusion followed her over to the picnic table in the shade of a large avocado tree, piled high with food and drink. Felix was already there, standing quietly in front of a mountain of presents from the other children and looking for a spot to add his to the pile. "Agua fresca is fine," Ilusion said. She sat down on the picnic table bench and pulled open her backpack. Each sculpture represented hours of eye-straining work with her paintbrushes. She pulled one out, carefully unwrapped and inspected it, holding her breath the whole time. Fortunately, it was whole, as were all the rest that she lined up next to her on the bench. She didn't realize until she was finished that the other mothers had formed a loose circle around where she sat and were watching her with expressions ranging from mild distaste to alarm. Only Maria Fabiola, who had picked Paco, her youngest, up out of his car seat and was cradling him in one arm, wore a kind smile.

Elvia stepped forward, holding out the cool drink in Ilusion's direction. "What beautiful wares,' she said with an almost audible swallow. "Did you... did you perhaps bring them as presents for Francisco?" Her eyes seemed to suggest that she prayed this wasn't true. "I'm afraid he might be too young for such delicate objects."

Caritina had boldly picked up one of the sculptures that depicting a young woman in a yellow dress surrounded by tall palm trees in which several bright red diablitos hid. They seemed to be watching the woman with big toothy smiles as they peeked out from behind the brightly coloured palm fronds. Clearly showing her disgust, Caritina was allowing the sculpture to dangle from her thumb and forefinger. "I don't understand all the diablitos in folklorico art. Diablitos in the trees, diablitos riding bicycles and driving cars, they're everywhere. You'd think that when that old monk forced the devil to kneel at the cross we'd be finished with devils."

"But, when the devil kneeled at the cross his knee made the spot where the Cupatitzio first started to flow underground," Maria Fabiola said. "We have the devil to thank for our beautiful river, here." She was laughing as she said it, but the other woman made a face and shook her head.

"The cross did away with all the devils," Caritina replied.

"And, yet the river remains," Maria Fabiola said.

Caritina sniffed and started to paw through the other sculptures. "Look! Diablitos in every one!" she said. "Hiding in every tree! I don't think Father Diaz would approve of any of these as a gift for a child."

"Oh no, no!" Ilusion took the sculpture out of the young mother's hand and carefully replaced it, along with the rest, in her backpack. "These are for sale,' she said. "Not a present."

Caritina looked offended. "Are you going to sell them here?" she demanded.

Elvia shot the other mother a look, part horror and part encouragement, although she seemed confused. "Where is my purse?" she asked. "Who would like another drink?" She stammered and tripped over words without saying much of anything. "I'm sure Ilusion is not trying to..."

"Look over there, you crazies," Maria Fabiola said, pointing with Paco's feet to the spot where Felix stood, still holding his big box. "There is little Felix with Francisco's present." She shook her head at the other mothers. "You all need to get out of the sun or switch to drinking cola rather than tequila."

Elvia let out a sigh of relief. "Oh, of course," she said to Ilusion. "It's Saturday, I forgot you'd be working." She clapped her hands and walked over to Felix. "Why don't you go play with the other children, Felix? You can put your present here with all the rest."

Ilusion tightened the strings that held her backpack closed and watched as Felix again looked over the mountain of presents. "No," he said at last. He hefted the box in his arms. "I think I will hand it to Francisco myself."

Again, Elvia looked a bit taken aback, she flashed a look back at the mothers as she took off following Felix's confident steps towards where the other children were playing. None of the other mothers seemed like they wanted to leave the shade of the avocado tree, so Ilusion forced herself to her feet and trailed after the younger woman.

Francisco Paz Marcelo was big for his age and he knew it. Why Felix had settled on him as a potential friend, Ilusion could not understand. In the Sunday church gossip circles, he was rumoured to be a bully and a terror in the playground, although his "little disagreements" with the other children were often glossed over at the

137

Jardin de los Ninos thanks to the generous donations given yearly by the Marcelo family to the Catholic church.

Now, as she walked over to where the group of about twenty nicely dressed children was playing Francisco was shouting at Juan Carlos, who stood playing some type of small electronic game while a group of children stood in rapt attention around him.

"It's my birthday! Let me play the game. Now!"

Elvia wobbled up to him on her heels. "Maybe if you ask nicely, mi cielo, Juan Carlos will let you play when he is finished."

"I don't want to wait for him to finish!" Francisco's face was turning deep red under his cowboy hat. "I want the game! It's my party. Today I get everything I wish for."

Elvia crouched down in front of her son, and tried to explain again, but Francisco pushed her away, nearly upending her onto the dry grass. "No," he said, determined. "Either Juan Carlos gives me the game or he goes home! I can have anyone's toys I want." With that he lunged into the circle of Juan Carlos's admirers and tried to rip the game out of the other boy's hands.

Several of the girls gave little screams of alarm, but Juan Carlos simply turned his back on Francisco's attack, lifted the video game high into the air and continued to play. Francisco made an angry, strangled sound, picked up a clod of dry dirt and flung it at the back of Juan Carlos's head. His aim was such that he missed the popular boy completely and hit Avelina Torres Sanchez right in the middle of her party dress.

Juan Carlos looked over his shoulder with a snicker. "You're in trouble, now," he told Francisco.

Elvia waded into the group of children. "Maybe, if we can't all share a toy," she said. "We should put it away."

Juan Carlos shrugged and turned off the game.

"No!", Francisco continued, incensed, "I didn't get my turn. I want to play with it now!" He came up to Juan Carlos, shoved his face in close and glared. "Give it to me!"

Juan Carlos gave an elaborate sigh. "I have to turn it off now," he said with a smile. "Your mom said so." He slid it into his back pocket and happily crossed his arms in front of his chest.

"That's not fair!" Francisco bellowed. The other children started to back away from him, sensing the approach of a tantrum. Elvia tried to distract him with suggestions for games they could all play together, but Francisco was having none of it and only repeated "Not fair!" louder and louder until he finally forced his mother to give up in frustration.

Francisco stomped his cowboy boots into the dead grass and threw himself to the ground, sitting cross-legged with a fearsome look on his face. "I don't want to play." He could barely get the words out he was so angry. "Everybody go home."

138

At that moment, Felix walked up to where the birthday boy sat pouting in the grass and placed his gigantic box on the ground in front of him.

Francisco's face curled into a sneer. "What's that?" he demanded.

"This is your present from me," he said. "You can play with it all you like. It's for you after all."

Ilusion caught her breath and covered her mouth with her hand. Oh Felix, she thought. Oh my poor, poor Felix.

Francisco's eyes narrowed as he stared at Felix. He reached out with his boot and gave the box a poke. "It looks ugly," he said. "Tell me what's inside!"

"It's big," one of the other children said. "Open it." Several other children joined in, and even Elvia gave an encouraging nod. Francisco, still glaring suspiciously at Felix, seemed to soften. He started to reach out a hand towards the box, while glancing around to make sure everyone was paying attention, only to discover that Juan Carlos had taken out the video game and was quietly playing it again for a group of five of his most loyal fans. With a wail, Francisco smacked Felix's present away and jumped to his feet. "I don't want your ugly. Stupid. Present," he screamed.

"Francisco, my love!" Elvia said in distress.

Felix stood in stunned silence, his arm half extended towards the box as if to protect it from Francisco's cruel words. "What?" he asked as if he hadn't heard correctly the first time.

"Are you stupid?" Francisco said. "I said I don't want your stupid Indian present!" With that, he pushed past Felix, who seemed incapable of getting out of his way and stormed over to the picnic table. Everyone else stood around in shock. Ilusion wanted to run over to Felix and carry him out of the hateful party, but was afraid to do such a grandmotherly thing in front of his classmates. Elvia covered her face in despair and the children stood staring at the ground or at one another out of the corners of their eyes.

With a deep breath, Elvia uncovered her face. "I know!" she said brightly, looking around at all the children, except Felix. "Why don't we get out the special piñata?" She attempted to herd the children towards the picnic table. "Let's try to cheer Francisco up. It's not right to be sad on your birthday. Come on Felix, you too!" She led the children back to the picnic table, leaving Felix standing alone in the grass next to his discarded present.

Ilusion crossed over to him. "That was a good thing you tried to do," she told him.

Felix sat down next to his present and put his head in his hands. Such an old pose for such a young child, Ilusion thought as she forced her old bones into the grass beside him. "Sometimes, a present is not appreciated the way we want it to be." She tried again. For the first time since Felix's mother had passed away, she felt unable to comfort him. It was a sickening feeling. "The main thing is that you offered the present with an open heart. I matters much less how it was received."

Felix turned his face away from her, in the direction of the cool breeze coming off the river. "I wanted him to be my friend," he said. "I wanted him to like me." He looked up at the branches of the avocado tree overhead. "But, he doesn't like me, does he? So what do I do with the present, now?"

Ilusion was about to answer when she was overcome with the strange thought that Felix wasn't talking to her, but rather someone that only he could hear.

∽∾

Back at the picnic table, the other children were enjoying a drink while Elvia had Caritina and her son, Juan Diego, bring out an enormous object covered in a brightly coloured blanket and place it underneath one of the avocado trees very near where Felix and Ilusion were sitting.

The other mothers were pressed into service bringing their children up to form a loose circle around the object. Juan Carlos was sulking because Maria Fabiola had finally put the baby back in the car seat and had discovered her son's role in the disruption. She'd given Juan Carlos strong words and had forced him to hand over the video game to a delighted Francisco, who now sat on the far side of the picnic table by himself.

"Francisco, mi cielo, come here and see what we have for you," Elvia called. She teetered around the covered object making motions as if to rip the blanket off and peering anxiously after her son.

"Leave me alone!"

"But, this is something you want very much, my love," her voice becoming shrill. "Come and see!"

"Go and play with your piñata, you big baby," Juan Carlos added.

Francisco made a face at the popular boy, stood up and dropped the video game to the dirt beneath the picnic table. Juan Carlos's eyes almost bugged out of his head and he took a step forward to rescue his toy, but Francisco was quicker. One large cowboy boot came down right on top of the game, shattering it and sending plastic splinters under the table. "I'm coming, mami!" he called. He wisely dashed around the table before Juan Carlos could reach him and ran to the spot where his mother stood. He wrapped both arms around her and kept her neatly in between himself and Juan Carlos, until Maria Fabiola grabbed her son by one arm and wrestled him into the circle with the other children.

140

While the other mothers hid their disproving frowns behind their cocktail glasses, Elvia smiled at her son as if he was the best-behaved boy in Uruapan. With a flourish she yanked off the blanket and revealed the largest piñata any of them had ever seen. Francisco's fake delight quickly turned genuine. Francisco's favourite thing in the entire universe was dinosaurs, and he loved the fearsome Tyrannosaurus Rex most of all. The piñata was the biggest, most realistic T-Rex that money could buy. It was nearly as large as some of the smaller second graders and came up to Francisco's shoulder. He clapped his hands. He hugged his mother again. He gazed at his T-Rex piñata with happiness and adoration.

Until Juan Diego climbed into the tree, with the piñata's rope held neatly in his teeth and looped the rope over a sturdy branch. He jumped down to the earth and leaned back, pulling on the rope and the majestic piñata rose into the air, all snarling teeth and tiny arms sticking straight out over a huge bloated belly filled with candies for the children.

Francisco watched his T-Rex rise off the ground, but his joy at seeing it spinning lazily in the breeze was brought short by the realization that the lifespan of a birthday piñata was not long. His mouth dropped open. "Wait," he said. "Wait! We don't have to play right now. We can have cake instead."

Elvia groaned. "Francisco, it's time for the piñata," she said. "Everyone is ready to play."

Francisco looked wildly around. There was the blindfold in his mother's hands and here came Juan Diego with the stick. A thought occurred to him. He took the stick from Juan Diego's hands. "I will go first," he announced to muffled groans from the other children. "It's my birthday, after all." He would pretend to try to hit the piñata, but miss until he could claim he was hungry and wanted cake. He tried to swipe the blindfold out of his mother's hands, but to his surprise she pulled back.

"The birthday boy goes last," Elvia told him. "Why don't we let Felix try first?"

Everyone looked around for Felix, who was still sitting quietly beside his present. He shook his head at them without raising it. Ilusion waved Elvia's offer of the blindfold away from her grandson. No, he would not be swinging at the piñata today.

"Let Juan Carlos go first," Avelina Torres Sanchez said. "He can do it. He'll break that piñata in one swing!"

The other children agreed and started to cheer loudly for Juan Carlos, who stepped forward amid Francisco's protests. Elvia put the blindfold on him, gave him three quick turns and plucked the stick away from her son before he realized what was happening.

Juan Carlos advanced on the piñata's last location, swinging the stick as Juan Diego lowered it to within his reach. Francisco tried to interfere and was almost smacked with the stick for his troubles. He stomped over to safety and watched nervously from the sidelines. Juan Carlos's swing just grazed one bright green T-Rex leg and the children let out an excited shout. Encouraged, the blindfolded boy let loose with another mighty swing that connected with the piñata, which made a hopeful crunch but remained intact.

"I will hold the rope!" Francisco said, his voice nearing panic. He wrestled the rope out of Juan Diego's hand and began hauling the T-Rex high up into the tree.

"You're cheating," Juan Luis shouted. "You have to bring the piñata back down!"

"It's my piñata," Francisco replied, pulling the T-Rex higher and higher into the tree. "I can do what I want. I'm king. I'm T-Rex!"

At that, Juan Carlos yanked off the blindfold and threw it to the ground. He lifted the stick over one shoulder as if it was a baseball bat and advanced on Francisco. "Let the piñata down," he said in a threatening voice.

Next to Ilusion, Felix stirred. They were far enough away that the two boys were no cause for concern, but she was very unhappy with the way this birthday party was turning out. Elvia, she noticed, had wandered back over to the picnic table to pour another drink and failed to notice her son's peril. "No," Felix said softly. "You don't need a stick to break a piñata."

"Who are you talking to Felix?" Ilusion asked.

Maria Fabiola stormed over from the picnic table. "Juan Carlos, you put that stick down this instant or you are going home. Do you hear me? This instant!"

After the tiniest hesitation, Juan Carlos threw the stick to the ground. "You keep your baby piñata," he told Francisco who stuck his tongue out at him. "I'm going down to the river. Who wants to come?"

At once a handful of the exasperated children followed him away from the piñata. Maria Fabiola came and stood next to where Ilusion and Felix sat, rocking little Paco back to sleep in her arm. "I guess the shouting woke him," she said.

"Yes, it did," Felix agreed, "Along with the bad words."

Maria Fabiola narrowed her eyes at Felix, but didn't reply. In her arm, Paco gave a mighty yawn and fell back asleep. She stood next to them watching as Francisco continued to taunt the remaining kids by lowering the piñata just enough so they had hope of hitting it only to haul it out of harm's way every time anyone came close.

"This is a terrible party," Maria Fabiola said, after a while.

Ilusion realized that no one would blame her, now, if she took Felix home. She stood. "I think we should be going," she said.

Maria Fabiola nodded. "I agree," she said. "I don't like those kids playing down by the river. It's too strong this time of year." Paco started to fuss and look around for food. "Ah, I left his bottle at the picnic table. Felix? Can you go down and tell them to come away from the river?"

Ilusion was about to offer to go instead, when Felix jumped to his feet. "I will go," he said. He picked up his present and started for the river.

"Felix, leave that here," Ilusion called.

"I'm taking it with me," Felix said over his shoulder. "If nobody wants it, I'm taking it home."

Maria Fabiola turned in the direction of the picnic table. "He's a good boy," she told Ilusion. "I'm only sorry he must grow up without his mother. Sesasi was a fine girl, nobody tells the truth about her."

Ilusion sat in shock. She hadn't realized that any of these wealthy Uruapan mothers knew her daughter. She wanted to run after Maria Fabiola, but as much as she wanted to know, she was afraid of the answers.

Felix took the packed dirt path away from the picnic area and made his way down to the river. It was much cooler beneath the thick shade trees that lined the Cupatitzio and he felt like he could breathe comfortably for the first time since Francisco had called him a stupid Indian. He felt his present jangling inside the box and knew that it had been damaged in Francisco's attack. He felt sad for all the hours he'd spent painting the diablitos hiding in the trees of his grandmother's sculptures. Each one of those diablitos had been like a friend to him, helping him get closer to having enough money to pay for the gift. He had given life to those sculptures as best he could, so the turistas would see them and want to give them a good home.

He heard the sounds of the other children playing and came down through a screen of bushes onto the banks of the river, not caring that the festive birthday paper caught on the branches and tore. Juan Carlos stood at the river's edge, angrily throwing rocks into it. The other children were looking for bugs in the dirt or hanging half out of the lowest tree branches.

"Hi Felix," Juan Carlos said. "What are you doing here?"

"Your mom wants you to come back to the party," Felix said.

"This party sucks," Avelina said. "Can't hit the piñata. No cake, no candy, no fun."

Juan Carlos threw another rock into the river. "You're right about that."

Felix set his present down on the damp dirt next to the edge of the river. "Yes."

Juan Carlos was in the middle of throwing his final rock when a

143

strange look came across his face. "Hey," he said. "Maybe, we don't need a stick to break the piñata," he said. "Everybody get as many rocks as you can, fill your pockets!"

"What?" Felix asked. "No! That's a terrible idea!"

"We'll hit that T-Rex out of the tree!" Juan Carlos shouted. He grabbed up two handfuls of the smooth river rocks and shoved them in the pockets of Avelina's party dress, ruining it. "Everyone get as many as you can!" The other children loaded their pockets with rocks, which were abundant on the banks of the river.

"No! That's not what they meant!" Felix said. "I'm sure that's not what they meant!"

"Come on Felix! Francisco's piñata is going to get it now!"

"No, stop!" said Felix, trying to delay the departing children. Juan Carlos jumped past him, but Avelina crashed into Felix's present, sending it down the bank and into the river. "No!" cried Felix. The big floated into the current and Felix was torn between stopping Juan Carlos and his gang and saving what remained of his gift. He looked back and forth between the two and realized he could do nothing to save Francisco's piñata, now, but he could save his gift before it floated away. He kicked off his good shoes and waded out into the mighty Cupatitzio.

∽∽

What was taking Felix so long? Illusion wondered. It seemed like hours since he'd left to find Juan Carlos and the other children. She knew she should get up and go looking for her grandson, but the heat and the disappointment of the day had sapped her old bones of strength. She wiped her robozo across her face and wished she had the energy to get herself another cool drink. In front of her, Francisco toyed with his piñata, making roaring sounds as he raised and lowered it from the tree branch. He shouted insults at the remaining children, who were either too tired or too hungry to fight back. One optimistic young boy had picked up the stick and now stared up at the T-Rex dangling too far to reach overhead.

Francisco leaned against the trunk of the tree holding the rope in one hand and a fresh roasted corncob in the other. As far as Illusion could tell he was the only child eating; she was sure that Elvia had snuck the food to her son while no one was watching.

There was a rustle in the trees opposite the one from which the piñata hung. Illusion looked up in time to see a smooth stone come flying across the clearing and ricochet off the avocado tree's trunk and land at Francisco's feet. Another stone quickly followed.

"Stop that!" Francisco shouted. He pulled the T-Rex higher into

144

the tree and tried to get it out of the thrown stones" reach. One of them hit the piñata square in the face, causing a part of the Papier-mâché covering to come fluttering down. "Stop it!" Francisco tried to lower the T-Rex to the ground, but the hit had caused it to jump and spin and tangle itself in the limb's side branches. It was now caught and hanging helplessly in range of the flying rocks. "I know that's you, Juan Carlos!" he said. "I know you are hiding in that tree. If you hurt my T-Rex you will go home!"

The rocks continued to pelt the piñata. The children who had been grumpy minutes before now gathered beneath it in excitement. Ilusion climbed to her feet. Even though it seemed that Francisco's piñata was finally getting its due -- it was no joking matter to be throwing rocks into a group of seven year olds. She raised her arms and shouted, trying to get the attention of the mothers at the picnic table, but they had turned their backs on the children and were enjoying their drinks. Gathering her heavy skirts, she ran as best she could for the trees.

"Children! Stop throwing those rocks!" She had reached the nearest tree and glared up at the branches. The nimble little monsters were hiding in the thick foliage as they took aim at the T-Rex in the avocado tree. "Juan Carlos, your mother will be very upset with you. Someone's going to get hurt!"

Juan Carlos's face appeared between the branches of the tree, high enough that Ilusion had no hope reaching him with more than her words. "The only thing that'll get hurt is that piñata," he called down to her and let loose another rock. The piñata was hit again and the children in the trees laughed loudly, pointing and calling out as the first few candies started to fall.

For one instant, as Ilusion stared up into the tree, she saw the faces of Juan Carlos and the other children, but it seemed to her that their faces changed. They became the laughing masks of the folklorico market, brightly painted with leering mouths and horns sprouting from their foreheads. The trees started to sway and spin around her. Too much heat, she thought, bending over her knees to catch her breath. "Take it easy or you will faint, Ilusion, and who will bring Felix home safe and sound?" She caught her breath and looked up again, but the things in the trees had become children again.

Juan Carlos threw his last rock. It passed cleanly through the T-Rex's belly, hit the trunk of the avocado tree and ricocheted into Francisco's forehead. Candy rained down on the overjoyed children. Francisco fell into a sitting position on the grass, his face a mask of shock that, in short order, crumbled into tears.

Alerted by her son's wailing cries, Elvia had at last roused herself from the picnic table and lead a charge of the mothers across the grass. Ilusion felt herself being pushed aside as Juan Carlos and the rock-throwing children broke from the trees and ran for the candy.

"Where is Felix?" Ilusion stumbled past the confused jumble of children and mothers and found the path that led to the river.

She found Felix sitting on the bank of the river. Next to him was what looked like the wet and broken box that once held his present. She hurried off the path and through the bushes. "Felix, what happened?" she asked, kneeling at his side even though her knees protested. "What happened to your gift?"

"It went into the river," Felix said.

"Oh, I'm so sorry, my love," Ilusion said. "I guess that will be one less birthday present for Francisco."

"He didn't want it, anyway," Felix said. "So the river took it."

Ilusion nodded. They sat in silence until she had gathered the strength to get to her feet. "Come on, let's go," she said. "Bring that with you." She pointed at the ruined box. "Nothing good ever comes from an empty box."

Ilusion made it back to the avocado trees, where Francisco was crying and bleeding all over his mother's lap. Elvia was having a fit, demanding to know who had hurt her child. Mothers were grabbing up their children and dragging them away before blame could be placed. Maria Fabiola was looking for her son, but Juan Carlos had climbed into the avocado tree and was busy untangling the piñata rope from the branches. Slowly and surely he freed it and began lowering the broken thing to the ground right in front of the spot where Francisco lay curled in ball with a paper towel held to the slight gash on his forehead.

Francisco had finally stopped crying when he noticed something drifting down out of the tree. He blinked away his tears and took a harder look. It was his T-Rex, battered, but returning to him! He jumped to his feet, knocking Elvia over in the process. "You're all right!" he exclaimed.

Juan Carlos jumped from the lowest limb of the tree and landed in the grass with a solid thud. Maria Fabiola spotted him immediately and set off to intersect his path as quickly as she could without waking Paco. Francisco had almost reached the remaining top half of his T-Rex when Juan Carlos made a mighty leap and landed on top of the piñata, crushing it under his shoes, jumping up and down on it for good measure. A few of the other children, emboldened by his actions, joined in and soon the poor piñata was ground into the dirt.

With a wail Francisco watched the destruction of the one thing he loved more than anything else in the entire universe until he could not take it any longer. He jumped up, grabbed the stick and charged Juan Carlos with it.

"Francisco Paz Marcelo!" Elvia shouted. She scrambled to her feet, tottered for a second, and lunged at her son. "You come here right now or this day is over. Do you hear me? Over!" Children scattered everywhere. Francisco swung the stick, but Juan Carlos jumped to one side and the stick connected with Elvia's forearm as she reached for him. She let out a cry and hunched over her hurt arm.

Felix emerged from the river path, still carrying his box. He walked through the crowd of children and their angry mothers, right up to where Francisco stood staring at the remains of his T-Rex. Felix set the box on the ground next to Francisco.

"I told you, I don't want it," Francisco said without any of his former anger.

"I think you do," Felix told him. "I think inside this box is everything you've ever wanted." He nodded.

"You're crazy," Francisco said, but his curiosity got the better of him. "What's in the box."

"Look inside and see."

Francisco moved closer to it. He reached down with one finger and pried up one of the flaps and took a quick peek. "I don't see anything," he said.

Felix leaned in a bit. "Look again."

Francisco stared into the box for a long minute. The other children watched, even Juan Carlos stopped trying to avoid his mother's grasp to look. "I see something in there," Francisco said at last. "It's far away though. What is it?"

"Maybe you should get inside the box and find out," Felix said.

Francisco pulled open the sides of the box. He put one leg over the side of the box, hopped a bit to get his balance and pulled the other leg in. "Something is in here!" he said crouching down and pulling the lid shut on top of himself.

"What's inside the box, Felix?" Juan Carlos asked as everyone looked on in wonder.

Felix shrugged. "It's just an empty box."

For one long second no one made a sound. At last, Juan Carlos threw back his head and erupted into laughter. Soon, the other children joined in. Smart Felix tricked Francisco into climbing into a box! What could be better than that?

Juan Carlos went over to the dead piñata and scooped it up. "Here why don't you play with your T-Rex in your empty box!" He yanked open the lid and threw the piñata inside, hoping to litter the birthday boy with the paper mache. "Hey," he leaned into the box.

147

"There's nothing in here."

"I know," Felix said. "It's just an empty box."

"No, I mean there's no Francisco in the box." Juan Carlos backed away and Elvia ran forward.

"What? Where's Francisco?" she asked. She leaned over the box. "Where'd he go?"

A loud and horrible sound came from the depths of the box. It grew in volume until it shook the ground beneath them. Elvia back-pedalled away from the box as quickly as she could in her high heels. Mothers grabbed their children. Ilusion ran to Felix's side. "What did you do?" she asked him. "What did you do to Francisco?"

Before he could answer, the sides of the box bulged outward and something emerged from the top. It was dark, dark green, the colour of old forests and it grew as it forced its way out of the top of the box, which flattened and collapsed around it.

It was a head, an enormous, impossibly large head with small beady unblinking eyes and a mouth filled with huge, curved teeth. It was too large to ever have fit into the box and now too large to be contained by it. It shot up against the branches of the avocado tree, snapping the limbs off as if they were twigs. The rest of the body flowed up from where the box had been: small forearms, followed by a grotesquely bloated body. The children started to run in all directions at once. Mothers screamed. One huge leg popped free and a foot larger than the picnic table slammed into the ground, shaking it violently.

Juan Carlos stood staring up at it. "It's a T-Rex!" he said. He looked at Felix with wild eyes for a moment before he took off running. The T-Rex struggled for a minute, but managed to get its other leg free. It stood in the middle of the picnic area, looking stupidly around and bellowing.

"It was just an empty box," Felix said, standing right beside one enormous clawed foot and staring up at the T-Rex. "Nothing was supposed to happen. It was a trick to get him to climb into an empty box." He seemed unaware of the danger he was in, so close to the shifting and stomping feet.

Ilusion grabbed him by an arm and rushed him around the back of the avocado tree and under the picnic table before the T-Rex realized food was directly underfoot. "What did you do?" she demanded.

"Nothing!" Felix said, hiding next to her as the T-Rex started moving towards the avocado trees and the children that were hiding in there. "I... I just thought it would be funny to put Francisco in the box." A quick guilty look passed across his face. "I didn't think anything bad would happen." He shook his head. "He said it was going to be a good joke. He didn't say what would happen."

The ground shook as the T-Rex charged into the avocado trees, grabbing them in its jaws and shaking them. Felix tried to cover his ears

148

at the screams of the children hiding under the trees reached them. Ilusion pulled his hands away. "What has happened to Francisco? Did that thing," she pointed at the beast, who was now pawing at the ground with one foot, trying to scare the children out from beneath the trees, "eat him?"

Felix shook his head. "No," he said sadly. "I think that is him."

Ilusion pressed her hands to her eyes. "Oh no."

"Juan Carlos is in serious trouble, now," Felix said with a small giggle.

"This is no laughing matter! You've turned a boy into a monster and it is going to eat those poor children!" Ilusion pointed across the picnic area. The T-Rex was thundering up and down, crushing cars in the parking lot and roaring loudly enough to shatter the windows in the surrounding houses. "Now, you turn him back!"

Felix lowered his head, he said nothing out loud and his lips never moved, but after a minute he looked up at her with a strange expression. "I have an idea," he said.

He climbed out from under the picnic table. The T-Rex was in the trees again and the trees were falling. Soon, all the children that had sought refuge there would be crushed or eaten. He found his grandmother's backpack, lying on the bench where she'd left it. He untied the strings and reached in and, keeping one eye on the T-Rex, carefully unwrapped his grandmother's sculptures and set them in the grass.

The diablitos looked up at him from their trees. He had breathed life into them in hopes that they would sell in the market, but he needed that life to be real now.

Ilusion watched him with fear in her eyes. Felix bent over each sculpture and spoke to it. She couldn't hear what he said, but as soon as he was finished he stood up and stomped on the sculptures. As each one was crushed beneath his boot there came a loud crackling sizzle and a human sized diablito appeared in the air before him. Ilusion covered her mouth to keep any sound from escaping her lips as the diablitos formed a neat floating line that faced her grandson. There were red ones with horns, black ones with white spots, blue ones with hissing cats protruding from the centre of their foreheads, even one on a bicycle with a gun made out of a dolphin. They bobbed on an unfelt breeze and squirmed and stuck out their tongues and rolled their eyes. Felix stood in front of them, a very small boy at the head of an army of diablitos. "You must drive the monster to the river!" Felix told them. "So Francisco can return whole again!"

With little yipping sounds, the diablitos swarmed the T-Rex. They scaled its sides and attacked it with their forks. The T-Rex thrashed and chomped, but the diablitos were too quick. They scurried over its back and head and pounded it with their cloven hooves until they forced it to turn from the avocado trees and crash blindly towards the river. The roaring was horrible to hear, loud bellows of fury as the monster ripped a path down the bank and into the rushing water.

A strange quiet filled the picnic area. For a long time, Ilusion stayed beneath the table whispering prayers, until at last some of the other mothers and children started to creep from their hiding places. Elvia was the first one out, calling for her son. Felix appeared to help Ilusion from beneath the table and sit with her in silence on the bench.

There was a movement at the edge of the path that led from the river and Francisco emerged, dripping wet and covered in mud and clay. His mother ran to him and gathered him in her arms.

"I do not want any more birthday presents," Francisco said.

Twelve Mile Limit – Gina Covelli

Mile marker twelve glowed green in the headlight beams. No one was ahead of us and no one was behind us.

"We're almost there," Nathan said, gripping the steering wheel of the jeep we were lucky to get. There were so few vehicles left in the QZ, and those were reserved for the Board of Directors. Everyone who ran was always on foot, and they were always caught. But Cora had a connection. She knew someone who knew someone who had a jeep and that guy knew someone with enough diesel to get us out of the QZ. It only cost everything we owned.

But we were going to make it. I relaxed against the backseat and looked out the window. The gold dirt and grey concrete of the QZ had already faded into a forest of rich greens that seemed to sparkle, even though the night was dark as pitch. I should have been concerned because of what the Directors always warned us. The toxic wasteland outside the QZ, created during the 100 year war that destroyed the world, had started to affect the border forest that surrounded the QZ. Some abstract group the Directors called "they" had dropped phosphorus in this part of the world, which is what made the foliage shine in the dark I guess. But then again, it could have just been the dampness of early fall reflecting in the headlight beam.

When I looked ahead of us the mile marker had grown from a small green square to something we could actually read. We would be the first ones to make it out of the QZ. The first ones to cross the border.

"There's something in the road," Cora said.

Nathan slammed the brakes and cranked the steering wheel to avoid hitting whatever Cora saw, but too late. There was a loud bang and the jeep swerved out of control and smashed to its side. Glass shattered, metal crunched, someone screamed.

Then nothing. Everything was still and the hiss of the cooling engine was the only thing I could hear. The jeep was on its side in the middle of the road and I was strapped into the backseat with my head resting on the cold pavement. My breaths puffed out in bursts of white steam I couldn't control. I stared at the edge of a shard of glass in front of me hoping the focus would slow my breathing. Once I was able to take a somewhat smooth breath, I wiggled the toes of my left foot, bent my right ankle, just to make sure I could move. I exhaled, long and steady, and closed my eyes. I heard someone moving ahead of me and lifted my head a couple inches and saw Cora.

It looked like she was asleep in the seat in front of me, but her head rested at an awkward angle and something dark and wet streaked through her soft, golden hair.

"Cora," Nathan said from the driver's seat. I couldn't see him but I could hear him release his seatbelt to get to her, his fingers fumbling with the latch. I didn't look away from the blood in Cora's hair.

"Cora, you OK?" Nathan asked. He leaned over her, touched her face and brushed shards of glass off of her. Her head moved a couple inches when he touched her and I could see blood on her forehead.

"She's bleeding," I said.

"I can see that, Ryker," Nathan snapped and tried again to wake her. I blocked out Nathan's voice as he talked to Cora – or to himself, I couldn't really tell – and adjusted in my seat, wincing in pain.

"Is she..." I started to ask.

"She's breathing." Nathan's voice came from outside the jeep. "Help me get her out."

I unclasped the belt, pulled myself toward the opposite door and shoved it open. I braced myself against the frame of the jeep as my head swirled before I climbed out onto the pavement. I shook my head to clear the dizziness and wiped at the blood on my face. Nathan grunted and cursed as he reached through the driver's door to get to Cora.

"We have to go through the windshield," I said, making my way around the front end of the jeep.

"Yeah, good idea." Nathan started toward the back hatch for something to break the windshield with but stopped when he saw me. "Shit, you OK, Ryker?"

"I'm moving," I said.

"You're bleeding too."

"It's fine."

"OK," Nathan said and disappeared behind the jeep. He came back around and handed me a blanket.

"Cover her up so the glass doesn't get on her," he said. I dropped the blanket on Cora and stepped back.

"I'm just going to sit," I said, my legs collapsing from under me. Nathan aimed the crowbar he'd found at the windshield and I turned my head, my eyes drawn to the green glow of the mile marker fifteen feet in front of us. On the other side, thick brush and hundred year old trees blew in a gentle breeze, carrying with it something that smelled sweet and wet. It must be what rain smells like when you're free, I thought.

I looked over my shoulder after the windshield shattered and looked down the road to the harsh, fluorescent glow of the QZ.

We almost made it.

PCR: Yes.

DDM: Now is your chance to thank and repay us for our hospitality. Tell me about Cora Welsh.

PCR: You've got her file.

DDM: I want to hear your opinion of her.

PCR: I don't have an opinion of her.

DDM: I find it difficult to believe you. From the evidence I've seen, the two of you seemed quite close.

[6 second pause.]

PCR: We weren't close.

DDM: Perhaps you need to go back into solitary.

PCR: I don't think that would help.

DDM: I disagree. A little time in your cell might inspire you. Clearly seeing the sun doesn't inspire you. [4 second pause.] You miss the sun.

PCR: Four days in solitary makes a man miss a lot.

DDM: You can stay here, see the sunrise. You could even return to your old room at the hospital. No more days in solitary. Just tell me about Cora Welsh.

PCR: There's nothing to tell.

DDM: Why are you protecting her? Did you love her? [10 second pause.] Answer the question.

PCR: No.

DDM: No, you won't answer?

PCR: No, I didn't love her.

Interview 004-PCR terminated at 5: 51 a.m.

Nathan laid Cora on the road and picked at the bits of glass in her hair, his lips pressed tight together. I ripped off the sleeve of my coat and pressed the material to the scrapes on my head and watched him from my seat on the pavement. I couldn't process what I was seeing – Cora so limp and fragile. She had this energy about her, this fierce energy that controlled space and time around her. Even when she slept. But the energy was gone now. It was like she stopped existing the minute her head hit the pavement. She was just a body, barely breathing.

"I don't know what happened," Nathan said. "The jeep was in perfect condition."

"We blew a tire," I said.

"There was no reason for us to blow a tire," Nathan said standing up and inspecting the road. He walked from shoulder to shoulder in a 10-foot radius of the jeep, shaking his head.

"Cora saw something," I said standing up beside him.

"I did too, but now there's nothing here. Just road."

"We all know the stories, about all the ways they stop people," I said and shrugged my shoulders. People tried to escape the QZ all the time, but it didn't matter how prepared they were or what route they took, they never made it. They were always stopped and captured and thrown in the nutter. And then it was like they never existed. Nathan didn't believe those stories. In fact, he didn't believe anything the QZ Board of Directors said. I used to joke with him that his disbelief came from having perfect genetics. Being in the top 1 percent of the population gave him the freedom to believe what he wanted because he was untouchable. The rest of us with crap genes? We believed the Directors and we followed the rules. We didn't have the luxury of perfection.

Nathan knelt next to Cora and checked her pulse for the tenth time since he got her out of the jeep.

"She'll be fine. She always is," I said and looked down the road toward the QZ. "We should get moving. The Snatchers will be here soon."

"You see them?"

"Not yet." I shook my head at the dark, empty road. They should have been speeding up behind us as we left the QZ. They should have had us surrounded by now. But they weren't there. No trucks. No Snatchers. Nothing.

Just us and a busted jeep.

Cora made a noise and Nathan whispered to her, his hand cradling her cheek, and I realized my error. There was nothing out here – no jeep, no road, no stars and moon – nothing at all except Nathan and Cora.

∞

QZ468
Interview 05-PCR
DATE: November 27, 2152
DD Ian Marshfield

DDM: Interview with Prisoner Charles Ryker, starting at 10:17 a.m. on November 27, 2152. Deputy Director Ian Marshfield presiding. How was breakfast, Mr. Ryker?

PCR: Grey.

DDM: What do you mean?

PCR: There was grey, soupy oatmeal and grey milk. I didn't drink it.

DDM: What do you prefer for breakfast?

[4 second pause.]

PCR: Bananas.

DDM: Bananas have been extinct for more than 50 years.

PCR: Yeah.

DDM: So why bananas?

PCR: Because your question is stupid. Meals have never been about preference and breakfast has always been grey, soupy oatmeal and milk.

DDM: Why not say pancakes or waffles, then?

PCR: It was the first thing that came to mind.

DDM: Interesting. Let's continue with this idea of word associations. I'll say something and you respond with the first thing that comes to mind.

[5 second pause.]

PCR: Why?

DDM: Just a change of pace. It could be fun.

PCR: Fun. [Snort.] Right. OK.

DDM: Let's begin with cake.

PCR: Dessert.

DDM: Sun.

PCR: Day.

DDM: Jeep.

PCR: Crash.

DDM: Black.

PCR: Snatchers.

DDM: Nathan.

PCR: Friend.

DDM: Cora. [6 second pause.] Cora.

PCR: Girl.

DDM: Why did you hesitate?

PCR: I don't know.

DDM: There's something about her that bothers you?

PCR: Are we done?

DDM: You loved her and that's why you're protecting her and why you helped her.

PCR: I think we're done.

DDM: I'll decide when we're done. What made Cora Welsh

155

special?

PCR: [inaudible]

DDM: Speak up, Mr. Ryker.

PCR: She called me Charlie.

DDM: Why would that matter?

[7 second pause.]

PCR: She's the only one who ever did. [5 second pause.] May I ask a question?

DDM: Of course. This is a dialogue.

PCR: [Laughter.] Right. A dialogue. So, what makes Cora so special to you?

DDM: What do you mean?

PCR: You keep asking about her, so she had to be important to you. Otherwise, why would the Directors waste so much energy questioning me about her?

[10 second pause.]

DDM: I believe we're done for today.

Interview 05-PCR terminated at 10:28 a.m.

Nathan was late again. Probably more meetings with the Director of Population and Breeding. He was always meeting with the Directors, almost every day for two years because they couldn't find him an appropriate match. It's hard to match perfect, Nathan would joke, but there was nothing funny about it.

I sat on a rickety barstool, sipping a pint of ale, and watching the second hand spin around the clock on the wall when she sat down in the chair I was saving for Nathan. Her hair was the colour of faded straw and it hung in wild curls around her shoulders like a lion's mane.

"Hi," she said to me as if it were completely natural for a woman to drink at the Sec-Bar.

"You're not allowed here," I said.

"Actually, I am," she said holding up her access pass. "I'm sorry if a beautiful woman ruins your night."

"I'm just surprised you'd have access to the Sec-Bar," I said and took a drink.

"That's because no one knows what to do with me."

"So they granted you access to whatever you want?" I asked, giving her my full attention.

"Sure," she said and rolled her eyes.

"I don't get it."

"Because you're just a Sec Officer. You're not made to understand people like me."

"What are you then?"

She flagged down the bartender who poured a pint of Bitter for her and looked at me with a smile that didn't reach her eyes and said, "An anomaly."

The bartender set her drink in front of her, spilling just a little of it on the bar.

"Thanks, Sam." She took a long swallow and then looked at me. "Why do you think bartenders are always named Sam?"

"What?"

"At all three bars in the QZ, the bartenders are named Sam."

"I only have access to the Sec-Bar."

"Maybe it's a requirement of the job," she said sipping her drink. "I'm Cora, by the way. Cora Welsh."

"Charles Ryker."

She smiled. "It's nice to meet you, Charlie."

QZ468
Interview 016-PCR
DATE: November 28, 2152
DD Ian Marshfield

DDM: Interview with Prisoner Charles Ryker, starting at 1:30 p.m. on November 28, 2152. Deputy Director Ian Marshfield presiding. I want to pick up where we left off yesterday. [6 second pause.] Tell me about your relationship with Cora. [10 second pause.] How close were you? [5 second pause.] Mr. Ryker, answer the question. [7 second pause.] Mr. Ryker?

Interview 06-PCR terminated at 1:32 p.m.

Someone pounded on my door, jerking me out of a blackout sleep. My head beat in time to the heavy thuds on the steel door and there was an unusual weight on my shoulder. I opened my eyes and saw Cora curled up next to me, her head nestled on my shoulder and her arm outstretched over my chest. I stared at the way her hair covered the pillow in gentle corkscrew curls and tried to remember how we ended up here.

Cora sat down where Nathan was supposed to sit. We talked. Nathan never showed. I walked her home. I lifted my head and looked around. We were in my apartment. She walked me home.

"Ryker, open up." Nathan was at the door.

"Whoever that is needs to go away," Cora said, rolling over and taking all her warmth and weight with her. I sat up and swallowed back vomit as my vision spiralled.

"You OK, man? Open the door." Nathan's voice gave away just a little bit of panic. I looked at the clock. For the first time in six years, I was late picking him up on our way to work. I pulled on my pants and went to open the door. Nathan, standing stiff in his uniform, shook his head when he saw me.

"You look like ass," he said.

"I don't know what happened."

"We have to be at work in twenty," he said, walking to the kitchen and grabbing a grey protein bar off the counter. "You better hurry."

Cora shuffled into the living room, wearing nothing but my shirt. Her hair frizzed in a wild mane around her shoulders and her pale legs glowed in the sunlight that filtered through the skylights.

"Good morning, Charlie," she said, kissing my cheek. "Who's your friend?"

Nathan didn't try to hide his surprise, staring at her with his mouth agape. Cora looked him up and down and smiled.

"That's Nathan," I said. "I have to--"

"Go to work, I know," she said. "I'll get my things."

Nathan stared after her as she went into the bedroom.

"I'll be ready in a minute," I said to Nathan and followed her. We got dressed in silence. I glanced at her every now and then, not sure what to do. I had no memory of how we ended up at my apartment or what we did when we got there, though I had a pretty good idea. I didn't know if I was supposed to say anything or do anything. After we were dressed, we left the room and found Nathan exactly as we left him.

"Um," I said.

"Don't worry about it, Charlie," Cora said. "Just a harmless fling."

Her eyes slid to Nathan and she smiled again, admiring his perfection. Tall, lean, muscular, crystal blue eyes and a jawline every sterilized chump wished he had. Most guys hated him for it, and I would have too, if it wasn't Nathan.

Cora took a few steps toward him and held out a hand. "I'm Cora."

Nathan shook her hand but looked at me. I shrugged and said, "She's an anomaly."

"What does that mean?" Nathan asked.

Cora shot me a glare, the muscles in her jaw tight. After a moment she smiled at Nathan but there was no emotion behind it.

"It means nothing," she said and made her way to the door. "See you, Charlie."

QZ468
Interview 07-PCR
DATE: November 29, 2152
DD Ian Marshfield

DDM: Interview with Prisoner Charles Ryker, starting at 5:27 a.m. on November 29, 2152. Deputy Director Ian Marshfield presiding. How are you this morning?

PCR: Tired.

DDM: Didn't you sleep?

PCR: Not really. The guy in the cell across from me yelled and threw his food dish against the wall all night.

DDM: Hmm. [5 second pause.] Well, this should be an easy session.

PCR: Yeah, right.

DDM: Tell me about your job.

PCR: My job?

DDM: You were security guard at the QZ Market. Did you like it?

PCR: Yeah. Actually, I loved it.

DDM: What made it so enjoyable?

PCR: There was a routine. A process, you know. Every day was the same and there weren't any surprises.

DDM: What was your routine like?

PCR: I'd wake up and get my workout in. Security guards had to meet certain fitness standards. I was never going to be the best because of my genes, but I worked at it all the same. Then, I'd walk to Nathan's place and he and I would get breakfast at the Sec-Bar. And then we stood at the main gates of the Market. Scanned people as they came in, scanned them as they left. Anyone caught with tagged merch was held for the Snatchers. Anyone who tried to run was shot. It was precise. Perfect.

DDM: You had a lot of authority.

PCR: Not that much.

DDM: But people were afraid of you.

PCR: Only if they planned on stealing.

DDM: How did Nathan like it?

PCR: He never complained about it.

DDM: Did he complain about other things?

PCR: Why would that matter? He's dead.

DDM: Answer the question, please.

[10 second pause.]

PCR: DNA. He complained about his DNA.

DDM: That's strange. What did he say?

PCR: His genetic screens always put him in the top 1 percent of the population. He knew what that meant.

DDM: And he didn't like it?

PCR: Apparently not. I guess I wouldn't like it either.

DDM: You were sterilized.

[7 second pause.]

PCR: Yes.

DDM: Why wouldn't you like to be in the top 1 percent?

PCR: Are you in the top 1 percent?

DDM: We're not here to talk about me.

PCR: You're not! You're genetically defunct. How'd you get such a high-ranking position with shitty genes?

Interview 07-PCR terminated at 5:38 a.m.

It'd been two months since I met Cora and I hadn't seen her since. I never talked about her but I thought about her. I'd wake up and miss the weight of her arm across my chest. Sometimes I dreamt about her, saw her smile at me, and I'd wake up almost in pain because it wasn't real. Maybe she wasn't real at all. She disappeared too quickly.

"It's a hot one today," Nathan said. We'd been standing at the gate for only an hour in the blazing sun, watching the steam rise up from the golden dirt floor of the QZ Market. My grey uniform was glued to my skin from sweat and the heavy weight of my rifle, protective vest and utility belt. My protective glasses kept sliding down the bridge of my nose.

"Sure is," I said, adjusting the heavy vest that weighed down my shoulders. I squinted at the sky above and wished a breeze would blow through and cool some of the sweat that baked on my skin.

"I've been meaning to ask you," Nathan said, and something about his voice made me stop watching the Market and look at him. He stood tall and stiff, his lips puckered as he watched an old man in a frayed denim coat pay for two mason jars of pickled venison at the butcher's white and red tent. Nathan finally finished his thought and said, "About that girl."

I turned back to the Market.

"Do you ever see her?" he asked.

"Nope."

"Not ever?"

I swallowed hard and tried to act like she didn't matter at all as I said, "It was just a harmless fling."

"She was pretty," Nathan said. "Not like anyone I've seen."

I nodded my head and waited for Nathan to continue. He was being too careful about his words and the way he said them that I knew he was hiding something. Five minutes went by in silence.

Just as Nathan opened his mouth to say something, the bell on the gate dinged. He tilted his head to the left, as if that motion would ease his annoyance at his thoughts being interrupted by the chime, and I slipped the scanner off my utility belt. I turned and almost dropped the scanner in surprise when I saw Cora, her grey dress clinging to her sweat-slicked skin and a canvas bag in her hand. She didn't seem to see me at all as she smiled at Nathan, who broke protocol and left his rifle hanging limp around his neck. I looked from him to her and decided the best thing to do was my job.

"Arms out," I said to her. She held her arms out so I could scan her from head to toe. No tagged merch. I took her ID card, registered it into the system and stepped aside so she could enter the Market. "You have one hour to complete your shopping."

"Thanks, Charlie," she said as if no time had passed from that day she sat next to me in the Sec-Bar, that morning she woke up in my bed. I returned my attention to the Market and did my best to ignore Cora as she made her way from tent to tent.

"She came by my place," Nathan said out of nowhere. "A couple days after she was with you. Just showed up at my door."

I didn't say anything.

"We just talked," Nathan said. "At first. But she kept coming back."

"You should stop talking about it," I said. "They could be listening."

"She's not like other people."

I watched Cora pay for a set of broken radios and walk to the baker's green tent. She took her time and looked up at the brilliant blue sky, as if the heat of the sun were the greatest joy of her life. She would smile at the other shoppers and bow her head as she thanked the vendors for their services. Every now and then, she looked at Nathan and smiled.

"You mad?" Nathan asked looking at me. I sighed and looked at a young, mousy woman who would probably never understand the joy Cora seemed to have, as she purchased a small glass jar of grey milk.

"Why would I be mad?"

"Well, we're friends, you and me. And she... I don't know." Nathan looked back at the Market. "You and me, we're friends."

"I know." I dug my toe into the ground. "I'm not mad."

That was true. I wasn't mad. I was something else altogether, and it wasn't Nathan's fault I felt that way.

∽

QZ468
Interview 08-PCR
DATE: November 30, 2152
DD Ian Marshfield

DDM: Interview with Prisoner Charles Ryker, starting at 8:06 p.m. on November 30, 2152. Deputy Director Ian Marshfield presiding. [9 second pause.] Why wouldn't you like being in the top 1 percent?

PCR: Because of what they'd do to you. You're a science experiment your entire life.

DDM: Is that what Nathan told you?

PCR: It's common knowledge.

DDM: Is that why Nathan convinced you to run? So he wouldn't have to be an experiment?

PCR: That might have been part of the reason.

DDM: And the other part? [12 second pause.] The other part?

PCR: I don't know.

DDM: We don't like when you lie, Mr. Ryker.

PCR: I know you don't.

DDM: You know the punishment for lying.

PCR: Yes.

DDM: So why are you choosing to lie?

PCR: I don't want to talk about it.

DDM: Your time with us is limited. [15 second pause.] Perhaps you need to spend some time in the cage.

PCR: I don't need to go in the cage. [6 second pause.] It doesn't help me to think.

DDM: I don't need you to think. I need you to answer the question. [17 second pause.] I'll just call the guards to take you to the cage.

PCR: Cora.

DDM: I'm sorry?

PCR: The other reason why we ran. It was Cora.

DDM: Can you explain?

PCR: Not right now.

DDM: We're growing very impatient, Mr. Ryker. A night in the cage will do you some good.

Interview 08-PCR terminated at 8:15 p.m.

∞

The Sec-Bar was unusually crowded. I was crammed into a corner and couldn't even reach the bar to get a drink. A drink I badly needed. I didn't know what happened to my life. One day everything was great, or as great as it could be in the QZ. I had my job, I had my friend, and I had the routine. Then this wild-haired siren burst into the room, and like a spotlight, she zeroed in on me. And in a snap, someone flicked the switch and she was gone. And with her, the only friend I ever had.

Nathan didn't look me in the eye at work. He didn't talk to me. He quit coming to the Sec-Bar with me. I stopped picking him up in the mornings and there were times when he was almost late to work. I'd ask him what was wrong but he wouldn't say. And he didn't need to. He spent all his time with her. Cora was the only thing he cared about anymore.

I was about to give up on ever getting that drink I needed when I saw Nathan squeeze through the door. He caught my eye and made his way over. I pointed to the bar, hoping he'd get the message to grab a couple drinks first. He didn't.

"Hey, Ryker," he said sliding into an open space next to me.

I gave him a nod but watched the bartender pour a pint of Bitter.

"Look, um," Nathan started. "I'm sorry about how things are. There's just a lot going on."

I looked at him and for the first time in almost four months I noticed the dark circles under his eyes.

"You're not sleeping," I said.

"I got the call. Apparently the Board of Directors found her."

"Oh." I had forgotten about that little threat. I just assumed they'd never find him a match. The women chosen to be breeders were always too fat, too slow, too ugly, too dumb. The woman they matched to Nathan had to be as perfect as he was and for two years, she didn't exist.

"Are they sure," I asked.

"Seems like it." He shook his head.

"And it's not Cora."

Nathan scowled at me. I probably shouldn't have said anything about Cora but I couldn't stop myself.

"I've got less than a month before they move me to the suites at the Department of Population and Breeding and turn me into some kind of Frankenstein whose only job is to impregnate the breeder and give blood and tissue samples for testing and replication."

"It may not be that bad," I said. Nathan laughed, but he and I both know there wasn't anything to laugh about.

"I hate this." He took a deep breath. "And Cora. I don't know what to do. I don't know how to leave her."

"Yeah," I said, as if I knew what he was talking about. And maybe I did a little. But I tried not to think about it.

Nathan tapped his toe on the ground and pursed his lips, deep in

163

thought. After a few minutes, he looked me in the eye and said, "If I do something crazy, you've got my back, right?"

"What?"

"We're friends, right? So you've got my back."

"I guess. What do you mean, 'something crazy'?"

"I don't know yet, but I won't let her go," he said. "I love her too much."

∞

QZ468
Interview 09-PCR
DATE: December 4, 2152
DD Ian Marshfield

DDM: Interview with Prisoner Charles Ryker, starting at 4:17 a.m. on December 4, 2152. Deputy Director Ian Marshfield presiding. Today's the day.

PCR: What do you mean?

DDM: We're going to talk about Cora.

PCR: We are?

DDM: It will be good for you to let it all out, get it off your chest.

PCR: It will?

DDM: I know you're tired. Four days and nights in the cage isn't easy, but the decision was made with your best interests in mind.

PCR: Sure.

DDM: Last time you said Cora was part of the reason why you ran. Can you explain that?

PCR: I don't know.

DDM: Are you lying again?

PCR: No. [12 second pause.] Nathan loved her. He saw her at the QZ Market and I don't think he saw anything else when she was around. A few weeks after they met, she stopped coming to the Market. A few weeks after that, he stopped going to the Sec-Bar with me after our shift. They just spent all their time together.

DDM: How did that make you feel?

PCR: I don't know. Lonely. Nathan was my friend.

DDM: Tell me about their relationship.

PCR: I don't know much about their relationship. They were in love.

DDM: They wanted to run because they wanted to be together. Is that correct?

PCR: Yes.

DDM: Why did they ask you to run?

PCR: Nathan and I were friends. And, well, Cora. [15 second
164

pause.] She was different. Not like other people. She existed on a different plane than the rest of us.

DDM: A different plane?

PCR: She wasn't part of the QZ. She was... I don't know what she was. [10 second pause.] Anyway, Nathan was a week away from moving to the suites at the Department of Population and Breeding, and Cora came by my apartment and convinced me that we had to run. All three of us.

DDM: How did she manage that?

PCR: She made me believe running would be worth the risk. [7 second pause.] And I didn't want to be alone.

DDM: You're alone now.

PCR: Yes.

DDM: Had you succeeded in your attempt to run, you would have been alone watching the woman you loved be happy with your best friend.

PCR: I suppose.

DDM: I don't understand why you agreed to go with them.

PCR: I don't know if you have the capacity to understand that. [5 second pause.] All due respect.

Interview 09-PCR terminated at 4:39 a.m.

⤨

I woke up to someone pounding on my door on my only day off I had that month. I pulled the blankets over my head and hoped whoever it was would go away. Or if it was the Snatchers, they'd just break the door down and shoot me.

But whoever it was kept banging their fist against the door. I threw the blankets off and made my way to the door, undid the bolt and threw it open only to see Cora.

"Charlie, I need your help," she said and walked in without invitation. She'd been crying. Women always get the same red rings around their eyes when they cry. It was a strange sight because I never imagined Cora as the crying kind. She walked right into my apartment and turned to look at me with her hands planted on her hips.

"I know about Nathan," I said. She sort of laughed and looked toward an odd corner of the room, as if looking at nothing helped her process the fact that she was going to lose him. "There's not much we can do. He's going to be relocated and we're both going to have to let him go."

"We have to run, Charlie," she said, looking at me. "You, me and Nathan. We have to get out."

165

"We'll be killed before we reach the border."

"Nathan and I will be executed if we don't run, so we have to take that chance."

"So run then," I said going to the kitchen to pour a glass of water.

"We can't leave without you."

I laughed. "You're kidding, right?"

She had to be. It's not like she wanted or needed me at all. I was just that harmless fling. Besides, she and Nathan were better just the two of them. They were connected by something that I couldn't understand. Maybe because of my crap genes. It was as if one brain controlled them – a right hand and left hand, completely in sync. They didn't even need to talk to each other. They acted and reacted in perfect harmony, and I was just in the way.

"It's not my call," she said, her voice slick and cold as ice. "I like you Charlie. You're a good friend, but I don't need you."

I set my glass on the counter and rolled it back and forth on its edge, doing my best to cover up the flash of pain that zipped through me. Cora sighed and leaned her hip against the counter to my left, watching me. I looked at her sideways and saw what Nathan probably saw – a woman they couldn't control, who found a way to enjoy life when she wasn't supposed to.

She licked her lips and folded her arms across her chest.

"Nathan won't leave without you," Cora said. "And considering...."

Cora sighed and the tick of the clock filled the void as I waited for her to continue. The tick beat louder and louder from a few seconds to almost a minute before I slammed my glass onto the counter.

"Considering what?" I asked.

"I wasn't sterilized, Charlie." She sort of shrugged as the realization dawned on me. "Nathan and I will be executed when they find out."

I shook my head and said, "They won't touch Nathan. He's too important to them."

"So, it's OK if I die?" She took a deep breath, released it in a slow exhale and took a step toward me. "Nathan wants to run but he won't leave without you. I know someone who will help us get out. You have to come with."

"If Nathan wants to run so much and can't go without me, why are you here and not him?"

"The Directors are watching him closer than ever. I haven't seen him in two weeks." She paused. "We could make it, Charlie."

I pursed my lips. She was crazy to think that any of us could get away. It wasn't just the Snatchers keeping us in, but all the rumours about what was beyond the border. Chemical wastelands, man-eating beasts, death traps. There was no way we could survive out there in the wild. I shook my head, wanting to tell her no, but couldn't form the word in my mouth.

"We have a chance, Charlie," she said putting her hand on my arm. "Please."

⚬⚬⚬

QZ468
Interview 010-PCR
DATE: December 11, 2152
DD Ian Marshfield

DDM: Interview with Prisoner Charles Ryker, starting at 5:15 a.m. on December 11, 2152. Deputy Director Ian Marshfield presiding.
[10 second pause.]
PCR: I must have made you angry last time.
DDM: Why do you say that?
PCR: Six days of solitary and six nights in the cage since our last chat.
DDM: Does that bother you?
PCR: Not anymore. [4 second pause.] What's with these little electrodes on me?
DDM: Those are little reminders that you're on borrowed time and cooperation is in your best interest. We've done our best to be accommodating and engage in a polite conversation with you, but we cannot wait any longer. All I have to do is push this button and you'll be hit with a series of electric shocks. [7 second pause.] Shall we continue our conversation?
PCR: If you like.
DDM: What did Cora want, exactly, when she came to your apartment?
PCR: She wanted me to help her and Nathan devise a plan to escape the QZ.
DDM: What did you tell her?
PCR: I told her Nathan was the luckiest shit in the QZ. I also told her that I'd help them.
DDM: Why?
[10 second pause.]
PCR: I couldn't abandon them. They believed they had this chance, really believed they'd make it. And when she came to my place, and almost begged me to run with them, I couldn't say no. [15 second pause.] They're better off now. Better than any of us.
DDM: But they're dead.
PCR: Right. Death can be better.
DDM: Do you really believe that?

167

PCR: I'm sure I'll find out soon.

[4 second pause.]

DDM: There are only a few questions left, Mr. Ryker. [9 second pause.] How did Cora and Nathan die?

PCR: In the crash. The jeep flipped and crushed them. [Electric buzz and screams, 4 seconds.]

DDM: It's not in your best interest to lie.

PCR: You saw the scene.

DDM: Where are their bodies?

PCR: Wherever the Snatchers took them. [Electric buzz and screams, 7 seconds.]

DDM: No one took their bodies because they weren't there.

PCR: You're making that up, trying to get me to say something so you can punish me again. They were there. They were crushed by the jeep. Whatever your Snatchers did to the bodies afterwards is your business.

[11 second pause.]

DDM: You're lying again.

PCR: I'm not-- [Electric buzz and screams, 13 seconds.]

DDM: Where are they?

[12 second pause.]

PCR: How long has it been since the accident?

DDM: What?

PCR: A month, right? Since the accident?

DDM: 36 days.

PCR: Yeah, that seems right. Good. You shouldn't be able to reach them now.

DDM: What do you mean?

PCR: They were there, the jeep crashed, and we all got out and looked at the mile marker. We heard the Snatchers coming and agreed to run for it. So Nathan and Cora took off. I stayed where I was.

DDM: Why?

PCR: So you would focus on me instead of chasing after them.

Interview 010-PCR terminated at 5:30 a.m.

Five minutes had passed and still no sign of the Snatchers.

"You can't wait for her to wake up," I said.

"She'll be pissed she didn't get to cross that line herself," Nathan said, scooping Cora in his arms. "Let's get moving."

"I'm not going," I said. I stepped closer to Nathan. "One of us has to stay behind."

"No. Ryker we need you."

"If we all go, they will never stop hunting us," I said, putting a hand on his shoulder. "We'd never be safe."

"They'll kill you," Nathan said.

"We're all dead anyways," I said. I looked at Cora, beautifully still in Nathan's arms, and sort of smiled and brushed a curl from her face. "I'll give you guys as much time as I can."

"You can't stay. I won't let you," Nathan said.

"Man, you don't need me out there. You'll have Cora and the two of you, you're better together. You're better just the two of you." Trucks rumbled off in the distance. The Snatchers were on their way. "Besides, who's to say a man-eating beast won't attack right after you get over the twelve mile limit?"

"Charlie."

"Just go, Nathan," I said. "Before they get here."

"I'll miss you."

"Yeah, now get out of here." I watched Nathan walk to the mile marker. He hesitated for just a moment, adjusted his grip on Cora, and stepped over the boundary. Nothing happened. No beast jumped out of the woods to attack. They weren't zapped with electricity. All the stories they told us to keep us in the QZ were lies. Nathan turned around and smiled at me. I lifted a hand, gave him a little wave, and then he turned and kept walking. I watched until they were gone, enveloped in the black of the night.

I smiled at the emptiness, knowing they'd be all right, and then turned to face the headlights of the Snatchers' trucks bobbing their way up the hill. I took a deep breath, sat down next to the busted jeep and waited.

Harold the Hero
- Paul R Davis

"Harold Jedidiah Peterson, get back in here and put your underwear on!"

Harold almost made it out the door and onto the bus with nothing but his jeans hiding his butt from the world. It was freeing, something his father said was a mark of pride. In fact, his father said if the boy was lucky enough, he'd run around his own house one day without pants or underwear. Mom did not appreciate Father's encouragement.

The boy walked upstairs, past his scolding mother, without a word. He was an awkward boy already, and there was nothing the other children could laugh at him for, no matter how low his jeans went when he ran. Braces gave him the name metal mouth. Thick glasses garnered the name bottle caps or four eyes. The freckles, so thick his face was more orange than paste, conjured the rumour he was half pumpkin. To top it all off, thanks to a TV show, his ginger hair had kids claiming with conviction that he was a soulless monster sent out of hell to torment others. But he did have a soul, and Harold reminded himself of that every day in front of the mirror, with his roly-poly belly hanging out. He had the soul of a hero, just like in his comic books.

Standing in front of the mirror, pondering what to do about the underwear dilemma, as he had it set in his mind he was going to show up to his fifth grade classroom commando, he thought about the heroes in his books. They all wore their underwear on the outside of their pants. Surely it would be partially acceptable. Mom did only give him the order that he had to wear underwear, not where or how.

"Harold," his mother screeched, "bus is rounding the corner. Get down here before I have to drive you."

The decision was made. Harold found a pair with minimal skid marks, as he could not be seen as a dirty comic book hero, and struggled to pull up the whitey tighties over his jeans. "Done," he whispered, admiring himself in the mirror as if some transformation overtook him. Then he ran.

He ran down the stairs, past the kitchen counter, picked up the lunch bag, and was out the door. Within seconds the bus was pulling up and he could hear Mom yelling, "What the hell are you thinking, Harold? Get back here right this second." The harpy ran out the door, but Harold was too quick.

"Go, go," he wheezed, getting on the bus. The driver, not paying attention and entirely unaware of the boy's fashion decision, did as Harold demanded.

Harold collapsed and pulled out his inhaler, taking several puffs. Children were already snickering, but the boy was too enraptwith the moment to hear the jeers. He made his way down the aisle, one seat after another denied to him, until he found an empty seat behind Cheryl Gordon. The day was starting out perfectly.

Cheryl Gordon was the vision of an angel, with gold hair that curled slightly, cheeks with a little chub, and blue eyes which looked as if heaven could be viewed when looking into them. Harold gawked until she turned around. She said, "What are you looking at, freak? Don't you dare touch me. And what the hell are you thinking, with your underwear on the outside of your pants?"

"Cheryl, I'm a hero, like from my books." The divine Cheryl acknowledged him, and it caused his heart to thump in his chest.

"Your heroes are freaks, too. Don't talk to me and stop staring. Take off your glasses so I know you can't see me."

Harold, being a very obedient boy, did as she said, and with a triumphant humph she turned back around. It was then, with his sight denied to him, that his heightened sense of hearing picked up the taunts aimed at him. Especially those from Ronnie and his thugs.

Ronnie said, "Four eyes really can't see. His underwear's on the outside. Bet he's not wearing anything under those jeans." He laughed, his friends laughed, and then Ronnie said, "Hey, Harold?"

Harold turned around, though he couldn't see anything. "Stop it, Ronnie."

"You don't want little Harold getting pinched, do you? Just looking out for you." The girls made an "eww" sound, gagging. The boys just laughed.

Poor Harold turned back around, looking at his feet as he muttered, "Not today, Ronnie. Today I'm strong and powerful. I'll kick your stupid teeth in."

Ronnie walked up the bus. "Harold thinks he can just mutter to himself? I'm sure it was something really nice, right? You wouldn't make fun of your good friend." Ronnie sat next to Harold and pinched the chubby boy. "Your heroes this fat?"

In defiance, Harold sat, saying nothing. He remembered in his classes if he just ignored the bully he would go away. He just wanted attention, and Harold would not stoop to that level. Not on that day. Not on his day as a hero.

"Fine, be boring." Ronnie ruffled Harold's hair then went back to his seat. The jeers did not stop, but at least Harold felt like his underwear gave him some power. Between Ronnie leaving him alone and Cheryl speaking to him, he knew it was going to be a great day.

At school, Miss Hessen collected the homework. It was one thing Harold was good at, and when he handed her his paper, she said, "Thank you, Harold. And how are you doing today?" She squinted, looking down. "Harold?"

Beaming, he said, "Yes, Miss Hessen?"

"Why is your underwear on the outside of your pants? Do your parents know?"

"I'm a hero, Miss Hessen." Then he whispered, casting a glance at Cheryl, "So far, it's gotten Cheryl to talk to me, and Ronnie left me alone."

"Sixth grade Ronnie?" she asked. Harold nodded. "Harold, you can always tell me. I can help you."

Harold shook his head, "Miss Hessen, the last time I told a teacher he picked on me, my head ended up in a toilet. I'm never tattling on them again. But I will stand up for myself." He scrunched up his face and made a fist.

"You won't hit him, Harold, will you? Violence is never the answer." She leaned over and put a hand on his head, briefly compressing his tangled curls.

His eyes lit up, "Miss Hessen, how could you suggest that? That would be horrible. I would never hit someone."

"Good." She patted his head. Her voice went flat, "But again, your parents know?"

"Of course. Mom watched me get on the bus."

"And she's happy about that? She told me about your little practice of not wearing underwear. I can't believe she's not upset about this."

"Oh, no, Miss Hessen. She wasn't upset." He thought a moment, reaching back into the vocabulary from their tests and the books they read. "Furious. I think furious is the word. She might even call and tell me to put them on the inside. Or just show up. But I think she has work this morning."

Miss Hessen stifled a giggle. "You're a good boy. A very honest boy." Harold blushed. If not for Cheryl, he would have fallen in love with Miss Hessen. "Do you want to put your underwear the right way?"

"No thank you, Miss Hessen."

Her body shook as she covered her mouth to stifle the full out laugh building up. "Are they at least clean?"

"Mom washed them yesterday. Cleanest pair I have."

"We'll let it slide for now. But if it's a distraction, you will go straight to the bathroom."

"Of course, Miss Hessen. I would never want to distract others from learning. I wouldn't be much of a hero then."

"No, no you would not. I'm glad you're so considerate." She continued on, collecting assignments, and Harold went back to his text book, readying for class.

Cheryl, who sat behind and to the left one seat, said, "Freak, it wasn't good attention on the bus. And I can hear you."

He looked back, slightly dazed. "Oh, I'm sorry if I embarrassed you by telling her. And all attention can become good. The more we talk, the more you'll realize we're meant to be."

"Meant to be what? I'm not wearing my underwear on the outside of my pants."

"That would be horribly inappropriate," he exclaimed. "What a scandal, to have a lady with her underwear on the outside. Women heroes wear one piece swim suits."

"Excuse me?" She slammed her pencil on the desk, and the tip snapped off. "Never mind. Look what you made me do!"

"I'll sharpen it. It's my duty." He puffed out his chest.

"Fine." She handed him the pencil. "It's the least you can do."

With pride at his first real heroic action of helping a classmate in need, he went up and sharpened the pencil, grinding the metal crank so the cylinders inside could gnaw away at the wood. Everyone watched him, and those who did not notice the underwear when he walked off the bus burst out in laughter.

Miss Hessen said, "No class, don't laugh. People are different. There are people with all sorts of fashion styles, and this is apparently the style in Harold's books. He is revealing his individuality, and we should support that."

The laughs were muted, but Harold knew they were still there. It didn't matter, though. The pencil was the first of many opportunities to show Cheryl what a great guy he was. He returned to his seat, and put the pencil on her dusk. Cheryl said, "Thank you." Then, when Harold smiled a little too brightly, she muttered, "Freak." Nothing could dampen Harold's joy.

"How did you get out of the house like that?" Franklin asked. Franklin was one of the few friends Harold had. All of their friends read comic books, and had either glasses or braces. Tim, another friend sitting with them, was a ginger as well. Aside from hair pigmentation, Tim would have been normal, sitting at the table with Ronnie and the other athletic kids. But the hair cursed the poor boy from a young age, stripping him of normality due to his mythologically missing soul.

"I ran. I ran faster than I ever ran, Franklin. Tim, you would have been proud of me. I sprinted so hard."

Tim said, "What about your asthma?"

"I've never held the inhaler so tightly as when I got on that bus. I thought my lungs would burn me up. If you slapped gram crackers, marshmallows, and chocolate on my body, you would've had s'mores."

The boys cringed and laughed. Then Franklin said, "Why do it? I mean, I think it's cool, but still."

"I want to be a hero. I'm going to be a hero."

"Will you stand up to Ronnie," Tim asked. "You know he's after you, especially today. I heard you didn't squeal when he sat by you on the bus."

"So what?" Harold shrugged, grinning. His chest ached with the pride filling him, his arms flexing of their own accord, as if they won some great battle. The compliment even went straight to his head, making him dizzy.

"He's going after you at recess. You know he'll try to get you then."

"Well, already ate my lunch money, so he can suck on pennies." The boys laughed again, and the bell rang, signifying it was time to brave the playground. When they lined up, Ronnie turned and looked at Harold, giving an evil grin. The sixth grader's teeth almost looked like they were sharpened for this very moment.

Harold emptied his tray as quickly as possible, got to the front of the line to go out, and looked behind him. Ronnie was giving him a head start, standing at the back of the sixth grade line. Then he made a cracking knuckles motion and said something to his friends. They all started laughing, and looked to the poor, freckled hero. At least they couldn't give him a wedgie. Then the bell rang and the doors opened.

Balls flew, bouncing off children and asphalt. A boy in front of Harold was struck in the head and dropped to the ground. Harold vaulted the crumpled mass and kept running, his feet slapping against the blacktop as he went for the jungle gym where there was a chance he'd get lost in the clamour of classmates enjoying the slides and plastic maze.

He took a puff from his inhaler when a scream stopped him cold. It was Franklin. "Ronnie, stop! Stop," he cried out, as Ronnie tripped him. Franklin skid across the ground. The teachers were too busy getting the balls out to the near riotous students to notice the injustice. But Harold saw it, and he knew what had to be done.

A ball was hurled at Harold, and he stuck a hand out to deflect it. It was no time for games. The child who threw it merely gasped at the manliness. Standing by Ronnie, Harold said, "Leave him alone."

"What are you going to do about it?" Ronnie put a foot on Franklin's back, and Harold's friend gasped for breath.

"Save yourself," Franklin said. "Run, before Ronnie gets you."

Harold pulled on the elastic band of his underwear and let it snap, glaring at Ronnie and his goons. "Today I made a decision. A decision to be a hero."

Miss Hessen was correcting papers at lunch when Harold took on the mantle of hero. She was not out there to see what happened, or where poor Harold was taken. But five minutes after class was supposed to start, when the stragglers with juvenile excuses finally sat down, Miss Hessen noticed there was no Harold. He was always prompt, sitting in his desk in the third row, reading up until the last possible second when Miss Hessen said it was time to take out their text book.

"Where is Harold," she asked. The children fidgeted in their seats. Some looked out the window to avoid eye contact. Others were unusually eager to delve into their textbooks for the next class, social studies.

"Franklin," she said, "he's your friend. Did you play with him at recess?"

Franklin shook his head, "Ronnie came at me. Then Harold came to help."

"And then?" Miss Hessen was concerned, though also a little proud of the boy. "Did he help you?"

"Yes. He got Ronnie off me." Franklin looked off to the side, staring at the pattern on the tile floor. His words were nearly muttered.

"What happened to Harold?"

He shrugged. "I ran. Ronnie would beat us both up."

"Did anyone see what happened to Harold?"

"Ronnie took him in the school. Don't know what happened." Some other kid piped up.

Miss Hessen glared and went to her phone. She dialled the front desk. "Hi, it's Miss Hessen. Could you send someone to check lockers? I think I have a student locked in one." There was a pause. "Harold Peterson. I think his locker is 115. Check there first. Thank you."

Harold was in the locker for twenty minutes before he was released from captivity. He spilled out onto the school secretary, and she jumped back up, brushing herself off. Harold clawed his way to his knees, then stood with effort.

The dark scared him and caused his chest to tighten. He thought it was an asthma attack, but the inhaler did nothing once out of his confinement. The school secretary escorted him to class, saying, "You shouldn't get yourself locked in your own locker. Kids will do anything to get out of class. I'd be surprised if you didn't get a detention."

The boy looked down at his feet, mumbling, "Sorry." Heroes died young or lived long enough to get detention, he thought. Maybe even a suspension. The thought made his skin shiver.

When he walked into the classroom, Miss Hessen gave him a smile. There was one part pity and one part pride in it, watching the whipped hero come back from failure. "I'm sorry, Miss Hessen. I couldn't stop Ronnie. Please don't suspend me. I didn't mean to skip."

Miss Hessen's eyes went wide, "Suspension? Harold, who told you there would be a suspension? You did what you could. Sometimes all we can do is help others. And you did that. Now turn to page 34."

Cheryl whispered to Harold, "You're brave." He blushed and turned around to look at her, stars in his eyes. She clarified, "I don't like you. I'm just saying, what you did for Franklin, it was cool. Even if he was a little tool and ran like a girl."

It didn't matter that she clarified. All he heard was, "You're brave."

That afternoon, Miss Hessen called Ronnie's parents, informing them of their child's behaviour, and Ronnie received a tanned butt. Every time his father smacked him, he swore he would get his revenge on the tattletale.

The next day, Mrs. Peterson watched her son put his underwear on, and then his pants. He cried, "But Mom, this is embarrassing. None of the other kids have to do this."

"None of the other kids go commando," she snarled.

"Tony does. He got pantsed last week, and we all saw his butt."

"That's why you need to wear underwear under your pants." She nodded her satisfaction that the boy's story supported her cause, and Harold realized he should be obedient to Mom. The heroes worked to aid the law, and one had to respect authority to respect the law.

Resigned to his new responsibilities as a fifth grader, he said, "Alright. I will always wear underwear on the inside of my pants, because you are my mom and I want to respect you."

Mrs. Peterson was taken back at her son's change in attitude; she knelt down and gave the boy a big hug and kiss. "You are a good boy. You just have your moments." She kissed his nose and went downstairs, shouting, "Lunch is on the table. Don't forget it."

"I won't Mom. I love you."

"Love you too, Harold."

As soon as he knew she was downstairs, he pulled another pair out of his dresser. All his heroes had an alter ego during the day. They lived a normal life to keep loved ones safe, and Harold didn't want harm to come to Mom or Cheryl, no matter how much of a pain both could be. So he would wait and change before recess, preparing for the confrontation with Ronnie.

He grabbed his lunch and his mom kissed his forehead. She said, "Have a good day, Harold."

"I will mom. It will be a super day." He grinned at his little joke.

On the bus, Cheryl moved over. "You can sit here, Harold. But don't get the wrong idea. I just think you look pathetic sitting all alone, and you were really nice yesterday."

Ronnie shouted from the back of the bus, "Looks like someone's in love. Too bad I'm going to beat the crap out of you and Franklin for being little tattletales."

Harold sat down, but his heart jumped and his face turned red when he heard what Ronnie said. "He's going to bury me," he whispered as he put his forehead against the seat in front of him, nuzzling the slippery grey plastic with burn marks stretching out the creased pattern.

Cheryl rubbed his back reassuringly, the circular motions reminding him of Mom when he had a tough day. She said, "Probably. But you stood up to him."

"Does that make me a hero, Cheryl?" He sat straight up, and she removed her hand. He peered into her eyes, breathing heavily as anxiety and developing hormones took over.

"Sure, Harold. Is there anything else I can do to ease your last day on earth?"

Harold pondered the question; he had no doubt it would be the culmination of his short career as a hero. He and Franklin would at least go on to the next life together. "Please hold my hand."

Their fingers interlaced, the touch of her skin making him smile. She muttered, "Really, last day on earth and he's not even trying for first base." She shook her head, leaving Harold to wonder what she meant. How could he reach first base if they weren't playing baseball?

Once he reached school, he darted off the bus, pushing in front of the other kids, leaving Cheryl behind. As soon as he let go of her hand, his hand felt cold, and his heart empty. But that was the suffering a hero had to endure.

Franklin was entering the building, and Harold sprinted to catch up, chunky legs pumping as his lungs tried to inhale quickly enough. He sucked in air, wheezing as he did, holding his sides when he was halfway up the stairs to the school, leaving him wondering what awful gym teacher thought up the torment of those stone obstacles.

"Franklin," he tried to shout. It came out more like his grandmother asking for something in her old age, when her breaths were short and there was never enough air to form a sentence. "Franklin," he said again, catching up to his friend at the doors and putting a hand on his shoulder. "We're dead, Franklin, but we have to make a stand."

Past Harold, Ronnie stepped off the bus, the fire in his eyes making Franklin take off. Once through the doors, Franklin said, "You're a hero, Harold. You can do this." And off he went.

Harold was not a hero at the time. He had to put his second pair of underpants on first. "I have to find a bathroom," he muttered to himself, though it caused those around him to chuckle and ask if he was about to pee his pants. Harold blushed, grumbling under his breath, but then smiled when he realized if he did pee his pants, at least he had another pair of underwear.

"I'm going to get you, Harold," Ronnie screeched, taking his time getting up the stairs. It was straight out of the comic book pages, the villain sauntering towards the outmatched hero, the hero at a disadvantage because he didn't have on his suit. The suit was what gave the power to endure. It would give Harold the ability to survive the oncoming onslaught.

"We can still be friends, Ronnie. Or at least, like, we wouldn't beat each other up."

"Each other? Do you remember what happened yesterday, tattletale? Remember how well you did?"

Harold tried to make his voice gravely, but all he managed was to squeak. "I survived. I will survive again. But this time, I'm ready. I'll take you down."

"You won't survive this one, Harold."

Ronnie stopped his slow walk up the stairs. He darted at the portly fifth grader, and Harold, after his eyes went wide and his mouth opened like a fish, dashed off into the crowd of elementary students. Ronnie pushed kids over, and Harold could hear books, folders, and papers slapping and sliding across the tile floor. Kids shouted at Ronnie, and some started to cheer on Harold, using language Mom expressly forbade.

The boy's bathroom door slammed open, heavy oak cracking as it struck the concrete brick wall, then with another slam, it was closed. Harold clicked the deadbolt, and stepped back as Ronnie ran into the door and howled. When Ronnie ran into the door, meeting unexpected resistance, Harold heard the nemesis crumple to the floor, which gave Harold time to rifle through his book bag. There were three other students in the bathroom, and they all cowered in a stall when they heard Ronnie's cursing. Harold put his underwear over his pants and prepared himself for the conflict resolution ahead. The teachers said conflict resolution was always to be mediated, but he wasn't sure where he would find a wrestling referee, and he was pretty sure the teachers expected them to use words. But Ronnie was not a man of words, at least not clean ones, and Harold was no longer afraid. He would not back down from the bully.

Harold unbolted the door and opened it to see Ronnie on the

floor with a circle of kids around him. He held his left arm, spinning in circles as his feet flailed. Every other word was comprehensible, some sour word or another that would normally end with soap in the mouth.

Standing over Ronnie, Harold put his fists on his hips, as he saw in so many comics, and said, "Ronnie, this is the price of villainy. The side of good is well calculated, intelligent, and not prone to running into doors without making sure they're unlocked."

Ronnie whispered something, and Harold had to get close to hear it. "I will kill you, freak." With a swift motion, Ronnie swept a leg under Harold, and the boy tumbled to the ground. As he flew through the air temporarily, his backpack and glasses went flying. He struck hard and saw stars. Touching his skull at the point of impact, Harold pulled his fingers back to see sticky crimson warmth staining his fingers. Ronnie really was going to kill him.

The sixth grader was on Harold in no time, punching the boy in the face. After the third punch, as Harold grimaced and opened his mouth, Ronnie punched Harold's braces. A tooth cracked, and the braces bent. Blood was on Harold's lips as the braces broke Ronnie's knuckles open. Ronnie jumped off Harold, holding his hand and cursing. Cursing seemed all Ronnie was capable of.

"The power of good is too much for you to overcome, cretin!" He wasn't sure what cretin meant, but the good guys always said it to the bad guys, and it seemed like a time of linguistic heroics as well as physical daring. Harold was on Ronnie shortly after, pinning the boy's hands to the side. "Stop your struggle. End this peacefully. I've won."

Harold's face was too close to Ronnie, and the older child head butted the hero. Stars exploded in Harold's vision, as he woozily moved off Ronnie and stumbled for a few paces before dropping. It was Harold's first fight, and it was difficult for him to tell how it was going, but based on all of his victories being accidental he assumed it was going poorly. He thought it was going especially poorly when a fresh set of explosions rang through his head as two fists came down on his back and brought him hard to the ground. The tiles were painted in blood, he noticed. He laid there a moment to take it in. Some was his. Some was Ronnie's. There was never blood in his books.

For a moment, in his existential crisis, Harold thought perhaps it wasn't worth it. Perhaps there were no heroes or villains, just people getting by in the world, and they could coexist and not bleed out on elementary school floors. At the very least, Harold was certain he didn't want to see his blood outside his body again.

Then he heard Franklin crying out, saying no over and over again. Ronnie moved on, feeling his fight with Harold was finished. And, indeed, if he had not gone after Franklin, Harold would have stayed on the ground, defeated, no longer having the will to be a hero. But Franklin was the point. The kid next to Franklin who just wet his pants, or spilled his apple juice, was the point. Considering Harold would likely be bleeding into the puddle shortly, he really hoped it was juice. Cheryl, standing at the forefront of the crowd gathered, bit her lip as she saw Harold bloody and bruised, was the reason he had to be a hero. Harold was not the reason he was a hero.

He stood up and ran at Ronnie. Before Ronnie registered the loud squeaks and taps against the floor, Harold slid, knocking out Ronnie's legs. If he was going to win, he would win by being smart, by using his environment to his advantage.

Ronnie dropped and howled. He struggled to get up, but he and Harold were intertwined just long enough that he only stumbled and sputtered. Harold was able to force Ronnie, who weighed less even though he was taller, to his stomach. Harold sat on the boy, pinning his hands. He looked to Franklin, "Get Miss Hessen."

Harold sat awkwardly in the principal's office. The lecture had been going on near an hour, with Mom and Dad there. Ronnie's parents also sat there. Ronnie's parents were not particularly pleasant, scolding the boy often. The father was even restrained and sent into the hall for slapping him upside the head a few times.

Meanwhile, Harold's parents sat there and listened, Mom's hand circling his back to calm him, a circle that seemed to isolate all the fear and anxiety of the moment. Heroes never had to deal with aftermath. When the city was destroyed and the bad guy was behind bars, they just walked off into the sunset. Harold tried to walk to his classroom after Miss Hessen took Ronnie off, but she barked at him, "Harold, you're joining us."

Obligatorily, knowing it was his duty to take responsibility, he went off to the office where he sat for half an hour waiting for his parents. It didn't take long, though, for Harold to realize why Ronnie was as mean as he was. Perhaps all villains had the same issue: no one was there to love them; nurture them; to give them a hug on a bad day. Ronnie's scowl increased with every shrill word from his mother, or strike from his father, and it made Harold's heart hurt. It made him realize what it meant to be a hero, and that his parents, even if he fought often with his mother, loved him dearly.

When the lecture finished, Harold was given a week of detention, which he thought was getting off light. Ronnie was suspended for a week, which Harold thought was strange. Why did the kid who started the fight get a week vacation from school? The conundrum shed away shortly when the two boys were finally walking to class, half the day already finished.

Harold went up to Ronnie and hugged the boy. "I know why you beat kids up. But you don't need to. You can have friends." Ronnie stood there, anger and confusion both flowing through his facial features. Harold had no delusion that there would be a positive response, so he walked away. He found solace in the fact Ronnie never bullied another kid. At least not as aggressively as he once did.

Once back in class after the ordeal, Harold took his seat and Miss Hessen went on with class as if nothing out of the ordinary happened. She would never acknowledge the moment directly, but once, walking out the door, she told Harold he was a brave and noble boy, even if misguided from time to time.

As for Cheryl, she showed him what first base was that summer, though she made it perfectly clear she would never fall for him. She sat by him in sixth grade and held his hand all through high school, where she showed him several more bases. They broke up when they went to separate colleges, as couples often do.

Harold lost significant weight and became muscular by sophomore year. He was the keeper of the halls, even though he stopped wearing his underwear on the outside of his pants. He rarely fought, and became a school mediator. But when he had to fight, he put down his opponent hard and privately. He never served another detention.

About the Authors

Laura Johnson

Laura Johnson is a fantasy writer and poet who hails from Toronto, Canada. Although her Psychology degree doesn't give her the ability to read minds, she does use it to flesh out her characters. Her writing lair is littered with dragon paraphernalia, emergency rations of dark chocolate, and enough books to fill a small library. At present she is working on a fantasy series that blends intrigue, mythology, and dark magic. Previously her poetry has appeared in *Folklore*, an anthology about Scandinavian folklore published by Nordland Publishing.

Shelley Roe

Shelley Roe writes fantasy, dystopian, and contemporary romance. She is currently working on a fantasy trilogy that she hopes to finish sometime this century. She likes dark coffee, fuzzy cats, and the Oxford comma. She can be found at https://www.facebook.com/AuthorShelleyRoe?ref=hl and @ShelleyWrites on twitter.

C.P. Roelke

C.P. Roelke predominately writes fantasy horror set in modern times, but he also enjoys branching out into other genres. This is his first publication. When not writing, he spends his free time exploring the Alaskan outdoors and playing board games with family and friends. You can follow him on Twitter by going to @cproelke

Thomas Atwood

I started writing when I was a kid. My dad used to get me Illustrated classics every Easter, and I'd imagine adventures for Robin Hood, King Arthur, Ivanhoe, and Sherlock Holmes in brand new adventures that weren't in the books. One day, on the advice of my English teacher, I started writing them down, creating brand new stories for my favorite characters. Shortly after that, I got into comic books in video games, and as a teenager my three best friends and I came up with the idea for a fanfiction series that span over sixty different short stories. On the advice of my girlfriend at the time I started writing original pieces, and after a few stumbles and roadblocks I started writing as a regular activity.

Beth Hammond

Beth Hammond is an author/illustrator who writes anything from YA fantasy to children's picture books. She is a wife, mother, and lover of life. Her early years were spent serving in the military, middle years spent raising babies, and figuring out her place in the world. Her later years are yet to come, and filled with hopes and endless dreams. She spends her days creating worlds through words and illustration. Find her new YA fantasy "The Sound of the Stones" at bethhammond.com.

Lindsay M. Toomey

Lindsay was born and raised in Hamilton, Ontario. She's married, has a small dog and smaller son. By day, she rents cars and by night, she sleeps.

She writes contemporary stories for the amusement of her friends and family and often includes them among her characters. Her first novel is unfinished as of yet.

John Ryers

John hails from Ontario, Canada with his wife and identical twin daughters. He began writing fantasy at a very young age, inspired by the impromptu stories told by his father at bedtime.

In 2012, John created the realm of Aeryeth, a fantasy world set in medieval times and ruled by the four prime elements. His debut novel The Glass Thief – the first book of a trilogy set in this world – is slated for completion later this year.

Find out more about John at: johnryers.com

Lilian Oake

Lilian Oake lives in Charlotte, North Carolina with her husband and four goblins. Over the years, she has finished six projects - two New Adult fantasy novels, two Young Adult fantasy adventures and two short stories. Four of her projects take place in the world she created, called Jaydur.

Lilian is best known for her Wattpad story, Nahtaia: A Faery's Tale, and her short, middle-grade fantasy, An Ogre's Tale.

Keep up with news and updates on Lilian's website and blog at lilianoake.com.

Joshua Robertson

Joshua Robertson currently lives in Alaska with his wife and children. In 1999, he began crafting the world for Thrice Nine Legends, including *Melkorka* and *Anaerfell*. He is also the author of the *A Midwinter Sellsword* and *Gladiators and Thieves* in the *Hawkhurst Saga*. His short story, *Grimsdalr*, is inspired by the tale of Beowulf. You can find his works at crimsonedgepress.com.

Shannon Hawthorne

Shannon Hawthorne is a short story sci-fi and fantasy author who lives with her husband and two daughters in Chicago. Having spent many years in the theatrical world as a director, vocal coach and improv comedienne, she is making the career shift to storytelling on paper. She is one of the six members of the Writer's Edge Podcast and enjoys being able to talk shop and nerd out with fellow writers on a regular basis. She loves baby elephants, orange tic-tacs and book hoarding. You can find her at shannonhawthorne.com.

Jasmine Brennan

Jasmine Brennan is a Mexican American writer born and raised in San Francisco. She studied creative writing at San Francisco State University and continued to write in many Bay Area groups and workshops. She is currently working on an Urban Fantasy novel based in California's Sacramento River Valley that details the start of a demonic invasion in a series of stories called The Fade Tales. The short included here is part of that shared universe. Jasmine currently lives in the East Hills of Richmond, California with her partner, Brent, and a handful of pets both domestic and wild.

Her much neglected website is at jasiland.com.

The FB page for her novel is at www.facebook.com/FadeTales

Gina Covelli

Gina Covelli is a fiction writer and poet. She earned a bachelor's degree in writing from Lakeland College in 2006 and worked as a journalist for almost 10 years in Wisconsin. She is the community relations manager at Lakeland College, and is working on a short story collection and her first novel. She lives in Sheboygan, Wis.

ginacovelli.wordpress.com

facebook.com/GinaCovelliWriter

Twitter: @gmcovelli

Paul Davis

With the experiences of mission trips to Guatemala, international travel, a Tough Mudder, teaching in Kentucky and Wisconsin, and a few forced experiences out in mother nature, Paul R Davis seeks to put the excitement of life in his books, inspiring others to seek adventure.

storytellerdavis.wordpress.com